At first, she only allowed her fingers to graze his shoulder, tentatively, uncertainly, but as the memory of his warm, hard flesh returned, she flattened her palm against him, savoring fuller contact. A hot wave of desire flooded over her, its sharpness followed by a willing languor.

The touch of his mouth was soft, but so achingly familiar that a quiver shot through her. This was Christopher, no longer a memory, a dream, but with her in this tent, breathing quick and hard, his body tense with longing for her.

He remembered her; he had forgotten nothing of what she wanted. He could please her as no one else ever could have. If there had been others, he would drive from her mind every thought of them. . . .

Dear Reader,

It is our pleasure to bring you a new experience in reading that goes beyond category writing. The settings of **Harlequin American Romances** give a sense of place and culture that is uniquely American, and the characters are warm and believable. The stories are of "today" and have been chosen to give variety within the vast scope of romance fiction.

Kathleen Gilles Seidel is a woman who understands that sometimes southern men are different from others. This is revealed in the character of Christopher Ramsey, the hero and husband of April Peters, the protagonists in *The Same Last Name*. It is a lovely story and you will learn a lot about romance and camping in the Adirondacks.

From the early days of Harlequin, our primary concern has been to bring you novels of the highest quality. **Harlequin American Romances** are no exception. Enjoy!

Vivian Stephens

Vivian Stephens
Editorial Director
Harlequin American Romances
919 Third Avenue,
New York, N.Y. 10022

The Same Last Name

KATHLEEN GILLES SEIDEL

Harlequin Books

TORONTO • NEW YORK • LOS ANGELES • LONDON
AMSTERDAM • PARIS • SYDNEY • HAMBURG
STOCKHOLM • ATHENS • TOKYO • MILAN

For Pam

Published April 1983

First printing February 1983
Second printing March 1983
Third printing June 1983
Fourth printing August 1983
Fifth printing January 1984

ISBN 0-373-16002-X

Copyright ©1983 by Kathleen Gilles Seidel. All rights reserved.
Philippine copyright 1983. Australian copyright 1983.
Except for use in any review, the reproduction or utilization of
this work in whole or in part in any form by any electronic,
mechanical or other means, now known or hereafter invented,
including xerography, photocopying and recording, or in any
information storage or retrieval system, is forbidden without
the permission of the publisher, Harlequin Enterprises Limited,
225 Duncan Mill Road, Don Mills, Ontario, Canada M3B 3K9.

All the characters in this book have no existence outside the
imagination of the author and have no relation whatsoever to
anyone bearing the same name or names. They are not even
distantly inspired by any individual known or unknown to the
author, and all incidents are pure invention.

The Harlequin trademarks, consisting of the words,
HARLEQUIN AMERICAN ROMANCE and the portrayal
of a Harlequin, are trademarks of Harlequin Enterprises
Limited; the portrayal of a Harlequin is registered in the
United States Patent and Trademark Office and in the
Canada Trade Marks Office.

Printed in U.S.A.

Chapter One

The three cars left New York City before dawn, getting away before the noisy tangle of a Friday morning rush hour. They swept north up Highway 87, following the Hudson River, this little caravan of small, expensive, imported cars, each piled high with camping equipment. Tents and sleeping bags were tied to the top-carrier of one; fishing poles poked out of the back windows of another; the third was pulling a small boat. As the May sun brightened the morning sky, the cars turned off the thruway, heading west, traveling swiftly across the tree-lined highways that wound toward the Adirondack Forest Preserve.

Mike McKenna was just finishing his midmorning coffee when the three cars turned into the main gate of the Frank Lake State Park. This grayhaired man, with lean, almost craggy features, was superintendent of the park, charged with the sometimes conflicting responsibilities of preserving the quiet beauty of the forest and providing camping and recreation facilities for the park's visitors.

From the window of the little stone ranger cabin Mike looked at the three cars suspiciously. He was never too pleased when a group of campers arrived to-

gether. If anyone disrupted the quiet pace of the campground, it was not the family parties or the small bands
of two or three backpackers, but the occasional groups
of college students, breezing in for a weekend of noisy
celebration. Like nearly every park superintendent
across the country, Mike liked to keep his eye on
groups.

"April, there's a group coming in," he said to the
park's one other full-time ranger. "Will you go out and
speak to them?"

"I'll be glad to." April Ramsey finished checking
one more item on the park's bank statement and stood
up. She was a slender girl with sparkling blue eyes, high
cheekbones, and masses of dusky curls. Perhaps it was
wrong to call her a girl. She was in her midtwenties, but
she looked much younger, so pretty and unspoiled, as
fresh as the forest after a spring rain, that people often
thought that she was barely out of her teens.

"If they are college students," Mike said gruffly,
looking at her affectionately, "let them know that we
won't put up with any nonsense."

April smiled at him—this was a familiar refrain—and
stepped out of the cabin where she and Mike lived and
worked. The little cabin sat back in a clearing, ringed by
tall pine trees, near the main gate of the park. In front
of the cabin the drive widened, and on a small grassy
island in the center of the asphalt was a little green hut
where campers stopped and registered for campsites.

As soon as her eyes adjusted to the bright May light,
April could tell that this was hardly a gang of college
students. College students came piled in a van or in
a station wagon borrowed from someone's mother.
These cars were too sleek, too expensive, too well-
cared for, to belong to students.

And the sandy-haired man registering for the group was clearly not a college student. As April crossed the drive she guessed that he was perhaps thirty.

"Can I help you?" she asked pleasantly. Faith, the girl on duty in the registration hut, was a college student herself, having just been hired for the summer. She had only started a few days ago and wouldn't know which campsites were the best for groups like this.

April's air of calm authority, something she had worked hard to achieve, made the man turn immediately.

"Yes, we—" he started to say and then broke off. "Well, hello," he drawled, a smooth smile appearing at his lips.

April was used to this: men being surprised that a forest ranger could have clear blue eyes and high cheekbones. But while April was studying to be a forest ranger, she had worked as a waitress, and men with too smooth smiles were all in a day's work. "Can I help you?" she repeated, her voice just a little crisper.

"Yes, my name is Ben Carleton," he said, his smile fading a little, "and I am here with a party of six. We'll be here for two weeks."

"How many tents do you have?" she asked, quickly reviewing a mental map of the campground, trying to decide where to send them.

"Three and a kitchen tent."

He had on the kind of mirrored sunglasses that April disliked. When she looked at his face, instead of seeing his expression , she only saw her own. Her dark curly hair was swept off her lightly tanned face by two gold barrettes, a style that was not only practical, but also emphasized the fragility of her finely etched cheekbones and the brightness of her blue eyes. A white turtleneck peered out from under her green uniform shirt, and tiny gold earrings were her only jewelry.

Although she had once been rather vain, April was no longer, and she did not spend any time admiring herself in the mirrored sunglasses. She took the map that Faith had given the man. "You certainly can take any campsites that you want, but with so many of you it would probably take you several hours to decide."

He suddenly laughed. "Oh, it certainly would. No, we'd probably spend the whole *day* in negotiations. We're all lawyers from New York City."

April smiled politely, a little surprised. It seemed odd that a group like that would be coming here for so long. They could probably afford to take any sort of vacation; why were they camping? Well, perhaps, they just liked the out-of-doors. It certainly wasn't any of her business.

"Why don't you go up to campsites fifty-three, fifty-four, and fifty-five?" As April pointed them out on the map, the man let his arm rest against hers. She stepped away discreetly. "You are on the water and the three campsites run together so it's a good area for groups." The Frank Lake campground was heavily wooded, and most of the campsites were each set in their own tiny clearing so that the trees hid each family from other people's tents. The staff was always glad to get fifty-three, fifty-four, and fifty-five filled. Most people didn't want them; they were too close together for three individual families.

"It looks good," the man responded. "I am sure that we'll like them."

"Did Faith give you a copy of the rules?" April asked.

"If this pretty lady is Faith"—the man gave the girl

inside the registration hut a smile that made her blush—
"then she certainly did."

"Then I hope that you enjoy your stay," April said
politely, thinking that there was a chance that some of
these big-city lawyers would get bored. Lake Placid, an
hour away, was the closest town with any entertain-
ment. During the ski season or the height of the summer it was a lively town, but the middle of May was a
quiet time. "I'll stop by later and see if things are all
right."

The man thanked her and turned toward his car,
then stopped. From the breast pocket of his corduroy
sport coat, he drew a piece of white paper. "Here is a
list of our names and the phone number of our law
firm."

April couldn't think why the park staff would want
such a list, but she took it and, barely glancing at the
neatly typed list, handed it to Faith.

"What should I do with this?" the girl asked as the
cars' engines started and the vehicles pulled away.

"I don't know," April answered. "Tack it to the
wall." The inside wall of the small registration hut
tended to be a collection of odd papers that no one was
quite sure what to do with. At the end of the summer
April just pulled everything down and threw it all out,
but the campers seemed to feel better if their lists and
notes were posted somewhere.

"Look, April," Faith exclaimed, apparently having
read through the list. "There's a man named Ramsey
on the list. Isn't that your last name?"

April was so unusual a first name that people working in the park never had to pay much attention to her
last name. That was fine with her. She had never felt
entirely right about keeping Ramsey. Once she had

thought about going back to her maiden name, but few of her new acquaintances had realized that she had been married, and she didn't think that she could stand to explain. And after all that had happened, she did not feel like April Peters anymore.

"Maybe this Ramsey is a relative of yours," Faith continued.

"I doubt it. It's a common enough name," April replied lightly, not wanting to explain that Ramsey was her husband's name, not hers.

"Even so, this will give us an excuse to go up and meet them," Faith said, turning to tack the paper to the wall. "There were some awfully good-looking men in those cars, and we can go up and find out if you are related to this Christopher D. Ramsey the Third."

April stopped dead. The scene before her stood out in bright relief, each detail sharp and clear. The scarlet impatiens bordering the gray concrete walk leading up to the stone cabin, the dark green door and shutters, the weathered picnic table sitting on the little mossy lawn, the spruce flagpole—a scene that April had looked at every day for a year, a scene that now seemed entirely unfamiliar.

Christopher D. Ramsey III. No, surely not. It couldn't be him, Not her Christopher. What would he be doing here with this group? That man, Ben Carleton, had said that they were all from New York. Why would Christopher be working in New York and not for his father's firm in Virginia?

But of course it was him. April shook her head and started up the shaded walk to the cabin. It had to be. There might be other Christopher Ramseys, but surely no other young lawyer named Christopher D. Ramsey III.

What an irony. He had tried so hard to find her once. Her minister had written her, begging that she let Christopher know where she was, and she had always written back "Tell him that I am all right, but don't tell him where I am." And now, long after he had quit trying, probably long after he cared, he would stumble on her.

April pushed open the rough plank door, and Mike McKenna glanced up from his cluttered desk. "Did you—April, are you all right?" His voice was suddenly concerned.

"Christopher's here."

During the long quiet winter, when there had been just the two of them, their solitude interrupted only by an occasional snowmobile or cross-country skier, Mike had come to seem like the father April had never known. So he now knew all about her, what she had been like at eighteen when she first met Christopher Ramsey, and everything that had happened after.

April had grown up in a small town in central Virginia. It was an old town, far enough from any city that it had not been taken over by housing developments and shopping centers. Change was slow there. Many of the names listed on the monument to the men killed in the Civil War could still be found on the rolls of the town's civic associations. It was a stable community, each person having his place.

During the last years she had lived there, April had had her little niche too. She had been the most popular girl in the local high school; everyone knew that. She had been Homecoming Queen and head cheerleader. She was never without a date on Saturday night, and she could go for three weeks without wearing the same skirt and sweater twice. She was lively, bright, and pretty, and the only thing that had seemed important to her was that people like her.

She had never had to cook a meal or clean the little house she and her mother shared. She had never had a part-time job even though the widow's pension that they lived on was hardly large. She never read the front page of the newspaper; she barely knew who the governor of Virginia was. She did get excellent grades, but she studied only because she would have been embarrassed to have done poorly. It didn't occur to her that someday she might need to know these things.

April now realized that she had been like that because her mother had wanted her to be. Mrs. Peters had wanted a popular, carefree daughter, and she had made sure that April had nothing more to worry about than what cheers to do at the weekly pep rallies. That April was so very unprepared to deal with an adult's responsibilities had to be, in part, blamed on her mother.

Much of what had happened that spring was also her mother's responsibility. Even April could understand that now, and certainly at the time, the Ramseys, Christopher's family, had blamed Mrs. Peters, seeing her as a social-climbing widow, out to get her daughter well married.

However much she now disapproved of what her mother had done, April knew that she had meant well. Mrs. Peters had wanted to see her girl comfortably settled, and she had only known one way to be sure of that. It had never occurred to her that April could have a career, that April could take care of herself.

Mrs. Peters had kept a tight rein on her pretty daughter. April wasn't allowed to go steady, and her curfew was the earliest of any girl in school. Boys never parked on country lanes with her or took her to drive-in movies unless they wanted to see the movie. They all knew that April was not the sort of girl to be fondled in the backseat of a car. But she was lively and fun, and her mother's strictness never kept her from having more dates than any other girl in school.

But suddenly in the spring of April's senior year, Mrs. Peters had dropped all the restrictions. Christopher Ramsey was home on spring break from his senior year at the University of Virginia. A little bored, he had asked April out to dinner. It had been a Monday night, and April had automatically refused; she was never allowed to date during the week. But to her surprise her mother had told her to call him back—she was also never permitted to call boys—and accept.

They had a wonderful time. Christopher was amused by April; she was so fresh and unaffected. April found him fascinating. Tall, with hair darker than her own and eyes of a startling green, he was assured and confident. His manner was relaxed and direct, without the nervousness of the high school boys she usually dated.

Mrs. Peters had let them go out every night that week. For the first time in her life April had no curfew, and she didn't have to tell her mother where she was. Christopher could pick her up after school, and she could stay out with him until two, even three, in the morning. Her mother would ask no questions. "He's a gentleman," Mrs. Ramsey kept saying. "You can trust him."

Although gentleman was not a word Christopher would have ever used—he would have shrugged the label off as somehow un-American—he was one in many respects. The Ramseys were from an old southern family, and Christopher had been raised in a more courteous tradition than most American boys. He called April's mother "ma'am," and when he spoke of April to people who did not know her, he referred to her as "Miss Peters." He stood up when she came into the room, touched the back of her chair when she sat down, and laughed at her when she popped out of his car without waiting for him to come around and open her door. Because these manners were automatic to him, they seemed effortless, never stilted or awkward. And his gestures appealed to April's girlish romanticism.

The boys April had dated before Christopher were just that: boys—skinny, awkward, all elbows and embarrassment. But the difference between eighteen and twenty-two is considerable in the male. Christopher was a man. Instead of dangling arms and sharp joints, he had broad shoulders and firm muscles across his back and arms. He was comfortable with his height, moving easily, attractively. Although April was not experienced enough to put the right words on her response to him, she found him enormously exciting. All she knew was that sometimes when she looked at him, she almost felt faint.

And she trusted him, just as her mother had told her to. Having never gone steady, April did not have the kind of experience that other girls had: the knowledge of just when to say no, of where a boy may touch you and where he may not. Other girls had heard all the lines and learned to ignore all the encouragements, but April had not, and during those soft spring evenings Christopher, twenty-two and experienced, had started to show her the kind of pleasure that her body could give.

And finally, on Saturday of that glorious week, they

had come back to the Peters's house after a basketball game. Christopher had watched her cheer, and she wanted to change out of her cheerleading uniform. Surprisingly the house had been dark and empty. April found a note from her mother, saying that she had gone to visit her cousin in Richmond and would spend the night with her so that they could go to church together in the morning.

Mrs. Peters had done nothing like that before, but April, bright and laughing, happy to be with Christopher, hadn't given it any thought. She had run upstairs and quickly showered. She had almost finished dressing and was just drawing on her blouse when Christopher had, without knocking, opened the door and walked into her room.

Try as she might, she could not forget that night. She had gasped when he had appeared, and she had quickly pulled her blouse around her. "No, April," he had said softly. "I just want to see you." He had come over to her and gently, his eyes holding her gaze, keeping her mesmerized, loosened her grip on the pale blue cloth. The blouse had fallen open, revealing her young, soft shape, still flushed with the water's warmth.

For a moment he had not touched her, a moment that reassured her, that stilled any fears. Then, wordlessly, he had reached up and just touched her neck, lightly smoothing the skin along her shoulders, and, without her quite realizing it, eased her blouse down her arms until it had slipped to the floor, a pool of blue on the cream-colored carpet of her room.

He had pulled her to him, and his hands, warm and strong, had caressed the soft curves of her waist and back. He had held her tightly, and the crisp lace of her bra and the buttons of his shirt had scraped against her skin. His kiss was deep, more demanding than ever, and April had hardly noticed when the clasp of her bra was undone. Timidly she had slipped her hand between their bodies, her fingers hovering at the buttons of his shirt. One button had seemed to undo itself; her hand burned against the warmth of his chest. And as he had shrugged off his own shirt he had eased her back onto the bed, his body pushing hers against the quilt, trapping her, pinioning.

Why hadn't she stopped him? This was a question she had pondered for many, many sleepless nights. Of course she was aroused at first, but April had plenty of self-discipline, and furthermore, between fear, surprise, and virginal discomfort, she ultimately got very little pleasure from his attentions. But part of the reason why she hadn't resisted was simply that it had been *his* attentions. Although she really did not know him very well, April was completely infatuated with Christopher, and knowing that it was she bringing the flicker to his green eyes was tantalizing. His intensity, his pleasure, his complete absorption in her, were simply irresistible.

And there was also a great deal of ignorance behind her behavior that night. Although they were alone in her bedroom, although her blouse was off and his hands and lips were caressing her creamy flesh, April did not at first understand that this moment was very different from all the other times Christopher had taken her in his arms. Before, he had always released her, and easing her hands from around his neck, he would kiss them and say, "It's time to get you home." And even when Christopher pressed her down on the bed, April didn't fully realize that it was not likely that this evening would end in the same way.

When she finally understood that this time was different, when Christopher's breathing changed, when his hands roved over her body, brushing aside her skirt, urging her to touch him. when he made no effort, as he had always done before, to hide from her the signs of his passion, when she was nearly frightened and wanted to pull away, April somehow thought that it was now too late to stop him. That was the impression that her mother had given her: almost as if men were brutish creatures, incapable of self-control or restraint.

Of course, April now knew what a foolish, ignorant, even insulting, picture of men this was. She now knew that Christopher would have never forced himself on her or any other woman if he thought that she was unwilling. Perhaps she would have had to ask twice, but if she had meant it, he would have stopped, no matter how difficult pulling away from her might have been.

And April now resolved that if she ever had a daughter to raise, she wouldn't just worry about her reputation. She would try to make sure that the girl had some sense too.

So Saturday night Christopher Ramsey had changed April's life forever, but as classes at the University of Virginia had started on Monday, he had to return to Charlottesville on Sunday. April, so stricken with guilt, so conscious of having done something very wrong, had almost been relieved. She did not know how she could face him again. Yet, as soon as he was gone, she had missed him terribly.

As inexperienced as April had been, she was not completely ignorant, and she had not been surprised when a few weeks later she had suspected that she was pregnant. What had surprised her was her mother's response. Mrs. Peters had made only the slightest pretense at being shocked or angry. Unbeknown to April, she had gone straight to the Ramsey family.

The Ramseys were important people. Mr. Ramsey's grandfather had founded what was now the town's largest law firm, and as senior partner of it, Christopher's father was nearly wealthy. Mrs. Ramsey spent her days with the country club set, playing tennis, raising funds for charity, dressing beautifully. They didn't want their only son to marry down, and they had first offered Mrs. Ramsey money.

But that had not been what she wanted for her daughter, and Mrs. Peters wrote Christopher, emphasizing that April had no father and that to take advantage of a girl in such a position was nearly criminal.

And so, without quite understanding how it all happened, April had found herself, the week after her high school graduation, watching Christopher's strong brown fingers slip a wide gold band onto her left hand.

He was starting law school in the fall, and they had taken an apartment in Charlottesville at the University of Virginia. April had been relieved to be leaving her hometown; married or not, she was still deeply ashamed, and she was tired of having people stare at her, sick of the sudden hush that fell whenever she walked into a room.

The first few months of her pregnancy had been difficult for her, and by the time she had finally stopped feeling sick, Christopher had started law school. He was busy, spending his days in classes and his evenings in the library studying. April couldn't help thinking about the year before, when she had been made Homecoming Queen, when she had been the center of so much attention and affection. Now she was a lonely, pregnant housewife.

But gradually thoughts of the baby began to fill the empty spaces in April's life. Her pregnancy had stopped seeming like a punishment and had become a matter of joy. She already loved her baby dearly and soon realized that, in part, she loved it because it was Christopher's too.

For she had quickly come to love her husband. When she had met him in the spring, he had just seemed excitingly adult, different from all the boys in her high school. When they married, they had hardly known each other. But living with him, seeing him every day, she saw the diligence, the decency, which he concealed under his casual manner. She sometimes felt like there were two of him: the fun-loving, relaxed Chris, always ready to laugh, and the Christopher who felt things deeply and seriously, but always hid those feelings from the outside world.

And she was clearly a part of the outside world. She seemed to arouse none of those serious feelings. He had never gotten angry with her. He had never been impatient with her queasiness or irritated with her first fumblings at cooking and cleaning. He had smiled politely at the little sweater she had knit for the baby. He had told her to decorate the nursery however she liked, and then told her what she had done was very attractive. This was a third Christopher, a new Christopher: young Mr. Ramsey, formal, polite, considerate, but uninvolved.

He didn't love her. She was a responsibility, a duty. He was fond of her, she knew that, and occasionally her enthusiasm, her rapture over a pair of tiny baby shoes, would make him smile, but he didn't think of her as a wife, a partner, a friend.

Only at night had it been any different. Wordlessly,

under the cover of darkness, Christopher would take
her in his arms, clearly delighting in her company at
those moments even if at no others. He was patient
with her and generous, willing to slowly teach an inexperienced girl about the splendors of physical love.
Even as her body changed, her waist thickening, he still
thought her beautiful. When the autumn grew cold,
the leafless trees black lines against a gray sky, he
would still slip his arms around her even if only to hold
her nestled to him as they slept.

Those nights gave her hope that once the baby came
the two of them could touch something deeper in him,
other than duty and desire. She wanted him to love her.

But the baby came too early. One gray November
morning, April had not felt quite right, and driving herself to the doctor's, she had had her first labor pain.
The baby's heartbeat proved dangerously low, and the
obstetrician had ordered an emergency cesarean.

His nurse had called the law school, trying to find
Christopher, but by the time one of the secretaries
thought to look in the library for him, the operation
was over. April was terribly ill with an allergic reaction
to the anesthetic, and the baby was lying in an incuba-
tor without much chance of surviving.

She remembered very little of the next few weeks,
just the overwhelming impression that no one cared
that her baby had died. She knew that Christopher's
parents were almost relieved and that her own mother
was not very deeply moved. What Christopher felt she
could not tell. He had been so careful: polite and formal. Sometimes she had thought he was trying to make
things easier for her. Other times she had concluded
that he too just must not care.

As she lay in the hospital bed, grieving for her little

daughter, April gave no thought to the future. Groggy from the medication, overcome with sadness, she lived in the moment, thinking nothing about what would happen when she left the hospital—until she realized that others were making plans for her.

One afternoon, as she woke up from a drugged sleep, she heard her father-in-law's voice, speaking quietly just outside her door.

The Ramseys were far too proper to neglect visiting her in the hospital. They sent her flowers, nightgowns, and books. She knew that if she hadn't been married to their son they would have liked her in a mild way. All the family discussions of her began "Of course, she is a lovely girl," and only the tone of their voices implied that she was not at all what they had had in mind for their only son.

That afternoon the Ramseys had come to the hospital with their closest friends, and the two men were speaking in the hall.

"What's to happen now?" the other man was asking.

"Well, nothing until the girl is well of course," Mr. Ramsey had replied. "I've not spoken to Christopher at any length, but certainly his mother and I are hoping for an annulment."

"An annulment? Is that possible?"

"We don't know yet. It will take pulling a lot of strings, but we would hate to see Christopher having to spend the rest of his life explaining a divorce."

"What does he say?"

"Well, his first concern is for the girl, just as it should be." April heard a chilling note of insincerity creep into those last words. "But if she is well provided for, as of course she will be, I think he will be reasonable."

All afternoon April lay against her white pillow, thinking of what had been said. They had married for the sake of the child; now there was no longer a child. Was there any reason to stay married?

April did not doubt Christopher's integrity. She knew that if she said "I want to stay your wife. Please don't make me go," nothing his father could say or do would make any difference to him. It might take him a moment, his eyes might widen in surprise, but he would say "Of course, my dear, I wouldn't think of anything else."

But why should he be bound to her for the rest of his life? He did not love her; it was hardly his fault that she loved him. Why should her love, her desire to continue the marriage, shackle him?

Later that afternoon, as she heard Christopher's voice speaking to the nurse, asking if she was awake, she had no idea what she would say to him, if anything.

In a moment he appeared at her bedside. He bent over and his lips brushed against her cheek. "How are you feeling, my dear?"

To this day April thought that his calling her "my dear" had given her the strength to leave Charlottesville. "My dear" was what his father invariably called his mother, and theirs was not a warm or affectionate marriage. They were quite compatible, but the only strong emotion they shared was their love for their son. April knew that the life would freeze out of her in such a chilled environment, so to have Christopher unthinkingly fall into his parents' cool formulas was more than she could stand.

She then realized that leaving would not be pure self-sacrifice, her sacrificing her happiness for him. She would never be happy in their marriage unless he loved her, and she honestly believed that without the baby there was no chance that he ever would.

Of course, she had not planned on going without talking to him. But she kept putting it off, not knowing what to say. If she said the truth, "I am leaving because I love you," he would never let her go. If she lied and said that she just didn't want to be married anymore, they would all sit around the mahogany table in his mother's blue-gray dining room, sipping sherry and discussing money. That she couldn't stand.

She put off talking to him until she was released from the hospital. But when on their first night back he had said, "You need your rest; I will sleep in the study," she had known that she wouldn't be able to talk to him. She could only have started such a conversation in the dark.

One of the nurses in the hospital had been from Buffalo, New York, and with no better reason than that, April had bought a bus ticket for Buffalo, a medium-size city on the shores of Lake Erie. She took half of the money in the checking account she shared with Christopher. It wasn't much, only a month's housekeeping money. She left him a note, promising that she would pay the money back and asking him not to find her. She said that he could reach her through her hometown minister and, knowing that he would track her down otherwise, promised that she would get in touch with him if she ever really needed help.

She got a job waiting tables, and the easy, friendly manner that had made her so popular in high school now brought in excellent tips. By the next fall April was able to start attending the inexpensive local community college. Although thirty hours a week of waitressing left her no time for the kind of fun she had once expected to have in college, she was almost certainly studying harder and learning more than if she had gone off to a Virginia college with all her friends as she had once planned.

Surprisingly she became a forestry major, drawn by the quiet peace of the wilderness. Her life so far now seemed to her as if it had been full of noise: all the football games in high school, the clattering dishes in the restaurant. And the natural world seemed so straightforward—so unlike the devious, petty adult world of her mother and the Ramseys.

Christopher had tried to get Reverend Clement to give him her address, and he had forwarded letters that she returned unopened and checks that she sent back uncashed. She had wanted to make it on her own. Even more she had wanted to stop loving him. She felt her only chance to do that was to have no contact with him, and the last communication Reverend Clement had forwarded had been the divorce papers.

April had tried to convince herself that the divorce was a good thing. Christopher was free to begin his life again, and now that she was no longer a legal part of the Ramsey family, she could get a scholarship and transfer from the community college to the state university.

The scholarship also had enabled her to take a lower-paying job in the summers. She could work in the state parks as most of the forestry students did. When she earned her degree a year ago, she had gotten one of the coveted positions as a ranger at Frank Lake.

Looking back, April had often wondered if she had been wrong to leave Charlottesville so impulsively. Perhaps she should have stayed and tried to make the marriage work; she certainly shouldn't have left without talking to Christopher. She knew that now, but she had been so young then; she hadn't known anything about being a wife. She hadn't even known how to start working on her marriage. If she were in such a situation today, she would have never left, but the past six years had given her a maturity and confidence that she simply hadn't had at nineteen.

It seemed so sad. She felt as if she had herself been a baby, given a fragile, crystal trinket to play with. It was not the child's fault when the ornament broke, but the broken pieces were still terribly, terribly sad.

Chapter Two

April shook herself, trying to break the grip of these memories. Mike was still looking at her with concern, and she moved across the room to sit near him.

Mike had been a ranger at Frank Lake for almost thirty years, and although the cabin belonged to the state, he had done a lot during the long winters to make it a home. The interior was paneled with split logs of white pine that had yellowed to a gentle glow. He had used the same wood to build the furniture, the table he was now sitting at, the rockers sprinkled around the two stone fireplaces, the bookcases, and the little bunks cleverly built into the walls. The floors were covered with thick, braided rugs that his sister had made.

Mike's bedroom, the kitchen, and a small bathroom were off one end of the room, getting their heat from one fireplace, while April's room and the bathroom Mike had built for her were behind the other fireplace.

It was a cozy little cabin. They now had electricity, but Mike had lived there so long without it that he didn't use it too much. The stove and hot water heaters were gas, and both he and April much preferred the soft light of the gas lamps to electricity's harsh glare. Once last winter they had lost the electricity for four days, and they had hardly noticed.

She looked at the familiar outlines of Mike's lean, craggy face. She knew that he didn't believe in divorce; in his mind she and Christopher were still married.

"So he's finally come." Mike pulled his pipe from between his teeth and peered into the bowl. "He's been long enough about it."

"No." April shook her head. "He was with that group. He doesn't know that I am here."

Mike raised his eyebrows and looked at her across the pipe. She had unfastened one of her barrettes and let a screen of dusky curls tumble across her face. "Now, you wouldn't be planning on hiding in here until he's gone?"

April fastened her hair and gave a slight laugh, acknowledging how revealing her gesture had been. "They'll be here for two weeks."

"Well, I know that you aren't asking for any advice, but it seems to me," he said in his slow, lazy way, "that you ought to get up there right now and show yourself off. You aren't going to have a moment's peace until that first sighting's over."

April smiled at him. "The question is how much peace am I going to have afterward?" She could be honest with Mike. She simply did not know how she felt about Christopher.

"We just can't know that, now, can we?" Mike returned.

April hopped up and dropped a kiss on his graying hair. "What would I do without you?"

"Probably chop a lot more wood than you do now," he answered blandly. "Now, get along with you. I've got work to do." He put his pipe back between his teeth and picked up a pen.

Despite her resolve to get this over with as soon as possible, April decided to walk up to campsite fifty-three. If she drove the park's pickup, she'd be there in a matter of moments; walking would delay things for at least ten minutes.

A narrow sandy road wound its way through the campground. The trail snaked through the forest, a pale brown ribbon between the dense, dark tangle of ferns, mountain holly, and wild raspberry bushes, whose fruit would delight the campers during the summer months. The towering firs hugged the road closely, and only a thin band of bright blue sky lit the road. To the right the wilderness went on, receding into darkness, while to the left the glitter of the sun sparkling off the lake marked the forest's end.

There were hardly as many campers as there would be after Memorial Day, but here and there April saw people settling in, collecting firewood, putting up tents of pale orange, ice-blue, and every shade of green, unfolding propane stoves, filling gas lanterns. April loved the way each little shady campsite became so different: Some were immaculately tidy, others a cheerful tangle of swimming suits, fuel cans, and lawn chairs. The backpackers' sites always looked so sparse, their tiny tents almost smaller than the picnic tables, the entrance to their sites unguarded by a car.

As she approached the curve in the road before campsite fifty-three, she could hear voices, a woman saying, "Ben, where is the tomato juice?" Then a man spoke, "Does anyone know where this pole goes?" Another woman's voice answered him, "Go ask Chris. He should know."

April stopped, almost feeling faint. "Go ask Chris." It was said so casually, so easily. These people must speak to him nearly every day; they were his friends. April had trouble imagining that there were people who saw Christopher, spoke to him, worked with him, and then went on with their own lives, perhaps not noticing what an extraordinary, absolutely unique person he was. She had cherished every memory of him during these six long years. Her heart had quickened just when she got a letter from him. She would gaze at the white envelope that she would not allow herself to open. "Mrs. Christopher Ramsey" would flow across the front in his bold handwriting, and then embossed in black letters on the envelope's flap would be his name so similar to hers. But the whole time that she had been fascinated by these envelopes, staring at them like a schoolgirl with a crush on a rock star, other people had actually been with him, talking to him, laughing with him, perhaps even loving him.

How foolish she had been, April thought, as she slowly started to walk up the sandy trail again. During these past six years she had always thought of Christopher as if he had been suspended in time, as if he had stayed the young law student she had left in Charlottesville. But just as she had changed, surely he had too. He would be twenty-nine now and thinking about whether or not his firm would make him a partner. He would have made friends, relationships; he might even be married.

Married! What if he were married? It wouldn't be unlikely, she had to tell herself; he was unattached, wealthy, and, at least in April's opinion, wonderful in every way. What woman wouldn't want him? He could easily be married. Either of those women's voices might well belong to his wife.

She tried to convince herself that that would be for the best. Things would be awkward for a moment, but then everything would be so clear-cut. The second Mrs. Ramsey would be a little curious; April would tell them what she had been doing; they would tell her how they met, and that would be that.

It sounded awful.

Through the trees April heard a little whimper. It was tentative at first, then it broke out into the loud, gasping squall of a baby protesting something amiss in his little world. For a moment her eyes widened and her heart stopped. What if that was Christopher's baby? She knew that she simply could not face what would be his second child.

But before she could decide what she should do, she realized that the baby's cries came from campsite forty-nine, not farther around the bend at fifty-three. Trying to regain her composure, she decided to stop and see if these people needed some help.

Threading her way around the battered red station wagon, she saw that the campsite had been taken by a young couple. The girl was trying to soothe the baby with animal crackers while her husband was struggling with the tent, an old, heavy, green canvas affair, much harder to put up than the new nylon ones and much more likely to leak.

April introduced herself and offered to help.

"Oh, thank you," the woman said, switching the baby to her other hip. "We've never been camping before. We borrowed this tent and I am not sure Joe knows how to put it up."

The baby had calmed and was gurgling happily. He stuck out a chubby fist and offered April the rest of his cracker, a now headless giraffe. She longed to ask the woman if she could hold him, but it made a great deal more sense for the woman to keep the baby and for April to help the man with the tent.

Although she and her mother had never camped, April had learned a lot about tents from working in a campground. She could now tell the kind of tent one was just by looking at the poles. This was an old-fashioned umbrella tent, with an awkward, inside center pole that held it up. You had to take the pole and crawl inside the dusty canvas and hoist the dark tent around you. But once that was done, the rest was not too hard.

When the tent was up, April looked around at their site and glanced in their car. They didn't have much equipment. She asked if they had brought a camping stove.

"A stove?" the man said blankly. "We were going to cook over the fire." Each campsite was equipped with a picnic table and a small stone fireplace.

"That will be fine." April smiled reassuringly, hoping that it would be. Some experienced campers did cook just on fires, but particularly in the morning many people were glad of their little stoves. Building a fire, getting it hot enough to boil the icy water, took longer than most people cared to wait for their first cup of coffee.

"Let me know if you need some more help," she said as they chorused their thanks.

Helping them, being able to master their tent so quickly, gave April a needed boost of confidence. Whatever was to follow, she was good at her job. She had a right to be proud of herself, of what she had accomplished by herself, and whatever Christopher thought of the girl that had left him, he would have to see that the woman she had become was quite a bit different.

The three campsites were the last ones in the campground. The trail just stopped at the tip of the large nearly triangular-shaped clearing. Two sides of the clearing were rimmed with trees while the third was the curving line of the lakeshore. There wasn't a beach here, just a short, rocky drop down to the water, but opening out onto the lake like this made these campsites the only really sunny ones in the park.

April could see people moving about the campsite, but she did not see Christopher. Ben Carleton, the sandy-haired man she had spoken to earlier, was helping a small brown-haired woman rummage through boxes of food. Another woman with long black hair was draped elegantly in a lounge chair. A second man, a lean, almost rangy blonde, was working on one of the tents.

They had good equipment. The three tents were nearly new, made of lightweight pale green nylon with large windows that zipped open from the inside. Around one of the picnic tables they had pitched a kitchen tent, floorless with walls of mesh that protected food from rain and insects. Some folded lounge chairs leaned against one of the cars, and the boat was loaded with lanterns, ice chests, a camping stove, and a small barbecue grill. They would be very comfortable.

As April walked past the three cars, parked in a careful line, Ben Carleton looked up and, lifting an arm in greeting, walked over to meet her.

"Hello," April said. "I just came up to be sure everything was all right."

"Things are fine." He smiled. "We've got two guys who know what they are doing."

"Well, that helps," April agreed, wondering if one of them was Christopher. She shook herself and tried to concentrate on talking to Ben. She didn't want Christopher, wherever he was, to first see her peering about like a nervous rabbit.

"Hello, I'm Beth Market," the brown-haired woman had come over. She was small and almost pretty, with lively brown eyes. "And I guess you've met Ben." She gestured toward the sandy-haired man next to her and then peered at the nameplate pinned to April's shirt. "Ben said that you suggested these campsites, Miss Ramsey. They are just perfect for us."

And as she automatically murmured, "Call me April," she saw the woman's expression change, a startled look coming over her face. Did the name mean something to her?

But before either of them could say anything more, Ben suddenly called out, "Hey, Ramsey, you've got a clanswoman out here. A girl with the same last name."

And through the trees April heard a laugh, still familiar after six years, and a voice saying, "Great. I could use some new relatives."

At first he was just a dark shape in the trees, then a figure carrying an armload of wood, and finally, as he stepped into the light of the clearing, Christopher, her husband.

She had not forgotten what he looked like. But she had forgotten what it was like to look at him. And just as she had felt at eighteen, so she felt now, clearly aware, absolutely certain that she was looking at a man.

He was in blue jeans, fitting so closely to his long legs that it was hard to imagine that the wide leather belt was anything but habit. He was wearing a flannel shirt, a dark black-watch plaid of navy and hunter green; it was open at the throat and rolled up at the sleeves. He looked tall and fit, with the clean, healthy look of a vigorous American male, seeming more like another forest ranger than a city attorney.

April turned toward him, thinking it unfair to be coy, and, in a moment that seemed to last an eternity, waited as his eyes got used to the sunlight.

The wood dropped with a crash, the logs banging against each other and then rolling across the sandy earth. Everyone turned curiously to look at him. Only Beth Market was still looking at April.

With a poise April never thought that she had, she walked calmly across the clearing to where he was standing at the edge of the trees. "Hello, Christopher," she said. "It's been a long time." She extended her hand.

It seemed silly to be shaking her husband's hand, but April couldn't think of anything else to do.

Automatically his hand met hers, but suddenly the casual touch convulsed into a tight grip that made her wince.

She looked up at his face, almost surprised that it was real, that his eyes had blinked with surprise, that there was a pulse beating in his throat. This man was alive: He had been a waxen memory for so long. And he looked much the same. His hair was even darker; he was probably in the sun less now, but his eyes were the same rich, dark green.

He was shaking his head slowly, disbelieving. "April, is that you?" he breathed. "What on earth are you doing here?"

Very conscious that everyone was looking at them, April tried to speak evenly. "I am one of the forest rangers on staff here." His eyes started to darken, but when she moved to pull her hand away, his opened readily, letting hers drop.

"Hey." Ben had come over toward them. "So you two *do* know each other."

April turned, suddenly shy. What was she going to say to all these people? How was she going to explain everything? But she was going to have to do the talking; Christopher was riveted, staring at her in disbelief, unconscious of Ben's question.

Before the silence became awkward, it was broken by Beth Market's soft voice. "I think that April is Chris's ex-wife. Am I right?"

April nodded.

The man over by the tent, the blond one whose name April didn't know, looked a little surprised. "Gee, Chris, I didn't know that you'd been married."

"Oh, yes," the black-haired girl said, "it's the deep sorrow in his past that makes him so silent and mysterious." Her voice was light and mocking. April glanced at her; her face had a cool and sophisticated beauty that seemed very out of place in the forest.

So the women knew that he had been married; the men had not. That seemed typical.

Christopher had knelt down, picking up the wood that he had dropped. That used to infuriate her—the way that he would turn to some little task, sharpening a pencil, folding up a newspaper, when she thought that he should be moved: upset, unhappy, or angry. She finally came to understand that these little chores were proof of his feelings: he was struggling to control his emotions, unconsciously buying himself some time.

And when he straightened, the wood secure under his arm, his face was still, his eyes expressionless.

"Yes, Steve," he said, walking over to the fire circle, ignoring the girl's remark. "April and I were married for less than a year, and we haven't seen each other since then. It's been six years."

"Six years!" Ben whistled, looking at April interestedly. "She must have been twelve when you married her, Chris. I think you can get disbarred for that."

"I was eighteen," April said, desperate to say something, not wanting to stand there and be spoken about like a small child. "Just out of high school."

"Just out of high school?" The black-haired woman tossed her long hair over her shoulder. "And only married for a year? Well, whatever happened to the baby?"

April was suddenly furious with this cool creature, furious at her insulting insinuation, even more furious because she was right. Not daring to look at Christopher, she said bluntly, "Our daughter died a few hours after she was born."

She immediately regretted saying it. Now an awkward silence did fall through the clearing. No one, least of all April, knew what to say.

Once again Beth Market stepped in. "April, it is just lovely to meet you. This is Julia Breeland"—she gestured to the other woman—"and that's Steve Webster over there. Our sixth, Josh Goodhue, is taking a nap."

"Yes," April said, trying hard to sound calm, "you must have left very early to get here so soon." She was very conscious that Christopher had left the fireplace and was watching her. She would have much preferred it to be the other way around so that she could look at him, watch his features, look for changes, for things that had stayed the same.

"Yes, we did," Beth continued, "and we were all about to be very decadent and have Bloody Marys. Can you join us?"

"Yes, it would please us if you could," Christopher added. His voice was deeper than she remembered, but still iced with the polite chill he had learned at his parents' country club. "It would please us if you could." People didn't talk like that. It made him sound so distant and unapproachable. Was he always like that? What had happened to the life and energy she had so admired? Was this why Julia Breeland had called him "silent and mysterious"? Or had the sight of her just momentarily frozen the warm laughter she had heard in the forest?

"No, I'm on duty." April had never been more relieved to have an excuse. She just couldn't sit down and make small talk with four strangers and her husband. "I need to get back."

"I'll walk down with you," Christopher said immediately.

She smiled politely in his direction, not really able to look at him, and spoke again to Beth, who seemed like a nice, generous sort of person. "There's a couple down the road with a small child. They don't have much equipment or experience. It would be nice if you could take them some hot water in the morning."

"We'll be glad to." Beth smiled. "Or at least Steve and Josh will. They are here to fish and plan on getting up at the crack of dawn."

And then suddenly she and Christopher were alone, walking along the narrow trail. She had forgotten how tall he was. The top of her head just came to his shoulder.

They walked silently for a moment, and then just for something to say, April asked, "How are your parents?"

"Very well, thank you," he said in the same formal tone. "I hear that your mother left town."

"Yes, she lives in Richmond now with her cousin."

"Do you get down there much?" His green eyes were watching her with the same distant concern that had chilled her during her bouts of morning sickness.

"About once a year." When April had left Charlottesville, she hadn't given her mother her address, being afraid that she would pass it on to Christopher. And Mrs. Peters, so angry at April for leaving, had at first wanted nothing to do with her. But the minister soon helped them reconcile, and now April wrote her mother polite little notes several times each month. "But it's a pretty long bus trip down to Richmond."

Suddenly Christopher's eyes flashed. "Bus? Good Lord, April, you don't take the bus all the way down to Virginia, do you?"

April faltered. His polite mask had dropped; this was the way he used to talk, straightforward and blunt. This was the Christopher she had first known, and she found it even harder to deal with him than with the polite stranger.

"Well," she ventured, "now that I am out of school, perhaps I can afford to fly."

"Out of school?" He sounded confused. Then he took her arm and steered her into an empty campsite. "We have to talk."

He sat her down at the picnic table. It stood exactly in the center of the clearing so that while the sun filtering through the green trees dappled the rest of the site with little shadows, the table sat in clear light. Christopher sat astride on the bench, facing her, one arm resting along the table. The light bleached the hair on his arm to a soft pale brown.

"Now, start at the beginning," he said. "Where did you go?"

Not "*Why* did you go?" Or "How have you been?" April took her cue from him and began to recite the events of the past six years. It seemed important to him to hear the details, and he would stop her with questions. "What sort of restaurant was it?" "How many hours a week?" "What kind of place did you live in?" But it was only facts, nothing about how she had felt, how lonely she had been, and now how fiercely proud she was of what she had accomplished by herself.

She kept trying to figure out what he was thinking. He had every right to be angry: Leaving without an explanation and refusing to read his letters had been very childish, she now saw. But he didn't seem angry; he almost didn't seem to care. His voice was flat and neutral, cool, almost professional.

But if he didn't care, why were they having this conversation? Why was he so insistent that she tell him each detail of those difficult years? It was almost as if he were her lawyer and she were some client with a case he was not particularly interested in, but for whom he was prepared to do his duty.

And suddenly April couldn't stand it anymore, sitting there, answering his questions like a schoolgirl. She had been married to the man. It might not have been one of the world's greatest marriages or even a very good one, but she had shared a home with him. She had seen him sprawled across the living room sofa with the Sunday paper; she had gotten out of bed before dawn to make him coffee so that he could read a few more cases before class; she had seen him sweaty and exhilarated after an intramural football game; she remembered the feel of his body on hers.

She would not sit here with him questioning her as if

she were his client. She broke off in midsentence and stood up. "I have to get back," she said abruptly.

He did not try to stop her, and she hurried down the trail. In the guise of talking to some campers, she glanced back.

He was standing in the middle of the road, a tall, still figure, his arms folded, watching her leave.

Mike was still sitting at his desk when April returned to the cabin. He looked up, waiting for her to speak, but she hardly knew what to say; she was much more shaken by seeing Christopher than she wanted to admit, even to Mike. So she just shrugged and went to the duty roster that was posted on the wall. She had to lead a nature walk at two, and then—

"So how's that husband of yours?" Mike prodded.

"He seems fine."

"Well, what's he been up to? Was he glad to see you?" Mike's voice was a little impatient.

April sank down in a rocker and stared into the empty fireplace. "Honestly, Mike, I don't know. He was surprised more than anything else. It was awkward with all his friends there, and then when we talked alone for a bit, it was all about me; he didn't say one thing about himself."

"He hasn't gotten himself another wife, has he?" Mike asked suspiciously, clearly quite ready to call the sheriff and have Christopher arrested for bigamy.

"No." April shook her head. "I mean, I don't think so. Surely someone would have said something if he had remarried."

He hadn't been wearing a wedding ring, but then he hadn't worn one when he had been married to her.

Mike tapped a pencil on the desk. "Then, maybe you

ought to take some extra time during these next two weeks and try to get to know him again."

It was April's turn to be suspicious. "What on earth would be the point of that?"

"You never know," Mike replied.

"Now, don't start hoping that something is going to come of him being here," April cautioned. "It was just an accident, and I am simply going to go about my business as usual."

"Well, suit yourself," Mike said and settled back down to work.

Chapter Three

"And what does Smokey the Bear say?" April was kneeling on the beach, one arm around a small dark-haired girl. Several other children gathered around her.

"Only *you* can prevent forest fires," the children chorused.

"That's right. And I want you to remember that while you are here." April stood up, brushing the sand off her jeans. "All right, that ends our nature walk. Does anyone have any more questions?"

Going about business as usual had been even more difficult than she had possibly imagined. Quite surprisingly Christopher, Ben Carleton, and the black-haired girl, Julia Breeland, showed up for the nature walk that April was leading that afternoon. The walk was really designed for children, but April found it hard to tell the simple stories and funny examples that the children enjoyed while Christopher was watching her, his face expressionless and controlled. His friends hadn't made it easier. Julia had seemed contemptuous throughout and Ben, obviously intrigued with April, with the fact that she had been married to Christopher relished asking her legal questions about land acquisitions and scenic easements that the children weren't interested in and she could barely answer.

She guessed from his undisguised interest that it had been Ben's idea to come. Christopher probably then felt as if he had to come too; that it might look odd and strained if he did not, as if he were avoiding April.

Why Julia Breeland had accompanied the two men was no mystery. She clearly had a message to deliver to April, and she delivered it. From the way that she stood next to Christopher, from the casual hand she extended to him for help when they all crossed a little stream, she was telling April that she had staked a claim on Christopher.

In fact, as soon as the walk was over, Julia touched his arm and said, "Shall we take the boat ride now?"

April knew that one of the things that had been drummed into Christopher when he was growing up was that he should never embarrass a lady. Of course, his mother and his grandmother had not counted on him having to deal with ladies quite as aggressive as this one, but still April knew that he would never say to Julia, "Perhaps later. I would like to speak to April now"—even if that was what he wanted.

Although, of course, April simply had no idea if Christopher did indeed want to speak to her.

So instead she found herself walking across the beach with Ben Carleton.

"So you were married to our wealthy friend from Virginia," he said immediately.

"Yes."

"Are you going to tell me all about it?" Without his mirrored sunglasses, Ben's sandy hair and freckles gave him a puckish, almost boyish look.

"Probably not," she replied.

His face fell. "Why not?"

"First of all, it is not really any of your business, and—"

"Oh, sure it is."

April ignored him. "And second, I am on duty and have to go check out some erosion."

"I'll come with you," he returned promptly.

"No, don't."

"Why ever not? I'm heaps of fun."

"I'm sure that you are," April answered patiently. "But—" Suddenly her control slipped for a moment. "Look, don't you think that all this is hard enough on me without having you hound me too?"

He grinned at her, apparently pleased. "Well, that answers one question."

April had immediately regretted saying what she did and refused to ask him what he meant.

He explained anyway. "You have seemed so cool I was beginning to think that seeing your ex-husband again didn't bother you one way or another. Mr. Ramsey, on the other hand, has certainly been wound up tight all day. We're all up there walking on eggshells."

"I'm sorry if I'm spoiling your vacation," April said tightly. "Believe me, it was involuntary."

"Oh," he said, suddenly alert, "would you have gone away if you knew he was coming?"

"I didn't say that," April snapped. "Now, please excuse me." And she hurried toward the trail that followed the shores of the lake.

What *would* she have done if she had known that he was coming? Would she have begged for some time off, or would she have stayed to face him?

April stopped herself; she was never going to make it through these two weeks if she thought about Christopher every moment. He hadn't even been here a day, and already she was completely exhausted from the stress of thinking about him.

Work had its usual calming effect. Erosion, the washing away of the precious topsoil, was something that rangers worried about almost as much as forest fires. For an hour April climbed down gullies and up rocky slopes, fording little streams, checking to be sure that the spring rains had not done any more damage than usual. Gradually she worked her way back toward the lake.

The cool forest, with its dark woodsy scent, was quiet. Occasionally a chipmunk darted up a tree, or a rabbit hopped across the path so quickly that April could only see a flash of its tail. The wind teased through the branches of the trees, and the water lapped up against the rocks that lined the shore.

As she worked along the bank, April became aware of another sound, the dipping of oars into the water. Whatever boat it was must have been coming closer to shore because she gradually started to hear the dull murmur of voices that eventually distinguished themselves into one male and one female. Soon an occasional word floated to her. People didn't realize, she thought, not really listening to them, how voices carry across the water.

"It *is* lovely here," a cool feminine voice sighed.

April lifted her head with a snap. That voice was familiar. She looked to the lake and saw that a small fishing boat had come close to the shore. In it, leaning against several life cushions, trailing one hand in the water, was Julia Breeland, watching Christopher row.

"I know," he said, lifting the oars out of the water,

letting the boat gently drift. "It's hard to believe that we were in the city this morning."

That, April thought, did not sound like a man who was "wound up tight" over seeing his ex-wife again for the first time in six years. The thought promptly depressed her: Maybe Christopher had been on edge, but being alone with Julia had soothed him.

She sighed, about to sink down onto the forest floor when she suddenly stopped herself, realizing that she was eavesdropping. They could not see her standing here in the dark woods; to stay would be inexcusable. But Julia's next words riveted her.

"She's very pretty, you know."

"Who?" Christopher's voice was blank. "Oh, April? Yes, she always was a pretty girl."

"She has such a freshness. I couldn't believe how good she was with the children on that little walk this afternoon."

Now, why was Julia complimenting her? April wondered. The other woman had made it so clear that she wanted Christopher for herself. So why was she praising April to him?

"But I suppose that it isn't surprising," Julia continued. "She's nearly a child herself."

"Does she strike you that way too?" Christopher asked almost eagerly. "She always seemed so young to me. That's the thing I remember the most about her—how young she was. And she just doesn't seem to have changed a bit. Watching her with those children..." His voice trailed off as if he weren't quite sure what his impression was.

"She didn't seem to have a great deal of sophistication, did she?"

Julia's voice was casual, but April suspected that this

was all very carefully planned. This was her ploy—to draw a picture in Christopher's mind of how young and childlike April was.

How clever she was! If she attacked or criticized April overtly, Christopher would feel honor-bound to defend his former wife. Obviously Julia knew him well enough to know that. But how had she guessed that April's age had been such a barrier during their marriage? Even April had not fully realized it until this moment. Had Julia just guessed it on her own, or had Christopher talked to her about it?

Julia's next remark answered that question.

"You never talked about your marriage."

"There's not a great deal to say," he answered. "It was very short."

"Obviously she was pregnant."

There was a brief pause. "Yes."

Julia's voice became teasing. "It was very wicked of you, Christopher, to seduce such a child."

"It was reprehensible in the extreme." April couldn't help noticing his odd word choice: How formal, even stilted, it was. This was how he talked when he had to discuss strong feelings.

Julia noticed as well. "Oh, Chris," she laughed. "I was joking. A man doesn't have to feel like it is all his fault anymore. Surely you don't feel like you ruined or dishonored her." Her voice was lightly sarcastic over the last few words.

"Well, I wouldn't put it like that," Christopher acknowledged, but it seemed clear that that was indeed how he felt.

"That's your southern background creeping through," Julia teased. "Things don't work that way anymore."

"They did in our hometown."

"Where neither of you live anymore," Julia pointed out immediately. "That's not how things work in Manhattan." She paused, her voice suddenly becoming more serious. "As you have every reason to know."

April bit her lip, a little knot forming in her stomach, as she realized what—or *who*—Christopher's reasons for knowing this must be.

"Well," he answered Julia, "the women involved are hardly eighteen."

"I should hope not," Julia said emphatically. "What on earth would a person say to someone that young?"

"Believe me, I do not know." Christopher's voice was weary, as if he had spent many tiring days trying to think of something to say to an eighteen-year-old.

April thought back, remembering the times she had met his law school friends and professors. They were, of course, all older than she, and her old-fashioned upbringing had taught her that a young person should not be forward in a conversation; she should let the older person choose the subject, ask the questions, direct the conversation into the channels that interested him. April's mother had told her that was the polite thing to do. But these people seemed a little inept, asking her when the baby was due, and then staring at her blankly until she would take over, asking them where they were from, finding out about their interests, doing things that she had been taught the more senior person should do. Under her direction, the conversations would go well, but at first, those people must have been wondering what on earth to say to an eighteen-year-old.

Julia's clear voice continued. April could imagine her, leaning against the cushions, flinging her black hair over one shoulder as she spoke. "You shouldn't be blaming yourself, Chris, not in this day and age. Even if you were technically the guilty party in the divorce, you know perfectly well what a legal fiction all that is." A note of passion crept into the cool voice. "I don't know why we can't have more sensible divorce laws."

April was a little taken aback by the intensity in her voice. Was Julia involved in a divorce? But before she could wonder, Christopher spoke. "Actually I divorced her."

"You did?" There was new interest in Julia's voice. "On what grounds?"

"Desertion." His answer was curt.

"She left you! How extraordinary. Why?"

"Pride, I suppose." April was a little surprised that Christopher had answered such a personal question, but his voice was almost dreamy, as if he had forgotten that he was talking to anyone. "I think she sensed that my father would try to buy her off," he continued, musing. "This all happened right after the child died. She'd only been home from the hospital for two days. I had to go to class; I'd missed so much while she was sick. I came back and she was gone. It was—" A tremor of feeling cut into the even voice, and Christopher broke off.

"No," said Julia in flat disbelief. "People just don't get up and leave a marriage without discussing it, without saying something."

"April did."

"How very childish." Julia's voice was curt, condemning.

"You can't blame her," Christopher said gently. "She *was* a child."

April bristled. Since when were eighteen-year-olds

children? Yes, she had been young, but she hadn't been a child. An eighteen-year-old in Virginia could sign contracts, buy beer, and vote—although, April acknowledged ruefully, thinking of herself at eighteen, it had been a good thing for the country that that hadn't been an election year. She would have hardly given much careful consideration to her vote.

Her flash of resentment at Christopher eased under this self-mockery. She was starting to find out how he felt when she left, why he wasn't angry at her. He simply hadn't expected her to be able to behave in a more mature fashion. She guessed that she was glad he wasn't angry or bitter, but she certainly wasn't pleased that this was the reason.

She heard the sounds of the oars being lifted back into the water. "I think we ought to get back," Christopher said. "It looks like rain.'

Throughout what was left of the afternoon and evening April felt guilty about having eavesdropped on this conversation. She had never eavesdropped deliberately before, and she knew that she shouldn't have done it. Nonetheless a part of her was glad that she had. With Julia planning on attaching herself firmly to Christopher, there seemed little chance that April would ever encounter him except in the most awkward situations. She knew she could not endure too many repetitions of the nature walk this afternoon, with Christopher watching her inscrutably. Now at least she knew what he had been thinking: how young she had seemed.

But how could he think that she hadn't changed? Of course, many people, at first glance, thought that she was a great deal younger than she actually was. But Christopher knew perfectly well how old she was. If she had been four years younger than him when he was twenty-two, then there was an excellent chance that she was still four years younger now that he was twenty-nine. Surely he couldn't think that she was still the same nearly mindless cheerleader that she had been at eighteen?

Hadn't what she had said this morning made any impression on him? Surely he understood that a person doesn't put herself through school by waiting tables without growing up a lot. If he thought for one minute, he'd have to realize that she had changed. But he had just told Julia that he didn't think she had changed at all. How could he be so stupid and blind?

That was unfair, April immediately checked herself, giving him the benefit of the doubt. He had not been at Frank Lake even twelve hours; he must still be dazed from seeing her again. Of course, he was stunned; in fact, he was such a private person that he probably never would have confided in Julia as he did this afternoon unless he was still reeling a little. He certainly hadn't had time to sit down and carefully consider what everything meant.

She tried to be hopeful. He couldn't be here for two weeks and not see that she had become a competent adult, a forest ranger. Maybe there would be some calamity, a forest fire or something, where she could prove herself, she fantasized, momentarily willing to sacrifice the entire Forest Preserve if it would make Christopher respect her.

Perhaps nature was just trying to save itself from April's fiery thoughts, but, as the afternoon turned into evening, it did start to rain. It just sprinkled at first, but as she was washing the dinner dishes she could hear it coming down in a light, but steady rhythm.

Christopher and his friends would be comfortable and dry in their spacious kitchen tent, she thought. The gas lanterns would throw a gentle light that would spill out from the tent, warming the edges of wet night, and they would all be talking and laughing. Would anyone else ask Christopher about her? How would he answer?

She tried to read for a while, but her mind kept drifting up to campsite fifty-three. They would have all put on sweaters; the evenings were cool in May. Did Christopher's aunt still knit him sweaters?

She finally gave up on her book and sat there listening to the rain; it was coming down harder, and as she and Mike started to close up for the night, water was streaming down the outside of the windowpane.

Mike banked the fire and stretched. "Anybody out there we need to worry about?"

With vans, RVs, and the carefully made nylon tents, most campers did fine in the rain; people who minded the little inconveniences caused by bad weather usually didn't come camping anyway. But April suddenly remembered the couple in site forty-nine, the ones with the baby and the heavy old tent. "Oh, yes," she said quickly, "there are some people I better go up and check on."

"Want me to go?" Mike asked. April sometimes had to fight with him to do her share of the park's dirty work.

"No." She shook her head. "I'm not a bit tired." If she went to bed now, she would just lie there, thinking of Christopher.

"Well, I am," Mike said. "We cleared the south hiking trail this afternoon. I thought it would take us two days, but those boys decided we might as well do it in one."

April pulled on her bright yellow poncho and hurried out to the truck. The rain was coming down hard; it would be a miracle if those people's tent weren't leaking.

She drove slowly through the campground, keeping the truck lights on dim, hoping not to disturb anyone. Most campsites were dark and quiet. People were snug in their warm sleeping bags, asleep or listening to the rain. As she came up to the bend where site forty-nine was, she saw bright lights, the headlights of a car, slicing a path through the rain. She turned into the site; the people were obviously trying to pack up and leave.

The woman was sitting in the car with the baby. April tapped on the window, and the woman rolled it down.

"Oh, hello," she said, almost in tears.

"Did your tent leak?" April asked.

"Oh, yes"—the woman sniffed—"and we couldn't get a fire going for dinner, and the baby would try to crawl away every time I'd set him down. It's just been awful."

April patted her shoulder. "We'll get you out of here in no time."

She hurried over to where the woman's husband was trying to take down the tent. Apparently someone had come to help; there was a person inside taking out the umbrella pole.

"You start putting your gear in the car," she suggested. "I'll help finish up the tent." Quickly she went to the tent and, stretching on her toes, lifted each corner so that the person inside could get the ribs of the umbrella pole out more easily. Then she held up the canvas so that whoever it was could get out.

It was Christopher.

The harsh glare from the headlights lit half his face,

outlining the strong set of his jaw and cheek. Although the rest was cast in shadows, April could see the flash of surprise in his green eyes.

For a moment they stood there in the biting rain, not speaking, she holding the awkward umbrella pole in her hand, he with the hood of his khaki poncho slipping off his dark head.

He recovered first and, pulling his hood up, took one end of the pole and helped her take it apart. He held open the wet bag as she slipped it in.

"Do you know how this folds up?" he asked. It was the first time they had spoken.

"In thirds, I think," she answered, and together they folded the sodden canvas. She went down to his end, and they tried to roll the tent up. Puddles had already collected on the canvas, and their hands got cold and wet, and their knees muddy.

"It will never fit in the bag," April said as they finished. "Let's just tie it up." She tried to hold the heavy tent as Christopher wound a rope around it. The canvas was too wet and loosely rolled to stand upright, and the tent sagged against her. The wet seeped through her jeans, but she was only conscious of the brush of Christopher's hand against her poncho as he repeatedly slipped the rope between the tent and her body.

Together they hoisted the tent into the trunk of the car. April shone her flashlight around the dark site, checking to be sure that they had got everything.

The man was starting up the car, and April went around to the window. "Would you like to come to the rangers' cabin and dry off a bit before driving home?" she asked. Mike always said that unless people were sick, he didn't really want them traipsing through his home. April understood and agreed, but that didn't seem to stop her from impulsively inviting people into the cabin's warm comfort.

But these people refused, saying that they only had an hour or so to drive and the baby was already asleep. They backed out and pulled away. April hoped that they wouldn't let this one bad night sour them on camping forever.

She and Christopher were alone in the dark, wet night. The rain pounded on the flat ground and on the picnic table, splashing off the rocks of the fireplace and the hoods of their raingear. "Well," he said after an awkward moment, "I think I'll get back."

April surprised herself. "Why don't *you* come down and dry off? It's a nuisance to have such wet things in a tent."

He hesitated. "Sure," he finally said. "Do you want me to drive?"

She must have looked surprised for he explained immediately. "I thought that you didn't like to drive at night."

When he had known her, she hadn't. "I've gottten used to it," she said. "In fact, I rather like it; the roads are so quiet and empty at night. But of course, you can drive if you would like," she added.

He looked at her curiously. "No, you know the road. And it certainly doesn't make much sense to be standing out here in the rain talking about it."

They got into the truck and April drove carefully, leaning forward to peer through the windshield. She pulled the truck in close to the cabin.

"Let's try not to wake up Mike," she said softly as they went in.

"Mike?"

"He's the park superintendent," April explained. "We both live here."

"You do?" His voice was very even: bland and controlled.

April glanced over her shoulder, a tiny sparkle of joy suddenly flaring within her. Christopher never spoke like that unless he was feeling something that he wasn't going to admit to.

Her blue eyes danced. "Christopher, he's nearly sixty."

"Oh," and after a moment, "it's certainly none of my business."

"True," she said, the joy dying into a cold, gray ash.

Mike had left one of the gas lights on for her and had built up the fire at her end of the cabin. The soft light touched the braided rugs, the arms of the rockers, the shelves full of April's nature books.

"Come on in," April said to Christopher. "If we go into my room, we won't disturb Mike so much."

April's room was not large, but she loved it. The bed was covered with a quilt that Mike's sister had made for her last Christmas. The soft squares were in rich jewel tones: jade, garnet, sapphire, amethyst. April thought it was the most beautiful thing she owned since her wedding silver, which she had left behind in Charlottesville.

The quilt gave the room its color. The bed frame, the chests, the nightstand, were all white pine, and her one comfortable chair was a pale rough-spun Haitian cotton. In front of the chair was a matching ottoman, and behind it, a beautiful brass lamp that the regular customers in the restaurant had given her when she graduated from college.

As pleasant and comfortable as April's bedroom was, the most extraordinary part of the rangers' cabin was her bathroom. Before she had moved in, the cabin had had only one small, chilly bathroom off Mike's bedroom. It had a shower but not a tub. The sink was chipped, and the mirror small and wavy. When funding had come through for a second full-time ranger, Mike had decided that a girl like April should have a nice bathroom. So with the money that he claimed was from the park's capital improvements budget—although April never did find any receipts or canceled checks indicating that state money had actually been used—he turned the storeroom into a bathroom.

Mike belonged to a large family that was sprinkled throughout the central Adirondacks. The family was full of plumbers, electricians, and carpenters, and one weekend last summer, they staged a noisy family reunion and built April's bathroom.

The room, paneled in cedar, was as large as her bedroom, with two casement windows opening out onto the forest, and space for a dressing table and a freestanding full-length mirror. One of Mike's brothers had salvaged the tub from an old hotel: It was six feet long and stood on elegant claw feet. He had reglazed it with a porcelain of a soft cream color. The sink, the tile, and other fixtures were of the same shade, as was the background of the wallpaper that covered the one unpaneled wall. The wallpaper had a small vine pattern of a dark jade-green, accented with occasional touches of melon. April planned to get towels in jade and melon someday.

She was almost embarrassed at how much she liked having a room such as this. Although she didn't spend anywhere near the amount of time on her appearance

that she had in high school, she still tried to look fresh
and well groomed. She just felt better if she did. When
she had worked here in the summers and lived in the
bunkhouse, it had been easy to get careless. But with
her pretty dressing table it was a pleasure every morning to spend a little time brushing her hair and putting
on a bit of mascara. After a day outdoors it was a quiet
luxury to give herself a manicure. She still had enough
vanity left that she didn't want her hands to crack and
her face to go leathery. And the full-length mirror that
greeted her every morning as she stepped out of the
shower had kept her from spending the long winter eating.

Behind some folding doors in the bathroom there
was even a small washer and dryer. She had just put
some clothes in the dryer that evening, and she took
out a robe of Mike's and handed it to Christopher. "If
you would like to shower and then put this on, I can put
your things in the dryer," she told him.

While he was showering, April pulled off her own
wet things. She slipped into a burgundy sweat suit,
changing quickly because Christopher never took long
in the shower, or at least he hadn't when she had
known him. She was just pulling up the zipper on the
jacket when the bathroom door opened and he said,
"Do you want to show me how to work the dryer?"

She took the wet clothes from him. The jeans were
as muddy as hers had been, and she hardly wanted to
put them in the dryer like that. "If you aren't in a terrible hurry, I'll run these through the washer," she said.
'It won't take long.''

"I'm not going anywhere," he answered. He started
to rub his head with the white towel, but it was too
flimsy and threadbare to do much good.

April apologized. "I'm sorry I don't have better towels. I am planning to use my Christmas money this year to get some."

"Christmas money?" he said blankly.

"Yes, Mother gives me money for Christmas now," she explained. "It's not as personal, but at least I can get something I need."

In the mirror she saw his face tighten and suddenly she realized how strange this must sound to him—having to wait nine months to buy new towels. He had always been used to money, and now between what New York law firms paid their associates and the income from his trust fund, he probably paid twice as much just in federal income tax as April earned at all.

He cleared his throat. "There's all the stuff from our apartment; it's stored at my parents'. Do you want me to have it sent up?"

"Oh, no," April gasped. Then a little embarrassed at having reacted so strongly, she tried to explain casually, "I just think I'd feel a little strange about using it, that's all."

"I can understand that," he said. "Although it *is* all yours, and it's probably pretty silly not to use it if you need it."

"It won't be the first silly thing I have done," April replied. But rather than explain that remark, she turned back to the washer. "Will this shirt run?" He had been wearing the dark plaid that he had on when she first saw him step out of the woods that morning.

"Who cares?" he said, giving up on the towel. Without asking permission, he picked up her comb and started to comb his hair.

"Apparently not you," she said, glancing over at him. He had to bend his knees a little to see in her mirror. She was suddenly curious about his life. "What do you do about your laundry?"

"Send it out."

"All of it? The sheets and towels too?"

"Every bit. I'm not really into laundry."

And this was the Christopher that she had first known, casual, even blunt, with none of the careful manners turning him into the distant Virginia gentleman who had once made her feel so unloved.

She started the washer and picked up his sweater. "I'll go put this in front of the fire; it won't dry completely, but it will start. Make yourself comfortable."

When she got back into the bedroom, he was in the armchair, his feet on the ottoman, his hands in the pockets of the robe.

"This is a comfortable cabin," he said, looking around. "I had no idea that the park service provided such good living facilities."

"I like it a lot," she answered. "Mike and his family added that bathroom; I don't think the state paid for any of it."

He ignored—or didn't notice—the slight defensiveness in her voice. "Did you really spend the winter here?"

"Yes." April went over to the bed and sat down, tucking her feet under her.

"How did you stand it?" he asked. "It seems like it would be a long, lonely haul."

This question was different from the questions this morning. This time he *was* asking about her feelings.

"Some days did seem to drag, but only a few. We had lots of work, trying to keep the trails open, checking to be sure that animals weren't caught in the ice. We took apart all the engines and motors on—"

"You? Took apart engines?" He sounded very surprised.

"Yes, me," April returned, and then added lightly, "I took them apart; Mike was the one who put them back together."

They both laughed. "That seems like a fair division of labor." Christopher smiled.

It was so comfortable, sitting here like this, warm and dry, talking to him, with the rain beating down on the roof. Christopher leaned back in the chair. "Go on," he said. "Tell me about the winter."

She spoke eagerly. "The snow was just beautiful, like in pictures you'd seen as a child. And it never got dirty or melted into slush like in Virginia. Of course, it was cold, but we had down parkas and insulated boots, and the cabin was often very warm."

"Didn't you get bored?"

"Not really. I think part of it was that, well, I was so tired after finishing school because of working the whole time and all. And then last summer was very busy around here—we were understaffed and seemed to go from one crisis to another. So it was nice to have such peace. I'm not sure I could do it year after year like Mike does." April was surprised how easy it was to talk to Christopher. "I think I might find it a lot harder this year. When the first campers came in this spring, I have to admit that I was thrilled to see them. Those poor people," she laughed. "I think I chattered their heads off."

"I don't imagine they minded," he said evenly. "And if they were men, they were probably just as thrilled to see *you*."

April blinked in surprise. "What a nice thing to say!" she gasped.

He just shrugged.

Still a little flustered by his compliment, April said quickly, "I took some pictures last winter to show Mother. Would you like to see them?" She hopped off the bed and, without waiting for his answer, opened one of her drawers.

The pictures were extraordinary to look at in the middle of May. Snow was drifted up to the eaves of the cabin and icicles the size of a man's arm hung from the garage and shop buildings. There was a picture of Mike shoveling a path through what appeared to be snow over his head. "I had him get down on his knees," April giggled. And he had taken a picture of her on a day of a gentle snowfall. Her face was turned upward toward the falling snow, her cheeks were pink from the cold, her lips were slightly parted, and her brown hair spilled out from her blue cap.

Christopher held that picture for a long time. "May I—" he started and stopped.

April had been standing by the chair, looking at the pictures with him. What had he been about to say? Was he going to ask for the picture?

"You've changed your hair since I knew you," he said instead.

"I've changed in lots of ways." April went back to the bed and drew her legs up, wrapping her arms around them.

"You still sit like that," he commented. She jerked upright; it was such a schoolgirlish way to sit. "Whenever I see someone sitting like that, I think of you."

"You do?" April had never imagined that he still thought of her regularly.

"Well, it's not often," he said, unconsciously dampening her interest. "Most people don't sit like that."

"I suppose not," she sighed. She realized that she

hadn't heard the washer in a while and so got up to put the clothes in the dryer. Then she went back to the darkened living room, now lit only by the fire to turn his sweater. As she rearranged it on the spark guard she noticed that it wasn't hand knit. It hadn't been a gift from his aunt; he had bought it in a New York store.

It was easier to ask her questions when he wasn't right there. "Christopher, why are you working in a New York firm?"

When she stepped back into the bedroom, he was sitting upright, and his face was arranged in a deliberately empty expression. He shrugged at her question. "Good pay, interesting work. Why does anyone work in New York?"

"No," she said, sitting down on the ottoman in front of him. "Why aren't you with your family's firm? Why didn't you go home?"

"You didn't."

April was startled by this crisp response. "It's hardly the same."

"Why isn't it?" Christopher asked. "Why didn't you go back?"

"And just try to pick up as if nothing had happened? I couldn't do that." April picked at the white fibers of the upholstery.

"Maybe I couldn't either."

But April couldn't see that their situations were at all the same. He hadn't loved her; he wouldn't have been as shattered by everything as she had been. He had a profession and a future—she hadn't had any of that.

"No," she said slowly, "you could have gone back. People weren't talking about you, saying that you had done something wrong and shameful like they were about me."

And it seemed for a moment, looking up at him in

the pool of light from the brass lamp, she saw more sympathy in his eyes, more genuine concern, than she had ever seen there before. "Maybe they should have," he said softly.

"What?"

He stood up and walked across the room, looking out the window into the rainy night. When he finally spoke, his voice was urgent. "April, you were the finest, prettiest girl that town had seen in a long time. You had so much life and spirit; you could walk into a dusty hardware store and set it ablaze with your laughter. Then that girl met me and in one week her life was shattered. You should have gone off to college with your friends like you had planned. Instead you had to go live among strangers with a man you hardly knew. And then after that the waiting tables, riding buses..." He slammed his hand against the wall. "Oh, God, April, if anyone should be ashamed to go home, it's not you."

And there on his face, his lips white and tight, his eyes glinting emerald, April could see all the feeling, all the passion, that had been missing in their conversation that morning.

But she could not bear to have him torturing himself, thinking that everything had been his fault. "Christopher," she faltered, "don't you understand that"— and she didn't know quite how to say it—"you were almost set up for everything that happened."

He leaned back against the windowsill and folded his arms. "So you understand your mother's role in all this now?"

"Yes," April said, surprised at how honest she could be. "What she did was wrong, and things can never be the same between her and me again, although I know that she thought she was doing it for my sake."

"I knew that," he said. "And that's what seemed so ironic. She was trying to help you, and it was the worst thing that could have happened."

The whole time they had been married they had never talked about any of this. "When did you finally understand my mother's role in it all?" April asked curiously. "It took me years to figure it all out."

His mouth twisted in a bitter little smile. "Oh, I knew the next morning."

"Christopher!" April's hand flew to her throat. "Then why—"

"Why did I marry you? That's exactly what my parents wanted to know. But look, there was no reason to punish you, although I don't know that our marriage didn't make you more miserable than anything any gossiping shrew could have said. Whatever your mother did, you were innocent; you didn't know what was going on."

"But why should you have had to suffer if the fault was *my* mother's?"

"Oh, April, come off it," he said impatiently, jamming his hands back into the pockets of the robe. "Your mother didn't force me into your bed. She just made it possible, that's all. I wasn't a kid; I was old enough to know what I was doing, to be responsible for my actions. It wasn't her fault; it was mine."

April couldn't speak; she just didn't know what to say. The timer on the dryer tinged.

"Your clothes are dry," she said automatically. "I'll go take them out."

"I'll do it," he said abruptly, and April knew that he needed to be alone for a minute.

It didn't seem right to her, not at all. The one thing that she had hoped for him was that he would be able to resume his life after she had left. It was the one consolation she had felt for her guilt. She and her mother had disrupted his life for a year; she had prayed that would be all.

But clearly his life was still altered by what had happened between them. He belonged in Virginia. His family had lived there for generations; his roots were in that red, rocky soil. And the town needed him, people like him, energetic and committed.

What had she done?

Christopher came out of the bathroom, buttoning the cuffs of his shirt. "Thank you for doing this; I feel much better." His hair had nearly dried, and although he was avoiding her eyes, he looked clean and comfortable.

"It was nothing," April replied automatically. "If you're ready, I'll drive you back up."

"I hate to make you go out again." This all sounded so stilted and formal to her.

"I do it all the time," she pointed out.

He held the door of the cabin open for her as she stepped outside. The rain was letting up; she guessed that it would be clear by morning.

"Will we be camping in mud for a week?" Christopher asked as she backed the truck out.

"No," she answered. "Our soil is light and sandy, and last month we dumped a load of straight sand on every campsite so everything dries out very quickly."

During their drive back they continued to talk about the surrounding terrain. April wasn't sure that he was particularly interested, but at least it was something to talk about.

When she had stopped the truck at his campsite, she rested her arms on the steering wheel and turned to him, saying, "It was awfully nice of you to help those people pack up. They just weren't prepared."

"It was just as nice of you," he returned.

"Oh, but it's my job," she answered lightly.

"I know," he said slowly, his hand at the door handle. "That's what bothers me." And with that, he slid out of the truck.

Chapter Four

So Christopher was bothered by her job. April simply couldn't understand why. She thought it was a wonderful job and that she was very lucky to have it. Many, many people always applied for each of the few ranger positions even though they could earn much more money in some other field. In fact, April knew that two of the summer staffers who would arrive after Memorial Day were fully qualified to be rangers and were doing work far below their skills just waiting for a full-time position to open up. So why wasn't Christopher pleased for her?

It was Saturday morning, and April had taken her folder of paperwork out to the picnic table in front of the cabin. As she had predicted the evening before, the clouds had cleared, leaving the sky a brilliant spring blue—it was much too nice a day to sit inside filling out forms.

April had to admit that when she first had become a forest ranger she had been surprised at how much paperwork the job involved. It seemed that everything that happened in the park had to be reported to the state in triplicate. But she had quickly learned that if she kept up with it, it was not bad. Mike had recently turned over the park's budget to her, and she was enjoying the responsibility. But today she was having trouble concentrating.

She had been so impractical when she had married Christopher. He had never complained, but she had not planned anything: menus, budgets, or errands. She had had to go to the grocery store three or four times every week because she never made a list. She would take clothes to the dry cleaners and forget about them. She never kept track of what she had done and had spent. If she ever had a home to take care of again, she thought now, things would be very different.

Suddenly she wanted to apologize to Christopher for how inept she had been; she wanted to tell him that she now realized how childlike she had been, to let him know that she would do better next time.

But what on earth would be the point of that?

April shook her head and took the cap off her pen, trying to force herself to concentrate. But before she could do more than pull out the form she needed, she was interrupted.

Julia Breeland and Beth Market were walking up the asphalt drive. Julia was wearing a pair of white designer jeans and a loosely knit lemon sweater. She looked fresh and immaculate, much more suited to the deck of a yacht than to a still damp forest. Beth was more appropriately dressed in faded blue jeans and a red pullover. She was carrying a white canvas laundry bag. "Hi," she said. "We were looking for the washers and dryers. Some of our stuff got a little wet last night."

"I'm sorry," April said, "but we're such a small park that we don't have those facilities." She would say those words several thousand times this summer.

Julia raised her eyebrows. "I thought that Chris said

something about your washing his jeans last night."

That must have worried her, April thought a little cattily. You don't usually wash a man's jeans while he is still in them. "We have a washer and a dryer in the cabin," she explained.

Beth spoke immediately. "Isn't that just like a man? Chris knows every law there is about public and private facilities, but he doesn't pay any attention whether a particular washer is one or the other." She laughed. "But the clothes are only damp. They will dry on the line."

"But surely"—Julia's voice was cool—"April will let us use her dryer. After all, we are her husband's friends." Her tone was just a little sarcastic when she said "husband."

"Of course," April said reluctantly. She knew that Julia was taking advantage of her, manipulating her, but it just didn't seem worth making a scene over.

April led them inside the cabin. Both women looked around curiously. Julia seemed indifferent to the cabin's charm, but Beth was enthusiastic.

"My grandparents used to have a cabin like this," she said excitedly. "My sisters and I would spend the whole summer with them."

It turned out that Beth was from New York State. She had grown up outside Rochester. In fact, coming to Frank Lake had been her idea.

"We all had such different reasons for coming. Josh and Steve wanted to fish, and Chris, as I suppose you know, wanted to backpack—"

April started in surprise, almost tripping down the cabin steps. She hadn't known that Christopher liked to backpack, the most solitary and rugged way to camp, in which a hiker carried all his food and equipment on his back and stayed out on the backcountry trails for days. Christopher had done nothing like that when she had known him.

Beth didn't seem to notice her surprise and continued. "And I wanted to sit in the sun and read romances. Ben wanted to drink and have a good time, so I suggested that we come here. It seemed to have something for everyone."

April noticed that she hadn't said anything about why Julia had come.

The three of them sat around the picnic table, waiting for the clothes to dry. Beth was admiring the flowers April had planted on either side of the walk. "I tried begonias last year," April remarked, "but the impatiens are doing better. There's just so much shade."

"I do miss having a yard," Beth sighed.

Julia did not seem particularly interested in gardening and interrupted. "Do you mind if we speak frankly?"

April tensed; remarks like that never came before something pleasant. Christopher's mother had always used that phrase before criticizing April for not having the right number of forks on her table or for letting Christopher sit down to dinner in jeans or something else that April thought equally unimportant. She wasn't so sure that Julia's remarks were going to be unimportant.

Nonetheless she spoke lightly to Julia. "You're at Frank Lake. It seems like the right place for speaking frankly."

As expected, Julia ignored her pleasantry. "Christopher is our friend; we want the best for him."

"So do I." April spoke with complete sincerity.

"He has talked to me often about your marriage—"

April knew that this simply was not true. Just yesterday Julia had said to Christopher that he had *never* talked about his marriage. Well, April could hardly object. After all, she had been eavesdropping, which was hardly more virtuous or ethical than Julia's lie.

Julia didn't seem to notice April's reaction. "Perhaps you are not experienced enough to realize it, but the childishness of your behavior has been quite unfair to him. Although"—Julia made no effort to hide the insincerity in her voice—"I am sure you are not doing it deliberately,"

"I don't understand," April said flatly.

"Oh, come now," Julia said as if April were being coy. "Even *you* must realize that by running away, by refusing to have any contact with him, you have managed to keep him feeling so guilty that no other woman has had a chance."

April gasped and stared at her, her eye widening. Guilty. Yes, of course. That was how Christopher felt. He wasn't angry or even hurt that she had left. He just felt guilty. That certainly explained everything that he had said last night; that's why he had left Virginia. He felt too guilty to stay.

And it wasn't just the guilt over having "ruined" her, as Julia had teasingly put it. He also felt guilty because he had disrupted her life so, sending her away from Virginia where she belonged. That's why her job bothered him. He probably felt guilty that she had to work. He would have been more comfortable if she had indeed allowed his father to buy her off.

When April said nothing, Julia's smug voice continued. "It's hardly fair, you know. You should give him a chance to develop a fulfilling adult relationship." She stressed the word *adult* as if April's marriage had been something else. "He certainly deserves to be happy with some other woman." Julia stood up, grimacing at the drop of sap that had fallen on the white jeans. "Now if you will excuse me, I'll go get the clothes."

As soon as she had left, Beth slid down the bench to face April directly. She spoke her name almost timidly. "I know that we hardly know each other well enough for me to be speaking like this, but please don't let Julia get to you. She's been trying to be the woman to make him happy, and that colored everything she just said."

Beth's eyes were warm, and April felt like she could talk to her. "Are they—" She faltered.

"Having an affair?" Beth seemed to understand how hard that was for April to say. "No, I'm sure they aren't. You see, Julia's been going through a divorce. I don't know all the details but apparently it's been quite ugly, with her husband continually threatening to contest it or to countersue her. As you can imagine, Chris was not at all interested in stepping to the middle of a mess like that. I guess he had to make it clear that until that was all over, he didn't even want to have lunch with her alone. But the rumor is that the divorce is final, or nearly so, which is why she wanted to come up here with all of us—even though she isn't exactly the outdoors type. So she isn't at all happy to be confronted with you."

"No, I can sympathize with her position," April answered honestly. "I just wish that she wasn't handling it quite like this. There's no need for her to criticize me."

"But you know," Beth suggested, "if what she says is true—that Chris still has guilt feelings about your marriage and that's what's keeping him from getting seriously involved with someone else—then, perhaps, in the long run, this will be the best thing for her. Surely seeing you again will help him resolve his feelings, get over some of his guilt. I know nothing at all about your marriage," she quickly assured April, "but you certainly seem to have landed on your feet. Good heavens, Steve Webster will kill for a job like yours. Anyway, seeing you again is probably the one thing Chris needs to stop feeling so guilty."

April agreed—although what she and Beth thought wasn't what mattered. "Well, how much of what she said was true? That he hasn't formed serious relationships?"

Beth clearly thought that this was a perfectly normal question for a man's ex-wife to ask. "He really does go out with a lot of women, but it isn't the way that I would ever want to date. He takes girls to expensive restaurants; he will have got fabulous theater tickets or something, but it's all like that, very formal and set. Nobody ever just hangs around his house with him on a rainy Sunday. Men, yes, but never a woman."

"That doesn't sound like him," April marveled.

Beth looked at her curiously. "That's interesting. My first impression of Chris was that he was so distant and careful, somehow guarded all the time. But I worked on a big case with him, and when he was working, he seemed like such a straightforward and warm person."

"Oh, he is," April exclaimed. "No, I mean he *was*." Her tone sobered. "It's funny; he used to be like that all the time." She thought back to the first week she had known him, when he would be leaning against his car, waiting for her to get out of school, how he would straighten and smile at the sight of her. "It was only during our marriage that he started getting so formal all the time."

"I think it's that contrast between the very formal face he hides behind and what he is really like that fascinates so many women. As if the way he looks—and his money, of course—weren't enough." Beth laughed. "Every time we get a new secretary at the firm, we all try to guess how soon she's going to get a crush on him. They all seem to. It really does irritate Ben Carleton; he'd like to think he was that attractive to women."

April noticed that Beth herself understood Christopher's charms but was remarkably unaffected by them. She supposed that Beth was involved with someone else. April was curious, but she wasn't going to pry. "Well, it seems like a shame that he can't just be himself."

"Of course, I don't know," Beth reflected, "but now that I've seen you, I would guess that he holds back sometimes because on some unconscious level he still feels married."

"What?" April gasped. "How could he possibly still feel married? It's been six years since we lived together and four since we were divorced. And he divorced me."

"I don't know," Beth repeated. "Maybe he just still feels obligated—just like Julia said. I imagine he doesn't love you anymore, but maybe Julia's right—he doesn't feel free to love anyone else."

As she went about her duties the rest of the day, April couldn't help thinking about this conversation. It now seemed obvious to her that Christopher felt guilty—she wondered why she hadn't realized it for herself.

But he shouldn't feel guilty; there was no reason to. Yes, their marriage had thrown April's life off its destined course, but she was glad of it. She was such a much better, stronger person now. The first years in Buffalo had been hard, very hard, but she did not regret them for one minute.

In high school she had had lots of friends; all the girls always said how much they liked April Peters. But now she understood that while she had had fun with those girls, they were all always competing with each other, trying to see who dressed the best, who dated the most. Only when she started waiting tables, meeting people who were working so hard to improve themselves that they didn't have time to compete with others, did she really come to understand friendship.

So she didn't want Christopher to feel guilty about the changes he had caused in her life. She didn't want an icy blanket of guilt to be freezing the warmth that she knew he was capable of.

It then occurred to her that Julia had made a major mistake in the boat yesterday. If she really wanted to free Christopher from the tangles of his marriage, then she should not keep reminding him of how childlike April was. Certainly such a strategy would keep him from loving April—although Julia clearly did not realize how very unlikely that was. But if he still thought of April as helpless, then he would continue to feel responsible for her. Only by seeing her as a capable, competent adult would he be able to break free of some of his guilt.

Of course, it was possible, April acknowledged, that Julia truly did not care whether Christopher was still tormented by guilt. She might be willing to take him—his name, his money, his person, whatever it was she wanted—without much caring how she got it.

But April cared very much about Christopher's happiness. And it did seem to her that if his guilt over their marriage was making him unhappy, then she was obligated to show him that she was a strong and independent person, able to take care of herself.

And as much as April really did believe that Christopher had a right to get on with his own life, one little part of her, she had to admit, was pleased that he had not fallen in love or married during these years, and she was eager to impress him with her maturity and strength, not so much so that he wouldn't feel guilty about her, but so that he would respect and admire her.

Every Saturday night during the camping season, the staff built a big bonfire on the beach and encouraged all the campers to come. They put up handwritten signs and usually went around late Saturday afternoon, talking to people while they were fixing their dinners, encouraging them to come down for the campfire.

April was usually too busy to do this although she really enjoyed talking to the campers. But today, when she saw Faith and Kim, two summer staffers, set out, she decided to go with them. She wanted, she admitted to herself, to see Christopher.

The three campsites at the end of the trail were the last ones they visited. As they approached the bend in the road, they could hear the sounds of evening activities: the clatter of pans, laughter, and an ax ringing.

Steve and Ben were sitting at a picnic table, looking at a map; Josh was cleaning fish; Beth was stirring something at the stove, and Julia was again in the lounge chair, a drink in her hand. It was Christopher splitting wood.

"Who is that?" Faith gasped.

April could understand her reaction. Christopher's shirt was draped across a stack of cut wood, and his chest and arms were tanned to almost a bronze. He had raised the ax over his head and was swinging it in a powerful arc, striking the wedge squarely with a sharp ringing sound, making the two halves of the log jump apart.

And for a moment other memories flooded back: Christopher standing over a bed, unbuttoning his shirt. He always did it with just one hand, making it seem so effortless, so arousing. The lamp on the nightstand would throw a gleam across his shoulders and then clearly illuminate, for a moment, his hand and arm as he would reach out to snap off the light.

"That," she said to Kim and Faith, "is my ex-husband." And without waiting for their reaction, she walked into the campsite to tell the others about the evening program.

Ben immediately said that of course they would all come. "Can we bring beer?" he asked hopefully.

"Certainly not," April answered immediately. "You aren't supposed to have liquor at all unless you're part of a family party."

"Oh, we are a nice, cozy little family," he returned. "Beth is our mommy and—"

"I am not either," Beth interrupted. April was a little surprised at the tightness in her face. April would have thought that she would have just shrugged, laughing off the joke.

"April, do you know anything about the backpacking trails?" Steve Webster turned his blond head up from his maps. "We're setting out tomorrow."

April was conscious that Christopher had not even looked at her. Was he deliberately ignoring her, or was he just concentrating on the wood? She wasn't quite sure what to do, but when Steve repeated his question, she sat down next to him and started pointing out the best trails. Suddenly they all heard a stifled curse and turned to look at Christopher.

"This piece was full of splinters," he said, looking at his hand with exasperation. "Does anyone know where the tweezers are?"

"I have a pair," April called automatically. The Swiss army knife she always carried had a pair of tweezers cunningly inserted in the handle.

Christopher looked up at the sound of her voice. "Oh, April, I didn't realize you were here." He picked up his shirt and came over to the table. "Can you get these blasted things out?"

He held out his hand—the strong, tanned hand that had slipped a wedding band on hers, that had taught her about ecstasy and passion, that had signed all the checks that she had returned. Two long splinters were piercing the brown palm. "It shouldn't be any problem," she said. At least it wouldn't be if she could keep her own hand from trembling when she touched him.

She unsnapped her red knife from her belt and taking a little box of matches from her shirt pocket, quickly sterilized the tips of the tweezers. She took his warm hand and tilted it toward the sunlight.

"How domestic," Julia said cuttingly.

April tensed at her remark and Christopher winced when the tweezers caught a bit of his flesh.

"Sorry," she murmured.

"It's okay," he said softly. "I understand."

She glanced up at him and his green eyes did seem to understand. He probably didn't like Julia's remarks any more than she did.

The splinters came out easily.

"Now are you going to kiss it and make it better?" Julia mocked.

April ignored her. "It should be all right," she said. "But it wouldn't hurt to wear a Band-Aid although I don't imagine you will, will you?" Christopher had never believed in fussing over little things.

"For a splinter? No way," he said, "but thanks."

Steve turned to him. "Your wi— April here suggests that we take this trail; it's a loop and should take us four days and three nights."

"That sounds perfect," Christopher said, and leaning over April, he looked at the map.

He had one hand resting on the picnic table next to her, and she was very conscious of his arm, almost touching hers, and of his bare chest behind her. She longed to lean back against him, to feel the hard strength of his body, the warmth of his skin. She tried hard to hold still, but when he leaned forward to look at the map more closely, her hair brushed against him.

He immediately stepped back and, taking his blue polo shirt off the table, slipped it back on.

April used the moment to stand up and excuse herself. She might not be doing a good job convincing him what a competent, self-reliant person she was now, but certainly he was convincing her that, physically at least, she felt exactly the same way about him that she had that spring evening seven years earlier.

And the rest of the afternoon, images of Christopher, shirtless, swinging an ax, haunted her, tormented her.

As soon as she finished the dinner dishes, she went down to the beach to help set up for the campfire. It was not the sort of thing that she usually did, leaving such work to the summer staff, but she sensed that

Mike was ready to settle in for a nice chat about Christopher, and she felt like she had already thought about him today a great deal more than was good for her.

But she soon discovered that she was doomed to yet another conversation, this one more awkward than any so far.

Ben Carleton was the first of the lawyers to come down to the beach. April suspected that he had probably excused himself from the evening cleanup.

But he was certainly eager to help her as she mixed the Kool-Aid that was served to the campers. "Go away," he cheerfully ordered the girl who was helping April. "I'll do this. Mrs. Ramsey"—his tone was mocking when he said that—"and I have things to discuss."

"We do?" April raised her eyebrows inquiringly.

"Yes, indeed," he returned, starting to tear open the Kool-Aid packages. "You are going to tell me all the dirt on your dear ex-husband."

"You know that I am not."

"Oh, come on," he said invitingly. "What's wrong with him? Did he beat you? Squander his whole paycheck every Friday on painted women?"

Suddenly April was tired of being patient with him. "Why do you want to know this?"

"I want to be able to look at him when he gets made partner next year and I don't, and have something to feel superior about," Ben said with boyish glee. "What frightens him? What are his secret weaknesses? What does he like in bed?"

That last question was delivered with a wide-eyed, innocent stare, but April still found it enormously offensive, and for a moment, behind Ben's boyish facade, she saw a man, intensely competitive, willing to use any ploy to try and make himself feel superior to other people. April was certainly not going to be pulled into any competition he felt with Christopher. It seemed so very sordid. But she didn't want to quarrel with him.

She knew what to do. "I don't know where you were brought up," she said, keeping her voice light and teasing, letting her words, not her tone, carry her message, "but in Virginia, we didn't ask people questions like that." She learned how to do that waiting on tables. It got the customer to behave himself, but didn't reduce the size of his tip.

It worked again. "Okay." Ben laughed, handing her a stack of paper cups. "You win, but when you are ready to spill his secrets, be sure and come to me first."

Secrets! April thought as she stirred the vat of lime-green Kool-Aid. Did she know any of Christopher's secrets? Certainly she knew some of his habits, that he liked his coffee strong and his food spicy—although those might have changed. And she did know that he liked the touch of her hand against his chest and that he would want her to— But that was a secret knowledge that she now undoubtedly shared with other women.

Suddenly April was very self-conscious about seeing him again. She felt she knew so much more about him than she had yesterday—about the guilt he felt over their marriage. And she knew more about herself too: that the brush of his chest against her hair made her mouth go dry.

But when the party of lawyers arrived, he and Julia were not with them.

April had to admit that she was disappointed. She guessed that an evening around a campfire with songs, children's games, and lots of Kool-Aid might seem just a little too tame for Julia. She must have convinced Christopher to stay with her.

But the others seemed to be having fun. Steve Webster borrowed a guitar from one of the staffers and in a clear baritone patiently sang all the simple songs that the children wanted to hear. It was surprising; in general, he seemed like such a quiet person.

And then she noticed Beth Market. The petite woman sat on a log, watching Steve, just like the others, but her expression was rapt, a gentle light softening her face, and April realized that Beth hadn't been telling the whole truth when she said she had come to Frank Lake to sit in the sun and read romances. She was here to be with Steve, and the romance was as much in her heart as in any book.

April wondered about the two of them. No wonder Beth had resented Ben's crack about her being everyone's little mother; that was not how she wanted Steve to think of her, not at all. Did he have any idea how she felt? What a wonderful wife she would make. She was—

A touch on April's arm startled her, and she jerked, almost spilling the Kool-Aid some child had given her to hold for him.

A strong hand grasped her arm, steadying her. It was Christopher. "Are you all right?" he asked. "I didn't mean to startle you."

"I'm fine," she answered. "I was thinking about something else."

"I gathered that." He smiled down at her. And to her surprise he gave her arm a little squeeze before releasing it. "Anyway, I am sorry that I'm late. I thought it would be a good time to shower. The showers are sometimes pretty crowded in the morning."

April noticed that his hair was still damp, and she couldn't help being pleased that he hadn't decided to spend the evening alone with Julia.

"I—we are glad that you could come down," she said. "Can I get you something?"

"What is that stuff?" He looked at her paper cup suspiciously.

"Kool-Aid," she said sweetly. "I'm sure that you would enjoy it a lot."

"How like you," he laughed, "to be drinking Kool-Aid."

April winced. Even his most casual remarks revealed how young he thought her. But what did he expect—that she would be drinking double bourbons, straight up, while on duty at a state park campfire?

This unpromising conversation was interrupted by a gruff cough.

It was Mike. As always he was in his green uniform, a pipe between his teeth. He took the pipe out and spoke to Christopher. "Are you her husband?"

Christopher looked startled. "I was," he answered, apparently too surprised to add his usual "sir."

April murmured an introduction.

"This is some fine girl you've got here," Mike said proudly and rumpled April's hair as if she were a five-year-old.

Christopher paused and then answered slowly, "I know that."

But, April thought, smoothing her hair and trying not to let herself be pleased, what else could he say?

"Well, I hope that she'll bring you down to the cabin sometime," Mike continued. April had not told him about Christopher's coming last night. "I'd sure like to get to know you better." And in his usual abrupt manner Mike turned and walked away.

April felt like she had to explain. "Don't mind him," she said, nervously playing with the knife that hung at her belt. "He thinks of us as still married. He doesn't believe in divorce."

Christopher was still watching Mike walk away. Without looking at her, he said softly, "I'm not sure I do either."

April was stunned. "What?" He was the one who had got their divorce.

Christopher was obviously regretting having said that much. "Oh, no, I didn't mean it like that. If people can't get along, they shouldn't stay married. But whenever you go to a wedding ceremony and really listen to the words, it's pretty clear that that's a promise you are only supposed to make to one person. But that's silly and romantic," he added briskly. "I know lots of people on their second marriages who are happy and settled. I guess it's just harder to make the promise when you know that you've already broken it once."

There was a tone in his voice that April had never heard before. Suddenly she realized what it was. Christopher thought that he had failed at something. As far as she knew, he had never failed at anything. As the Ramseys' only child, he had had a lot of pressure placed on him to be the very best at everything he did, and he drove himself hard to live up to these expectations. And he had always succeeded at everything—until he had tried to be a husband and his wife decided to get on a bus for Buffalo rather than live with him anymore.

Paradoxically this failure had probably given him more self-confidence. The one thing he had never known about himself before was how he would cope with failure, how he would react if he didn't succeed. Now he knew that he could pick up the pieces and go on. It probably made him much more tolerant of other people's weaknesses, much more sympathetic to their confusions and failings.

And looking up at his face, a shadow of pain darkening his eyes, April knew that the attraction that had been reawakening in her since the moment he stepped out of the forest, carrying an armload of wood, was not merely physical. She loved him.

"Well, hello, April." Julia Breeland came up and slipped her arm through Christopher's. "Now, don't you look sweet?"

April looked exactly like she had every other time Julia had seen her, except that this evening the white turtleneck she had on under her uniform shirt was a light sweater.

"Some of the children are looking for you." Julia's elegantly manicured fingers moved against Christopher's arm. "They want you to play some little game with them."

Seething at Julia's patronizing tone, April excused herself. She couldn't say that her job was giving her much of a chance to impress Christopher with what a competent adult she had become. Besides taking the splinter out of his hand, which anyone could have done, all she had done was play games with children. Oh, well, she sighed, that was part of her job too sometimes, and it wasn't fair to the children to act like she didn't enjoy being with them just because Christopher's green eyes were following her.

The campfire broke up early. Many of the people had young children, and campers, in general, kept early hours. Ben Carleton came over to her. "We've decided to continue the campfire up at our site," he said. "A slightly more adult version of it, that is. Can you come?"

"Yes," she said, unable to refuse anything that would give her a chance to be with Christopher. "I can't leave until things are cleared up here, but I will be up later."

"Do you need help?" Suddenly Christopher was at her side.

"Sorry, Ramsey," Ben put in. "You are our champion fire-builder, and we've just invited people to a campfire. You better get up and start to work. I'll stay down here and help these pretty ladies."

Christopher just shrugged and called to Steve. Beth, April was sorry to see, did not leave with them.

Ben had asked most of the staff so the beach was cleaned up much more quickly than usual, and they all trooped happily up to campsite fifty-three. April was a little relieved that the campsites were at the end of the trail; she was afraid that there might be more noise than the other campers would tolerate.

Christopher and Steve had built a bright fire and set out all their lanterns so the little enclave was a friendly oasis in the dark night. Josh and Julia had put out several jugs of wine, a cooler of beer, tin plates of good cheeses, cans of smoked oysters, and jars of little pickles. The staffers were surprised at how much food and drink there was, and each automatically thought of what it cost and held back. But Steve Webster said quietly, "Look, we all put ourselves through school too, and we know what it's like. But we've got money now; don't be reluctant to let us share."

Although it wasn't entirely true—a trust fund had

certainly paid Christopher's tuition—it was the perfect thing to say, and April saw a quick look of pride flash across Beth's face.

The two groups mingled happily. Ben flirted with some of the girls, and another one moved shyly in Christopher's direction. Beth, who looked several years younger than she actually was, was surrounded by the young male staffers, all of whom seemed a little frightened by Julia's cool beauty. Julia was trying to attach herself to Christopher, but he was being uncommonly attentive to a young staffer.

April found herself standing next to Steve Webster. He handed her a plastic glass filled with white wine and started to ask her about being a ranger. He was genuinely interested, sometimes sounding almost envious of an outdoors life.

"What a terrific job you have," he sighed. "You aren't cooped up in an office; you do something different every day. It sounds wonderful."

"It is." April smiled and unthinkingly continued. "Beth says that you would probably kill for a job like this."

"She did? I wonder how she knew that." Steve sounded very surprised, and April regretted her hasty remark. She just didn't know enough about the way things stood between them to be interfering. So she quickly returned to talking about her duties.

But the whole time she was talking to Steve she couldn't help glancing at Christopher. He was leaning against a tree, a beer can in one hand, his wool Pendleton shirt open over a navy turtleneck. He was looking down at the young summer staffer who had come to talk to him. He was asking her questions, listening to her answers, relaxed, sometimes amused. But it was clear that she seemed very young to him, pleasant to talk to, but still very young.

April felt a little sick. She was not at all envious of the girl, as Julia perhaps was. Quite the contrary. April didn't want those tolerant, amused smiles, and she felt sick knowing that that was probably how Christopher had smiled at her so many years ago, and how, if Julia had her way, he would smile at her still. That was not what she wanted from him. Not at all.

Ben and Faith, the summer staffer who usually worked registration, soon came over to talk to April and Steve. Faith, a forestry major, asked her a few questions about her education, and Ben finally said, "Doesn't Cornell have an excellent forestry program? Why didn't you go there?"

April and Faith both laughed. Cornell, an Ivy League school in upper New York State, did have one of the best forestry schools in the country—it was also one of the most expensive. "Money," April said lightly.

"Well, I can understand that," Steve put in. "I didn't have any either."

Ben looked at April curiously. "Yes, but I thought Chris's family was just dripping in money."

April said nothing, and slowly the two men realized that Christopher had not helped her with her education. They both looked startled and Steve even seemed a little disappointed in his friend.

An unpleasant light gleamed in Ben's eye. "So that's his secret," he said softly. "He's vindictive. I must say that I am surprised." Suddenly he called out to the others, "Hey, guys, did you hear this? Our aristocratic friend, Mr. Ramsey, would not even give his wife enough money to pay for her education. He made her do it herself. Really, Ramsey, is that how all you southern gentlemen act?''

April gasped. What a dreadful thing to say. How painful, how humiliating, for Christopher. And it was so unfair! He had tried to help her.

She looked over at Christopher. He had straightened and was still holding a beer can in one hand, but the other was knotted in a tight fist, and in the light from the lantern April could see his eyes glittering.

But he said nothing; he didn't try to defend himself or explain that everything had been as April had wished. He stood there silently, letting people think that he had been selfish and ungenerous.

And April wondered if in some strange, confused way he thought he deserved punishment like this. She tried to say something, anything. "But I didn't want—" she faltered.

Again Beth Market sensed her difficulty and quickly changed the subject. Ben, clearly aware of how offensive his remark had been, tried to cover up with more of his light chatter.

As the tension eased a little, people moved back to the tables for more beer and wine. April felt that she had to say something to Christopher, to apologize somehow, and she murmured an excuse and moved across the clearing toward him.

Suddenly some music blared loudly.

April whirled and stiffened. Josh Goodhue and one of the staffers had gone down to the bunkhouse to get some cassettes, and they had turned on the tape deck in one of the cars.

April hurried over to the car, hardly conscious that everyone was watching her. "Evan, turn that down," she ordered. "It's much too loud for this time of night."

Evan immediately reached in the car and snapped off the music.

"I *am* sorry," Josh apologized. "I just didn't think."

"You can certainly have music," April said quickly. "Just not that loud." She sent Faith down the trail to see just how high the volume could be without disturbing the other campers.

Once the music was adjusted, and Faith started jogging back, April realized that Christopher and his friends had been a little startled at how quickly the staffers followed her orders. She was a ranger; they were summer help. It was a distinction that perhaps hadn't been appreciated before.

"I'm sorry," she said, conscious in particular of Christopher's gaze, "but most campers go to bed pretty early." She wished she didn't feel so awkward; after all, she had only been doing her job.

"Well," Ben said, breaking the silence, "it's too nice a night to be in bed, and this is dance music." He grabbed Faith as she jogged back into the site. "I for one intend to dance." He put his arm around the girl's waist and embarked on an elaborate sequence of dance steps that she couldn't begin to follow.

Other staffers immediately joined them, but the lawyers, April noticed, hung back. It occurred to her that Josh and Steve were waiting to see what Christopher was going to do. After all, none of them had any idea how things stood between April and Christopher—whether they were enemies, friends, or entirely uninterested in each other. They certainly weren't going to ask her to dance if he felt he had a right to dance with her first, and if he didn't want to dance with her, to associate with her, well, he was their friend, and their loyalty was to him.

It was an awkward moment that seemed to go on and on. April sensed Beth beside her; she was probably equally agitated, wondering whether or not Steve would ask her to dance.

Suddenly Christopher put down his beer and came over, extending his hand. "Come, April, it's been a long time since I've danced with you."

And as she moved toward him she noticed Josh walk toward Julia, leaving Steve to say awkwardly, "You wouldn't feel strange about dancing with a colleague, would you, Beth?"

Almost timidly April laid her left hand on Christopher's shoulder. His arm slipped around her waist and his other hand closed over hers. The clear sound of the music circled through the moonlight and the trees. And in the soft light from the lanterns it didn't seem to matter that even the girls were in jeans and boots.

But the dance floor was hardly what it should have been, and just as Christopher was guiding April into a turn, she stumbled on a tree root.

His arm closed around her, holding her so that she would not fall. "Are you all right?" he asked quickly. Without releasing her, he laughed, "I guess I got a little overambitious. I don't usually have to avoid tree roots."

April wrinkled her nose at him. "You city folks just don't know how to take care of yourselves in the wilderness."

"Maybe not," he said softly. "But I think I can manage to take care of you." April felt the arms around her tighten, pulling her to him. She lifted her face and hoped that in the shadow of the tree he would kiss her.

But she heard him make a startled, confused sound,

and then step away. "What was that?" he asked, his hands on her shoulders.

"What?" She glanced down to where he was looking and had to laugh. "It was my nameplate." The plastic tag that she wore on her breast pocket had poked into his chest.

"Well, for heaven's sake," he laughed, "what sort of woman goes out for a night of dancing in this kind of rig?" And then lightly, his fingers just grazing her breast, he unfastened her nameplate. He turned her around to face the light. "What other sort of armor do you have on?" He hooked a finger in her belt and unfastened the knife that dangled there. He dropped both the knife and the name tag into his pocket. "It's like dancing with a prison guard." And when he gathered her back into his arms, it was to hold her much more closely than before.

April's shape had changed since high school. She had been a slight girl then, but having a baby had left her with fuller breasts and softer hips. Her rigorous outdoors life kept her slender, but her body was quite clearly a woman's. And now, dancing with Christopher in the dark of a spring evening, she had to wonder if he noticed.

Suddenly she thought that this might be the way to show him that she wasn't a child anymore. She could let him know how she felt to have his arm around her waist. She could press herself against him, letting him feel her body tremble with the responses, the desires of a woman.

As quickly as she had this notion, she had to dismiss it. It wouldn't work. After all, she thought, remembering those dark, wordless nights in their bedroom in Charlottesville, her *physical* maturity had never been questioned. Anyway, she reminded herself, the point of this plan was supposedly to set him free, to make him able to care for another woman. Seducing him seemed, at best, an awfully roundabout way of doing that.

The music was soon over, and people changed partners. Josh clicked on a lively, big-band tape, and everyone tried hard to remember how to Charleston and jitterbug. When a slow dance finally came on, April was a little disappointed to find herself dancing with Ben. She couldn't help remembering the brush of Christopher's strong fingers against her breast, and she wished that he was her partner again. Ben wasn't pleasant to dance with. He persisted in trying to hold her too close, and the dance was devoted more to the little struggle between them over that than it was to actual dancing.

As soon as the music faded and she had broken away from Ben, Christopher came over and dropped her nameplate and her knife in her hand. "I should have given them back earlier," he said evenly. "It looked like you might have needed the knife during that last dance."

So he had noticed how tightly Ben had been trying to hold her. "Christopher, could we talk for a moment?" She still wanted to say something about what had happened earlier, about that awkward moment after Ben's remark.

"Of course," he answered. "It's pretty late. Do you want me to walk you back?"

April had walked down the trail hundreds of times alone, on darker nights than this one, but she didn't say anything, and silently, without explaining to anyone where they were going, they started down the trail.

Christopher was walking with his hands in his jeans pockets, and wordlessly, without taking his hand out of his pocket, he crooked an elbow a bit, inviting her to slip her hand in. She did, and his strong arm pressed her hand to his side.

Why had he done that? April wondered, her fingers sensitive against the soft thick wool of his shirt. It wasn't the sort of formal gesture that she used to hate, when he would direct her walk with a cool hand touching her back. Nor was it a romantic gesture, arousing and seductive. No, it just seemed intimate and familiar as if he were admitting that they had shared a past, a past that made it silly for him to treat her like a client as he had yesterday, or like a child as he had today.

She wanted to walk this way forever, silently, down the dark trail, her hand nestled in the warmth of his arm, but he was clearly waiting for her to speak.

"Christopher, I want to apologize," she finally said.

"For what?" He glanced down at her, obviously a little surprised.

"For what Ben said."

He shrugged, and she could feel his shirt shift beneath her hand. "It's hardly your fault he had such a quick tongue. He's always like that."

"No, no," she said immediately, unconsciously tightening her grip on his arm. "I want to apologize that he was able to say it, that it was true. But, you see, when I left Charlottesville, I thought that the best thing I could do for everybody, for you and for me, was to just disappear, for me to learn to take care of myself. That's why I sent the money back." She took a breath and tried to speak more slowly. "But I think I now see that that was selfish, that you probably would have felt a lot better if I had taken the money."

"I certainly would have." Christopher kicked at a pebble lying in the trail, and her hand was jarred away.

"Do you know what it feels like when a man's wife won't even take his money?" He suddenly looked at her, his voice impatient, angry. "God, April, what was I to think? I knew that your mother wasn't giving you anything. You had no skills; you had never worked. I simply had no idea how you were going to support yourself."

"And you felt guilty about it?"

"You're damn right I did," he said abruptly. He pushed a lock of hair off his forehead and sighed. "April, you were just a kid."

"But don't you feel better now, now that you've seen me again?" she asked eagerly. "I have a good education and a job that I love. Don't you see that you don't have anything to feel guilty about?"

"Are you kidding?" he scoffed. "At least before I could hope that you had met somebody, that you were married with a house and kids, everything you ought to have. And now I find out the truth—that this whole time that I have been sitting around with more money that I have time to spend you were waiting tables and riding buses. It doesn't exactly make me feel wonderful."

"But what about now?" she pleaded. "That part of my life is over. Things are so much better for me now."

"But, April"—he shook his head—"what comes after this? You yourself said that you don't know how many winters you can take. Or what if something happened to Mike, and the next superintendent is married and needs the whole cabin?"

"I don't know what will happen next," she said impatiently, "but I know that whatever it is I will be able to cope with it. Why can't you believe that?"

"But you shouldn't have to cope all by yourself." He seemed as exasperated with her as she was with him.

"If I were a starving poet or something, it might be one thing, but I am not." He jerked at his collar in frustration. "Good Lord, April, what am I supposed to do every time we have bad weather for the next twenty years, sit in my home and think about you taking down other people's tents?"

"Well, I just don't see that you have any choice," she said angrily. "Not only am I not your responsibility, but you don't have any say over what I do." She suddenly stopped and covered her face with her hands. "Oh, Christopher, I don't want to fight with you."

She felt his arms go around her, holding her gently. "I don't want to fight with you either. I just want you to be well and happy. I really do." His voice was low, tender. "It's been such a shock, seeing you again, finding out how hard your life has been. I just don't know what to think."

April rested her cheek on his wool shirt, listening to the reassuring beat of his heart. She felt so comfortable with his arms around her. She didn't care what she had just said about looking out for herself; this had to be better.

He stepped back from her so that he could look at her tearstained face. "But I do know one thing," he said.

"What's that?" She sniffed.

"I haven't said how good it is to see you." His voice was gentle. "And not just because I was worried about you. It's just good to see you. I had forgotten how pretty you are, what fun you are to be with. I guess I had forgotten how fond I am of you. You are a very special person." He cleared his throat and took her arm. "Now let's get you home."

Chapter Five

So Christopher was "fond" of her. Well, Christopher was probably fond of baby animals, his favorite hiking boots, and several professional football teams. But April now knew that she didn't want him to be fond of her. She loved him, and this casual affection was not at all what she wanted.

Christopher, Josh, and Steve left to go backpacking the morning after the campfire, not to return for four days. The campground felt empty to April, and she had trouble losing herself in her daily round of duties. It worried her; if she felt like this during May, what would the winter be like?

Julia Breeland and Ben Carleton were apparently also getting a little restless, and several times, April saw his sleek silver car sweep out of the main gate, taking the two of them into Lake Placid looking for some excitement.

April spent much of her free time with Beth Market. They did not confide in each other, sharing their feelings about Christopher and Steve, but they didn't have to. Each realized how the other felt, and April certainly knew that if she ever had to talk about Christopher she could talk to Beth.

Instead they talked about things that Beth laughingly described as "things girls are supposed to talk about." She was apparently tired of only talking about law, and she and April had several happy conversations about sewing projects, skin care, wallpaper, and Beth's dearly loved nieces. It did make April wonder what a woman like Beth was doing in such an exhausting, demanding job. Why wasn't she working for a firm that demanded less, that would give her more time for herself.

"Well, I don't really know," Beth answered when April finally asked her. "Maybe it's that it's so easy to lose yourself in your work, so you don't have time or energy to think about what your life is really like, how empty it is." And then suddenly she looked at April and spoke more directly than she ever had before. "I think that's why Christopher has done so well at the firm. He works so hard, and working hard gives him an excuse for not having much of a personal life. I honestly think"—now she faltered a little—"that Steve is the only person he is at all close to."

April knew what else Beth was thinking: that his work was only Christopher's excuse for not having a fulfilling relationship. His guilt over April was the reason.

Beth asked April to come up to the campsite for dinner on the night that the men would return from backpacking, and April was very tempted. How she would love to see Christopher coming out of the forest, exhausted and exhilarated, happy to be back to the comforts of running water and fresh fruit, but reluctant to leave the challenge and beauty of the wilderness.

But she said no. She felt sure that Christopher must have done some thinking while he was hiking the trails. He must have tried to sort through the guilt he had felt for six years and the affection that seeing her again had reawakened. She had no idea what his conclusions might be; for all she knew he might ruffle her hair and want to buy her a balloon, or he might start treating her with more cold formality than ever before. She knew it was better to wait for him to come to her.

But it wasn't easy, that long evening, staying in the cabin, trying to write her mother, all the while remembering that Christopher was only moments away. She didn't need an excuse to drive up to their site and ask about their trip; she could just go. It would be a natural thing for her to do; no one would think it at all odd. But she resisted the temptation, and she did not go.

The next morning she saw Josh and Steve first. They were coming down to the boat landing to tell Evan, the boat dock attendant, about the fish they had caught in the mountain pools. They had had a wonderful time, they told her.

"We're ready to go right back out," Josh laughed.

"Surely not *today*." April smiled, hoping for both her sake and Beth's that Christopher and Steve were not quite as eager to go out again as Josh was.

"No, not today," Josh admitted. "Actually we are going to take some canoes and go up the inlet late this afternoon, have supper, and then come back by moonlight."

"That's a fun trip," she replied. The narrow channel that fed into Frank Lake wound back into the forest for several miles before the falls that brought the water cascading out of the mountain. Canoeing up the inlet and then drifting back was a popular activity among the campers. The park rented out canoes so that everyone could do it.

"Ben Carleton doesn't want to go," Steve said.

"And we would like to take an even number so that no one has to sit in the middle of a canoe. We were all wondering if you would like to come with us. If you aren't on duty, of course."

April hesitated.

"It was Christopher's idea to ask you," Josh added quickly.

April wondered if he knew how she had to hear that before she could agree to come. "I'd love to."

"Oh, by the way," Steve said as the two of them were turning away. "Chris came down the trail with us. I think he's looking for you."

In a moment Christopher appeared, walking down toward the water, his arms swinging lightly. The morning was still cool, and he had a beige down vest over a blue and beige checked shirt. He caught sight of April and his step quickened.

"I heard that you had a good trip," she said as soon as he was near.

"Yes, thank you, we did," he answered.

April's heart sank. It was the voice she had heard on the first day, his careful lawyer voice, cautious and formal. Why had he come looking for her, why did he want her on the canoe trip, if he was going to be like this?

"I assume that you're on duty," he continued in the same tone. "But do you have any free time today? There are some things I would like to discuss with you."

"This is as good a time as any," she said awkwardly. "But I've got a nature hike scheduled in twenty minutes or so."

"It shouldn't take that long. Why don't we sit down?" He gestured toward a log bench facing the lake.

Obediently April sat down on the bench and folded her hands in her lap. She had no idea what he was going to say. What could he say? He couldn't tell her to get out of his life. She already was. He wasn't likely to rant and rave at her for leaving Charlottesville without talking to him; she knew that he wasn't angry about that. What was he going to say?

"I want you to come back to the city with me."

"What?" April gasped. She couldn't have heard right; he couldn't have said that.

Christopher held up a hand. "No, think about it for a minute," he said calmly. "Don't reject the idea out of hand, because it really does make perfect sense."

April shook her head, speechless.

"I have given it a lot of thought," he said with deliberation. "What are you going to do if you can't face another winter here? Ranger positions are hard to get; you aren't going to be able to transfer to a place less isolated. Mike says you—"

"Mike?" April cried. "Mike? What does he have to do with this?"

"He came up and talked to me the morning before we left. April, he's just as concerned about your future as I am. And both of us agree that while you are really great at this job it's not the sort of life for you in the long run."

"Isn't that for me to decide?" She was starting to seethe at the idea that the two of them had sat down to decide what she should do, just as her mother had made all her decisions seven years ago.

Christopher hardly heard her. "Of course, Mike wants to see us get married again, and if that's what you want, then, of course, we will. But you and I both know that I can never give you what you need and deserve.

But if you come to New York, it's likely that you will meet someone who can."

April just couldn't believe it. Was he offering to fix her up? Introduce her to some nice young man? Get her married again and off his conscience?

"My brownstone is much too big for me," he went on, seeming completely insensible to just how outrageous his words were. "I bought it as an investment. You can settle in there for as long as you want. A man I know brought his younger sister up from North Carolina to stay with him, and since we have the same last name, that's what most people will think. Of course—"

That was the last straw. "Have you lost your mind?" April interrupted angrily. "Your sister?"

"Well, that part isn't important," he said smoothly. "What—"

"It isn't?" she demanded. It sounded important to her.

He ignored her. "What matters is that I will be able to help you, keep an eye on you."

"I don't want you keeping an eye on me; I don't want your help." April was furious.

"I'm sure you don't mean that. After all, starting over in a new city is difficult—"

That he could be so calm made her angrier still. "Don't tell me about starting over, Christopher Ramsey. May I remind you that it was *me* who got off a bus in Buffalo and had absolutely no idea where I was going. I didn't even know whether to turn right or left when I walked out of the bus station."

"Don't remind me," he said, bitterness creeping into his tone. "I know what you went through."

"No, you don't, or you wouldn't suggest that I need looking after. I've walked into a restaurant and asked the man behind the counter for a job, and I could do it again.''

"What you can or can't do isn't relevant.'' Christopher's voice was taking on an impatient edge. "What matters is that you don't *have* to do it. If you have to start over again, why not let me make it easy for you?''

"Maybe I don't want to start over again just yet. I've only been here for a year. And, anyway, even if I were leaving here tomorrow, I wouldn't go to Manhattan. I don't want to live there. I don't want to be cooped up in all that concrete, living in some little box.''

"My home is hardly a little box.'' He was now angry too.

"And I am supposed to live there until I 'meet someone.''' April's voice was heavy with irony. "What are you going to say to my gentlemen callers? 'Hello, pleased to meet you, this is my ex-wife, but I am pretending that she is my sister. I don't want her anymore but perhaps you will.'''

"April...'' The anger had drained from his voice.

But April hardly heard. "Oh, Christopher, come on. If you really had a sister, would you want her to come to New York and hang out for a husband? Wouldn't you want her to have a little more pride than that?''

He made a noise of protest, but she was not through. "Well, that's what you had in mind—hanging out for a husband. You just didn't put it that bluntly. Or were you planning on buying me one? You could probably afford it; you seem to think that you can afford everything else.'' Even in her anger April knew how very untrue that was, but she just didn't care. "Now, I may not be one of *the* Virginia Ramseys,'' she stormed, so angry that she had apparently forgotten her own last name, "but I've got my share of pride. And it isn't just pride. I don't want another husband. I have had one husband already, and that experience certainly didn't make me want to go looking for another one. If that's what husbands are like, I have had enough of them."

She didn't mean that. Dear Lord, *why* had she said it?

"Oh, April." Christopher's voice was quiet, pained. "What have I done to you? Have I really made you feel this way?"

No, of course he hadn't. Her anger immediately washed away. She stared out at the lake, biting her lip, trying not to cry. The lake looked so thoroughly ordinary, just as it looked every morning at this time when the sun topped the trees to sparkle across the dark water. How could it look like it always did, when Christopher had just made this ridiculous, preposterous suggestion that she come to New York and live with him as his sister?

What could he be thinking of? What confused depths of guilt had this plan sprung from? And with what arrogance did he assume that he knew what was best for her?

She knew that he was looking at her with concern and that she would have to say something. She looked first down at his hands, tensed against the denim of his jeans, but before she could steel herself to look at his eyes, she heard her name called.

"April, your nature hike people are all here."

"Excuse me," she said to Christopher. "I have to get back to work."

His fist clenched angrily, but he said nothing.

This was not the short children's walk, but a three-hour hike designed more for adults. The hike went back into the woods to a spot that had been burned out twenty years before, and the leader had to know a great deal about how a forest recovers from a fire so that he could describe to the campers what it had been like just after the fire and how, even now, there were still signs in the type of vegetation, in the way that it grew, marking this area as one that had once burned. Several summer staffers went with April, learning how to lead the hike themselves, so she had to concentrate, not just to answer the questions that people were asking today, but to try and anticipate for the staffers what other sort of questions they might be asked all summer long. She was glad that the hike was so demanding; otherwise she would have done nothing but worry about Christopher's extraordinary suggestion.

When the hike was finally finished and she walked back up to the cabin, she no longer had any choice about what to think about. Thoughts of Christopher and what he had said came flooding to the front of her mind.

Surprisingly she was no longer angry. She was still shaken, but not as much by what he said as by her response to it. She had not known that she was capable of being that angry.

Perhaps it was the hike that had put their problems into perspective. She had described a forest fire to the campers, trying to get them to see the hot, angry flames leaping from tree to tree and the frightened animals desperately running, searching for safety. She had talked about the charred black land and its long, slow return to green, how it gradually, serenely, healed itself, taking its time, knowing that it had forever. Somehow this eased the angry flame that was churning within her.

Perhaps she also wasn't angry because she had to admit that Christopher was, in part, right. She didn't want to be a ranger all her life. Yes, she would never want to quit doing things outdoors, but she didn't want to grow old, leading nature walks for other people's children. She wanted children of her own.

But she didn't see what she was going to do. Certainly going to New York in the middle of the summer, pretending to be her husband's sister, was hardly the answer. What had he said? "Mike wants to see us get married again, and if that's what you want, then, of course, we will." She sighed. That was exactly what she wanted; she would even live in the city if that was the only way to be Christopher's wife. "But you and I both know that I can never give you what you need and deserve." He would marry her out of guilt, but he could not promise to love her. April unhappily kicked at a pebble. That was not the sort of marriage she wanted; she had already had that.

As she turned up the walk leading to the little stone cabin, April stopped and knelt down, pulling a few weeds that had come up in her flowers. This was what she would like someday: not to care for a whole forest, but just to have her own little garden with flowers and some vegetables she could can and some fruit she could make into jam. She shook her head, brushing the dirt off her fingers, reminding herself how unrealistic that was. A life with Christopher would be in the middle of Manhattan. She could undoutedly buy some exotic houseplants, but she couldn't have a real garden. Just some houseplants, not a garden filled with children and love.

The front door of the cabin was open to the May sun, and just as April reached for the handle of the screen door, she heard voices.

"She's pretty independent," Mike was saying. "You've got to admire her for that."

April froze. Mike was talking about her. Dear God, had Christopher come up to report?

Indeed, it was his voice answering. "Is she? I never thought of her that way."

Suddenly April was furious again. He was acting as if she were eighteen again. This was like a parody of some old-fashioned proposal—the young man talking to the girl's father, the girl not having much to say about her fate. Well, this woman had a great deal to say. April grabbed for the door.

She stopped herself, slowly letting her hand drop off the handle. Storming in there angrily, railing at them, undoubtedly ending up in tears, was hardly the way to impress Christopher with her maturity. Trying to seduce him had probably been a better idea than that, and it had been one of the worst ideas she had ever had.

So April instead crossed the road and went over to the bunkhouse and spent a distracted half hour chatting with one of the summer staffers.

She didn't return to the cabin until it was time to get ready to go on this canoe trip she had promised to go on—not that she was very eager to go anymore.

Christopher was gone by then, but Mike didn't try to conceal that he had been there.

"So your husband wants to take you to New York?" Mike said when she came out of the bedroom, having put a swimsuit on under her clothes.

"Stop calling him my husband," April snapped.

Mike raised his eyebrows and looked at her interestedly. Why did he always read so much into normal aggravation? she thought irritably. She would have to calm down, or who knows what outlandish ideas would come into his head.

She opened one of the pine cupboards and took out some insect repellent and a flashlight. "Yes, he suggested it. Isn't it the most extraordinary thing you've ever heard?" She tried, without complete success, to keep her voice light.

"No."

She turned on Mike. "What do you mean, *no?*" she demanded.

"Now, don't get so huffy," he said. "But it isn't so surprising. Most men want their wives to live with them."

"But, Mike," April cried in exasperation. "I am not his wife anymore, and that is not why he wants me there. Didn't he tell you? About how—" She faltered. It sounded so ridiculous, she couldn't bear to repeat it.

"Yes, he did. He thinks you'll meet more people in New York than you will out here."

"Not people, Mike, *men.* Surely you don't think I ought to go."

"Why not? Everything he says is true. You can't do this year after year. If there wasn't such a shortage of positions, you could transfer to a larger park, but you're a fool if you count on that. It's more likely that the state will be cutting back on rangers, not creating more. So go back to New York, make a life for yourself with him. I don't see that you would be all that unhappy, and you might end up making yourself a right happy woman."

She sat down. "But, Mike, he doesn't love me."

"Are you sure about that?"

"Of course," she said immediately. "He has actually

suggested that I come to New York so that I can meet someone else. He's not talking about the two of us making a life together."

"Well, that's what he *says* he's talking about."

April suddenly felt defensive. "Christopher is as straight a person as there is. If he says that's why he wants me in New York, then that's why he does."

Mike pulled the pipe out of his teeth and slowly began to fill it, again looking at her as if her sudden defensiveness was very revealing. "I'm not saying that it's deliberate. I think he's fooling himself about why he wants you there."

April's mouth dropped open. "No, Mike, you're wrong."

"Could be," he answered. "I suppose you know a lot more about it than I do." He flicked on his lighter and, sucking on the pipe, lit it. When he got it going, he took it out of his mouth and looked at her. "May I say something?"

April had to smile. "Just what have you been doing for the past fifteen minutes?"

He ignored her. "I can understand how you were pretty taken aback when he asked you to go to New York, but it sure sounds like you said some things that you had no business saying."

April sighed. She knew what he was talking about, and he was absolutely right. She had sounded like a man-hating old maid.

Mike continued. "You've got the man believing that you're all frozen up inside, that he hurt you so badly that you won't ever make a man a good wife. It's not true, and it's not fair to let him go on believing that your marriage soured all the good parts of you."

"You're right," she said, rolling up a towel and moving toward the door. "Of course, you are. I'll say something to him. They've asked me to canoe up the inlet this afternoon. I'll talk to him then."

The five lawyers were already down on the beach when April got there. They were sorting through life belts and paddles, each person trying to find a paddle the right size. As April came around the green wooden posts that marked the end of the road, she saw Christopher look up at her, his eyes dark with concern, and she knew that he was still worried about what she had said that morning.

She felt awkward under his gaze as she picked up a paddle and went to speak to Beth. If only he would stop looking at her like that.

Evan was carrying the three canoes to the water's edge. As he flipped the third he called out, "There. You're all set."

No one moved.

April guessed that at least half the group was wondering how they should pair up in the canoes. She assumed that Julia wanted to go with Christopher, and she had to admit that she did as well. Riding in the canoe together would give her a chance to explain what she had said this morning, how she really hadn't meant it. But if she couldn't ride with him, she would probably have the best time with Beth, but surely Beth would want to ride with Steve. What Christopher wanted, April did not know, whether he wanted to ride with Julia, herself, or neither of them. Perhaps he didn't care; perhaps he was only interested in canoeing. If that was the case, she reflected, he should go with her. The first summer she had worked at Frank Lake, she had had Evan's job, as boat dock attendant, and she had become an excellent canoeist. But how would Christopher know that? To him, she was nearly a helpless child.

Well, she thought, turning over a bit of sand with her paddle, she was the guest; she'd let them sort it all out. She would go in whatever canoe she was told. The only person she actively didn't want to ride with was Julia, and that was hardly likely to happen.

Josh Goodhue started to speak, which made sense to April. He seemed to be the least involved in all the emotional turmoil that surged through the group. "Why don't we put the inexperienced people with some of the better canoeists?"

Julia seized the suggestion. "I'm sure that I am the worst, so I should go with Christopher."

"But, Julia," Steve Webster protested, "April was the boat attendant here once." She had told him that the evening of the campfire. "She's probably the best, so maybe you should go with her," he continued helpfully, apparently completely oblivious of all the emotional currents swirling around him, currents that were probably far stronger than anything they would encounter in the water.

"No," Julia answered coolly, "I'll be fine with Christopher."

"All right," Josh said briskly. "Then, Beth, you—"

Beth interrupted. "I'll be happy to go with you, Josh."

April stared at her. Why did she do that? Surely she wanted to ride with Steve; why hadn't she waited to see if that was what Josh was going to suggest. She must be worried that Steve would think that she was throwing herself at him. That was hardly likely, April reflected. Steve seemed to have very little sense of himself as an attractive man, which probably came from all those years of having no money and not being able to date much. He didn't expect women to react to him the way they reacted to Christopher. Beth probably could have crawled into his tent at night, and he would have managed to think up some other reason why she might be there.

What a dilemma. Beth was too proud to encourage Steve in any but unconscious ways, and he would almost certainly miss the significance of the soft glances that sometimes escaped from her eyes.

"Do you want the bow or stern?" Steve had come over to April.

"It doesn't matter to me," April lied. The person who sat in the back, or the stern, of the canoe guided it while the person in the front just followed orders. It was more fun to stern, and April had gotten very good at it. She wouldn't mind one bit to have Christopher see just how good she was.

Fortunately, Steve was not the sort of man who would insist on taking the stern himself. "Well, if you know what you're doing, then you take the stern. Maybe I can learn something. I've backpacked a lot, but I haven't been in a canoe since I was a kid."

The bows of the canoes were in the water so Steve got in first. April pushed their canoe off, easily swinging herself into the stern seat as the canoe glided across the water.

"You did that without getting your feet wet," Steve marveled.

"Of course," she answered, then noticing that the others were still on the beach, taking off their shoes. "Straightaway," she ordered unthinkingly.

Steve turned his blond head around to look at her blankly. "Huh?"

She laughed. "Straightaway is the command for—Oh, never mind, just paddle forward."

He grinned. "I'm afraid that you're out of our league. Look at Julia."

Julia was holding her paddle all wrong. Her upper hand was curled around the shaft, and her lower arm was bent. If she didn't straighten her arm, she'd be exhausted in half an hour.

"I'm sure Christopher will show her what to do," April murmured, noticing that his stroke was perfectly competent.

The inlet was about three quarters of a mile around the shore, so they set off across the lake. The late-afternoon sun cast a sparkling path across the water, and the green trees rimmed the shore, dividing the lake from the sky. There was no wind, and the water was like glass. As April lifted and turned her paddle at the end of each stroke, the beads of water dropping off it splashed a delicate little arc across the glassy surface.

She and Steve paddled well together. He was stronger than she was, but because strokes from the stern always have more power they were equally balanced, and their canoe moved straight, not drifting off to one side as happened when one paddler was stronger than another. April had to do almost nothing to keep them on course, and the canoe glided through the water with seemingly effortless speed.

"Good heavens," Steve said soon. "You do know what you're doing. Look at the others."

April turned to look. Although considerably behind them, Josh and Beth were doing all right although Beth was unconsciously biting her lip, obviously having to concentrate intently on her stroke in order to do it right. The other canoe was having problems. Julia's stroke was so weak that Christopher's easily over-powered her, sending the canoe steadily to the left. In order to keep them straight, he had to use his paddle as a rudder, which slowed them down, or to change sides every few strokes and paddle for a moment on her side. Changing sides like that was extremely tiring.

"J-stroke," April murmured.

"What?" Steve asked, glancing back at her.

"Nothing. It's just that there's a stroke to be used when the stern is much stronger than the bow. Watch." April added a little hook on the end of her stroke, and in a few moments their canoe started to move more at an angle. "If he'd do that regularly, they would stay straighter."

"Then let's go back and tell them."

"No," April said quietly. "People usually don't like unasked-for advice."

"Not Chris," Steve said immediately. "He is so con-fident about what he does know that he doesn't mind at all admitting what he doesn't know. That's absolutely the first thing I noticed about him. Not many people are like that."

Not many *men,* April amended silently. But she turned the canoe and steered them back to the others.

As they neared Christopher's canoe she told Steve to stop paddling and easily brought their canoe up to the other one, turning just at the right moment so that they shot alongside Christopher's canoe in a perfect parallel line, with only a few inches betweeen the two canoes, but absolutely no danger of collision. April had to ad-mit to herself that she was showing off.

Steve held the canoes together as April quickly explained the J-stroke to Christopher. As Steve had predicted, he did not at all resent the instruction. He concentrated on what she was saying, watched her do the stroke, and, after trying it several times himself, asked a few questions.

"And if you tell Julia to put her paddle in deeper," April said very softly, knowing that Julia would resent advice from her, "she'd have more power."

Josh and Beth were curious about what the others were discussing, and their canoe would have rammed into April's if she had not quickly reversed her paddle and poled them away.

"I think we could all do with some instruction," Josh said. "Why don't we stick together and have April give us some pointers?"

"But April is supposed to be off duty," Christopher said quickly. "She shouldn't have to give us canoeing lessons."

"I don't mind," she said immediately, almost resenting that he felt like he had to step in and protect her from being taken advantage of.

Wanting to avoid another confrontation with him, she quickly started talking about the basic stroke and watching each one of them. By the time they reached the inlet, everyone, even Julia, was doing much better.

The stream that fed Frank Lake was, as mountain streams go, an easy one. It didn't have many twisting curves or patches of swirling white water. Still it was not like canoeing in the lake. They were traveling against the current, and the water danced over rocks and around boulders. But usually the difficult spots were shallow and the less experienced canoeists could easily push off the rocks with their paddles.

It was a fun trip, with people talking and laughing as they had near misses or as they didn't have near misses and crashed into the rocks, the aluminum of the already battered canoes ringing out over the rush of the current.

After an hour April called the expedition to a halt. They were now to where the inlet was winding down from the mountain. The current was getting stronger, rushing from the falls that were a little ways upstream. The water swirled around the rocks, now foaming and spitting in white froth. Only experienced white-water canoeists could travel through it easily, and April was also sure that Beth and Julia might be tiring.

"This is a nice place to stop," she said, not bothering to explain that she didn't think they ought to travel any farther for fear that the men would resent her concern for their safety. "We'd have to go around the falls before finding another pleasant place to eat, and I don't think that we want to bother with portages." The falls were treacherous enough that even the most experienced canoeists unloaded their canoes and carried everything on a little path that ran along the water.

"I'm ready to stop," Beth said. "I know that this water isn't deep, but for the last ten minutes I've been worried that somehow I was going to end up in it."

"Don't you trust me?" Josh demanded teasingly from the stern of her canoe.

"Not a bit," she answered lightly.

"I don't see the problem," Steve said as they all pulled their canoes up on the bank. "April and I didn't have a single close call."

"And you're taking credit for that?" Christopher asked him. "I seem to recall that during the fanciest stuff you weren't paddling at all."

"A chain is only as good as its weakest link," Steve returned. "And so as the weakest link, I am taking all the credit."

Everyone laughed—everyone except April, who was surprised at the sudden tightening in her throat, the burning in her eyes. Christopher had noticed how well she had brought her canoe up to his.

They had stopped at a place where the channel of the stream suddenly deepened and narrowed, leaving a broader bank between the water and the forest. The sun had long since dropped behind the trees, but the sky was still light, so they moved about in a soft, shadowless world, unloading the canoes, starting to fix supper.

April was surprised that they had brought steaks for dinner. She had expected cold sandwiches or, if they decided to build a fire, perhaps hot dogs. But this group had no reason to economize. For a moment it made April aware of how different she was from them. None of them, except Christopher, had family money; they supported themselves, but they all earned enough that the little luxuries of life—steak, real perfume, theater tickets—could be purchased unthinkingly. Beth and Julia probably had lovely towels in their bathrooms.

The smoky scent of the steaks sizzling over the coals blended with the clean fragrance of the forest, and April reminded herself that, however much money they all had, this moment was rare and unusual for them, just an occasional holiday from their exhausting, demanding city lives. She lived here, always surrounded by the forest, by its majestic beauty, its green peacefulness. That had to be worth a great many lovely towels.

As she sliced into her steak, the red juices oozing from it, April had to wonder if any other country had meat as wonderful as this beef raised on good midwestern corn, grilled over a fire built from the wood of the Adirondacks.

No one else seemed roused to patriotism by their dinner, so April ate in silence until Steve asked her if she had ever been on a long canoe trip.

"Just overnight," she answered. "Last summer a couple of us did portage around the falls. I would love to take a full week some time."

"You wouldn't know it from my canoeing skills," Josh put in, "but my Boy Scout troop spent a week in northern Minnesota when I was a kid."

"In Canoe Country?" April breathed. "Was it as wonderful as it sounds?" The Voyageurs National Park was several hundreds of thousands of acres with nothing but lakes and forest. No roads cut through it. It didn't even have the little patches of civilization that dotted the Adirondacks. The only way into the park was by boat. Ever since she had started leading an outdoors life, she had longed to go there.

"It's even better," Josh answered. "It irritates me now that I was just a kid and didn't appreciate it. It—"

"Hey," Christopher interrupted. "Instead of going backpacking in the Rockies like we planned, let's go up there in September and try our luck on the water."

"Yes, let's," Steve said enthusiastically. "It's so flat out there that we don't have to be expert canoeists, and I imagine there are outfitters we can rent equipment from."

Immediately the three men started making serious plans, their faces alight with enthusiasm, leaving all the women feeling a little left out and awkward.

"Can you take a week off in September?"

April suddenly realized that Josh was speaking to her. "I usually do," she answered unthinkingly. After Labor Day the campground grew quieter, and the park could survive with just one ranger.

Josh turned away from her and announced to the others, "Then I think we should take April with us. Keep us from getting stuck on the rocks."

A week in Voyageurs! It sounded like heaven. Paddling through the beautiful, unspoiled forest of the north, building campfires at night that would shine as little beacons on the dark shore...

April simply couldn't help what she did next. She forgot their angry confrontation of the morning, and her eyes went straight to Christopher's as if she were asking his permission.

The answering light in his was warm. "It's a perfect idea. April, you simply must come." His voice was as inviting, as enthusiastic, as she could possibly want.

"Beth could come too, and the girls could chaperon each other if they think they need to," Josh continued. "Although, Julia, I'm sorry, but I just don't think it would be your cup of tea."

Beth immediately clutched at April's arm and whispered eagerly, "How hard is it? I don't think I could go backpacking, but could I do this?"

"Yes, yes, you could," April breathed, caught up in the excitement. "Easily. It's not nearly as hard as backpacking." It all sounded so lovely. Not just to spend a week in Canoe Country, but to spend a week there with Christopher, smiling at her, his eyes warm—it was like a cherished dream.

His eyes lingered on her now as if he understood her thoughts, but when he spoke, it was in response to Beth's concern. "There'll be five of us, Beth. So we'll only take two canoes, and it'll be much easier on you to be the third person in a canoe. I know I'd be delighted to have you in mine." The slight undercurrent of old-fashioned gallantry in his voice suggested that all three of the men would be simply honored to have the chance to make things easier for her.

Beth threw him a grateful smile; at least the smile started in Christopher's direction. It somehow ended up in Steve's. April was almost equally pleased that Christopher had not thought he needed to make special arrangements to make things easier for herself—and even more pleased that he was making no effort to include Julia.

"Then it's settled," he said decisively. "We'll fly up on a Saturday and—"

The word *fly* brought April back down to reality. Plane tickets, at least one night in a hotel, probably two, renting canoes and Duluth packs, buying all the expensive freeze-dried food—while it was nothing compared to the cost of staying in a resort, it was still out of the question for April.

"I'm sorry," she said abruptly. "I'm very flattered that you asked me, but I can't go "

"Oh, why not?" the others chorused.

"I can't afford it," she said bluntly. Why should she be embarrassed that her job paid so little?

Christopher's features were suddenly tight. "Damn it, April," he cursed. "Don't be such a fool. I'll—" He checked himself, unwilling to talk about money with her in front of the others.

"Now, wait a minute, Chris," Steve said. However blind he was to the way people felt about each other, money was the one thing Steve did understand. "Of course, any of us would pay April's way in a second—"

"*I* sure as hell would." Christopher's voice was crisp.

April was startled. He hardly ever swore; now he had done so twice in less than a minute.

"I know," Steve answered. "It's not that much for

us, and her company would easily be worth it. But I've been in her shoes, being the one without money. You work and work to save for something, and then someone offers it to you, easily and glibly, making a mockery of all your efforts. I've been there." Steve's voice picked up an intensity, colored by the memory of difficult times. "I know what she is going through, and you don't. You've got no right to swear at her. Just shut up and leave her with her pride."

"I don't see that it is any of your business whether or not I give my *wife* a plane ticket," Christopher said angrily.

"Oh." Steve had so obviously, in the intensity of the moment, forgotten Christopher's and April's marriage. "When you put it like that..." He sounded so dumbfounded that Christopher's anger immediately dissolved.

"It does change things a little, doesn't it?"

The confidence in Christopher's voice, the certainty with which he spoke of what he could do for her, infuriated April. Especially after everything he had said this morning. "Not for me, it doesn't," she announced. "I am not your wife anymore so stop slinging your money around."

Across the awkward silence floated Julia's cool voice. "Goodness, people with money in this country do have to put up with a shocking amount of abuse from people who don't have it."

"Yes," Beth said in her calm soft voice, making the conversation general. "But that's never going to change. And I, for one, am glad to live in a country where we can criticize people like Christopher Ramsey without worrying that they can throw us into prison or foreclose on our mortgages."

"Foreclose on a mortgage! That's much too tame for me," Christopher returned lightly. He too wanted the subject changed, believing that he had a far better chance of forcing April to accept a gift from him if they were alone. He towered over Beth and then, to her surprise, scooped her off the ground, and holding her small body easily in his arms, started threatening to tie her to the railroad tracks, run her through a sawmill, and other grisly fates that said a great deal more about the old silent movies he had seen than about his true character. "But first we are off to the woods!"

"No, no, not the woods," Beth giggled in the high false voice of a melodrama heroine. "Anything but the woods!"

"Okay." Christopher seemed to be a very biddable sort of villain. "How about the water?" He carried her over to the bank and, extending his arms, dangled her over the water.

"Chris, no," she squealed. "Put me down."

April turned her head, knowing perfectly well that Christopher would never toss Beth in the water. At any other time the sight of him and his friends teasing and laughing would have fascinated her, but she was still smarting from the proprietary air that had been in his voice when he had spoken about her. Her eyes focused on Steve. He was watching Christopher and Beth, a surprisingly desolate look on his face at the sight of her cradled in Christopher's arms. If Beth could see that look, April thought, she would probably think a good soaking was a very small price to pay for it.

April leaned toward him. "Thank you for that support a minute ago," she said softly. "Christopher is a little hard to stand up to sometimes."

Just at that moment Christopher swung Beth to her

feet and with his arm around her shoulders, looked down at her affectionately. He lightly kissed her cheek.

It was just an impulsive bit of friendship, a tribute, if anything, to the simple, uncomplicated relationship that he had with her, compared to the complexities that colored his dealings with April and Julia. April understood perfectly and didn't feel the slightest touch of envy. That kind of pure liking was not what she wanted from him.

It wasn't so clear that Steve understood as well. "Yes," he said slowly. "I suppose girls do have trouble resisting Chris."

Suddenly everything felt so complicated to April, such a dark tangle of misunderstandings and confusion. No one seemed certain of how he himself felt, to say nothing of having any idea what someone else might feel.

No, she was wrong. Christopher Ramsey knew how he felt. He liked his ex-wife, felt obligated to her and responsible for her, and was perfectly willing to act quite brotherly toward her as a way of redeeming his own guilt. There could be no doubt about that. His bizarre proposal that morning had made that quite clear.

Suddenly April started pulling her shirt out of her jeans. "I'm going in the water," she said to Steve. "Would you keep an eye on me?" She was not so distressed as to forget the basic rules of water safety.

He seemed startled: The sun was down and the evening was cool. "Do you want me to go in with you?" he asked, regardless.

"No. I'll just be in for a second."

As she had hoped, the sharp shock of the icy water drove everything out of her mind. The dark whirlpools of twisting emotion stilled into frosty peace. She only stayed in briefly and was out again so quietly that almost no one but Steve noticed that she had even gone in.

She hurried back across the bank and picked up her towel and clothes. As she started toward the dark trees to change, she heard Josh call her name. "April, are we doing this right?"

He and Christopher were over by the canoes, holding paddles, apparently practicing one of the strokes she had shown them earlier that afternoon. Josh was craning his head around. "Where did she disappear to?"

"I'm right here." she hurried over.

"Have you been in the water?" Christopher asked carefully. His voice had taken on the familiar bland tone that she knew was hiding some strong response.

"Obviously," she answered. Under her clothes she had been wearing a two-piece bathing suit. Around the park, she usually wore a simple one-piece suit, the kind serious swimmers wore. She felt she always had to be prepared in case she had to rescue someone, and she didn't want to be burdened with tight straps or anything that might slow her down. Of course, a one-piece suit was too much of a nuisance under clothing, and so she had worn a two-piece. While it was not a skimpy bikini—she had, after all, had a cesarean section when her baby was born—it did call more attention to the soft curve of her waist and the swell of her breasts than did her other suits.

Was that why Christopher had spoken like that, so carefully? Was he suddenly aware of her body? No, she told herself, he probably just thought that she was an idiot for going swimming when it was so cold. "Let me see you do the stroke again," she said calmly.

The men complied, pulling their paddles through the air.

"You've got your hand too low. You'll get better leverage if you pull it up a bit." And unthinkingly, just as she would do for one of the children she had taught canoeing to, she reached her arm around Christopher and moved his hand up.

Christopher was much larger than her usual pupils, and the gesture brought her breasts pressing into his back and her arm against the hard warmth of his hip. The sudden contact with him sent a flash of fire through her chilled flesh. When she forced herself to pull away, she couldn't help it, but her arm drifted against his leg, feeling his jeans move against his thigh.

"Come on, April, get away from me. You're all wet."

But he said it after she had already stepped away—as if it had taken him a moment to frame the right words. And though the words were casual, just exactly what anyone might say at such a moment, his voice was anything but easy. A deep tremor ran through it, revealing how difficult he found it even to speak at all.

"I'll be right back," she said and slipped back into the woods to take off her wet suit.

April hadn't really expected to go in the water. A May evening in the Adirondacks was not exactly swimming weather. As a result, she had brought no underwear with her. But she had no intention of paddling for two hours with a cold, damp suit under her clothes, and so she slipped her jeans and shirt back on over her naked flesh and went back out onto the little shore.

The men were still working on the stroke, a difficult one designed to move a canoe sideways through the water. It was an emergency stroke, designed for avoiding rocks and dangerous patches of water. It was not necessary in most canoeing, but these two men obviously liked learning new things, mastering new skills.

"Now, remember," April said as she watched them practice, "you will mostly use the stoke in an emergency so get used to putting all your strength behind it." She took Christopher's paddle and demonstrated.

The paddle was, of course, too long for her, and as she gripped it, holding it out in front of her, her arms were stretched more than usual. She was standing in front of the lantern and did not realize how the light shone through the loose weave of her shirt, outlining the white curves of her breasts in an inviting silhouette. As she demonstrated the stroke her breasts moved freely inside the shirt, causing the fabric to ripple gently, hinting of the vibrating softness underneath.

"It's a good thing we won't need that stroke much," Christopher said curtly, but as he took the paddle from her the back of his hand brushed against her, lingering against her breast just long enough that she could not be sure that the touch had been accidental.

"Anyway, I think it's time we headed back. Let's get started," he called out to the others.

Steve was talking to Beth, sitting at a distance as if he didn't feel he had the right to sit next to her. He immediately stood up and started over to April, obviously planning to canoe home with her.

April decided to assert herself "Josh," she said loudly, "you don't really have that stroke right. Why don't you and I go in the same canoe and work on it?"

And as she watched the look of pleasure suffuse Beth's face, she was surprised to hear Josh whisper, "Nice work. I was wondering how to do that."

As they loaded up the canoes, April realized that she

hadn't been paying a great deal of attention to Josh
Goodhue. Ben Carleton, of course, forced himself on
her attention, and she was interested in Steve because
of the way Beth felt about him. She had not given
much thought to Josh. But suddenly she realized that
behind his gray eyes lurked quick insight and sympathy. She thought back. It had been Josh who had several times maneuvered Beth and Steve together, so
subtly that no one had realized what was happening.
The evening of the campfire when Christopher had extended his hand to April, Josh had immediately gone
over to Julia, nearly forcing Steve to ask Beth to dance
with him.

April was suddenly very curious about just exactly
what Josh understood, but the trip down the river was
with the current and easy enough that all the three canoes stayed together, and there was no chance for a
private conversation.

Once they were back out on the lake, however,
Josh's and April's canoe quickly outstripped the others.
Julia was hardly paddling at all, and Beth was so absorbed in her conversation with Steve that her strokes
were erratic without any definite rhythm.

When they were out of earshot, Josh spoke softly.
"Funny, but Beth certainly concentrated a lot more on
her stroke when she was with *me*."

April laughed lightly. "I imagine that she did."

It was a beautiful night for lovers. The moon was
nearly full, its lustrous sphere casting a path of diamonds across the lake. In the dark sky over the open
water thousands of stars glittered, tiny points of radi-
ance on black velvet.

April found it easier to ask questions that she would
have never dared to ask in the sunlight. "Josh, was it

your idea for all of you to come camping rather than just you, Christopher, and Steve to go backpacking?"

He twisted around, his gray eyes dancing in the moonlight. "Whatever made you think that?"

"You know exactly what is going on, don't you?"

"What can I say?" He shrugged and smiled. "I have scads of sisters and just seem to know more about women than do lots of men."

"You are a very dangerous man."

"People quake in their boots when I walk by."

April laughed. "Actually I suspect you are very sweet."

"Sweet! My dear Miss— Well, whatever your name is, don't you know not to ever call a man 'sweet.'" His voice was suddenly serious. "Actually it's a little awkward sometimes when you know that you know something a woman would rather have a secret. So I just always say to myself, if this were one of my sisters, and somebody knew this about her, what would I want him to do? I've got a sister who is like Beth, a little shy, not really able to assert herself when it comes to men. She was made very unhappy once, and I think the guy never knew that she cared. And he probably wasn't as much of a nitwit about such things as Steve."

"I have noticed he's a little slow to pick up hints," April acknowledged.

"A little?" Josh laughed. "It's hard to believe that he is simply an amazingly good attorney. He and Chris are quite clearly the best associates the firm has. You can believe it of Chris; he just seems like he would be good at whatever he does. And actually Steve is doing pretty well out here. Did you see his face when Chris picked Beth up? We are making progress," Josh said in a satisfied way, but then his voice became serious again. "I probably sound like a real busybody. Maybe it was interfering too much to arrange for them to vacation together this way, but I kept thinking that maybe if my sister had some time with this man outside of their office, she would be a lot happier today. And I hope if Beth has got any brothers, that they feel the same way about her."

"That's so lovely," April breathed. "I would adore having a brother," she went on, quite forgetting that someone was trying to take that place in her life.

"Well, I'd offer my services if I didn't think that somehow or another it would lead to having to shoot my friend Christopher Ramsey."

"What?" April gasped.

Josh laid his paddle across the canoe and turned to face her. "You aren't wearing much under your shirt, are you?

"No," she admitted. Josh's casual tone made his embarrassing question surprisingly easy to answer.

"Back when you were showing us those strokes, well, I thought it looked pretty nice, and if *I* did, then Chris— Let's just say that since then old Christopher the Third hasn't done a lot except try very hard not to look at you. And"—he smiled—"excusing your lady-like ears and all, I don't suppose looking is really all that he wants to do."

"Oh." A warm glow flooded over April. She had been so careful all day not to look at Christopher, knowing that she would only see concern in his eyes, their emerald depths mirroring the anxiety he felt over her careless, hasty words that morning.

Fortunately Josh seemed to know enough about women not to expect her to say more than that "Oh."

"I've been with the firm for two years," he continued,

"and I've worked with Chris the whole time. We've been in a lot of tense, pressured situations where our people have goofed up or the clients have changed their minds in the most annoying sort of way, but until Steve told him to shut up and stop bothering you, I have never seen him lose his temper. Never."

"He loses it with me about every other time we speak," April pointed out.

"I'm not surprised," Josh said cryptically. "But sometimes it must be a relief after all those stiff, genteel manners he is capable of hiding behind." He smiled gently when he heard April sigh. "Anyway, meeting you certainly does explain a lot about him."

"Does it?" April knew perfectly well that she shouldn't be so curious. Christopher's grandmother would not have thought such curiosity befitting a lady, but old Mrs. Ramsey hadn't known much about a canoe gliding through moonlit waters.

"Sure. We've all wondered about his wife."

"Oh, did you know he had been married?"

"He never talked about it, but I think his résumé says that he is divorced; anyway everyone knew."

"Steve didn't." April remembered that first morning when she had gone up to their campsite.

"April, for heaven's sake, don't you realize that Steve doesn't know *anything*? If he did, do you think any of us would need to be here right now?"

April laughed and hoped that Josh would return to his initial subject. "I'm not sure that our marriage lasted long enough for it to explain much about Christopher," she said invitingly.

"Don't be a goose," he said bluntly. "It's no wonder he has such high standards in women. You aren't an easy act to follow."

"What a nice thing to say!" She was quite genuinely pleased. "But no," she spoke more slowly, "I was the most thoroughly ordinary eighteen-year-old when we married."

"I doubt that. Anyway, you've got poor Julia Breeland in a tailspin."

"I do?" April had a lot of trouble imagining the cool and elegant Julia as anything but very poised.

Josh looked at her intently for a moment. "You do know that she is after Chris?"

"I am not Steve," she returned by way of a reply. "Of course I know."

"I think she's worried that you don't make her look so good."

"Surely she always looks very good," April said, thinking of Julia's fragile features, her designer jeans, her beautiful black hair.

"No, I'm not talking about looks, but about things that Julia has the sense to know are more important than physical beauty." he explained. "She's a bit of a gold digger. She knows it and does a good job of hiding it, but she had to realize that your refusal to take money from Chris, even if it does irritate the hell out of him now, is someday going to make her look pretty bad."

"It certainly does make him angry now," April sighed.

"April, I wouldn't worry about it if I were you. I know that Chris really respects Steve for having made it on his own. His feelings aren't just an idle 'good for you' thing either. His admiration for Steve is very deep. So when Steve made it so clear that he considers you as going through exactly what he did, well, Julia can't be too pleased to hear that."

"Oh," April had not refused Christopher's money in order to earn *his* respect; it had been the only way she could respect herself.

"Another thing," Josh continued, again not discouraged by April's minimal response, "is that Julia is so out of her element here. She's amazing in the city—she always knows a wonderful little place to lunch, and it sometimes seems like the entire taxi system believes that it exists just for her convenience. But she's inexperienced out here and has come as close to looking awkward as I have ever seen her. While you—you could probably wrestle a bear to the ground and stand up smiling."

"I wouldn't go that far," April laughed.

"Well, no," Josh admitted, "but it must seem that way at times to Julia. I think she really agonized over whether to come. She knew it might be taking a risk—and I don't think she likes to take risks—but apparently her divorce is almost final, and it was time to begin on Chris in earnest."

"What was he like?" April asked curiously.

"Who? Her ex-husband? Nobody knows. Although I must say it would be interesting to meet him. Maybe it would explain why she is as she is."

Josh and April had been drifting so long that the others had caught up, and they had to cease their conversation, a conversation that April had found very interesting. She wondered if Josh had been right about Julia. If so, the black-haired woman was certainly more impressed with April's abilities than Christopher seemed to be. Well, in any event, Julia couldn't have liked being so pointedly excluded from the canoe trip. In fact—

April stopped, her eyes widening, staring at Josh's

back. Who had excluded Julia from the trip? Josh. And who had suggested that April be invited? Again Josh. It had also been Josh who had quickly assured her this morning that Christopher had wanted her to come along on this trip today, knowing that she needed to hear that before she could come. And he had suggested that she not let her canoe get so far ahead of the others. "I just seem to know more about women than do lots of men." What did he know about her?

"Josh?" Her voice had a worried, almost frantic edge to it.

"Yes, April?" When he turned, his eyes were so smooth and expressionless that April had to conclude that there was nothing at all on his mind, that he had not sensed any of the secrets she was trying to conceal—except that she couldn't get rid of the lingering suspicion that that was exactly what he wanted her to believe and that it wasn't one bit true.

Oh, well, she sighed, there wasn't a thing she could do about it, and it seemed much more likely that her secret was a great deal safer with Josh than it was with Mike McKenna.

Slowly all three canoes paddled toward the beach, the trip almost over. April had not forgotten that she had planned to explain to Christopher that she had not meant what she said that morning about hating men. Perhaps she would still have a chance when they were putting away the canoes.

But even that didn't seem likely, for the beach was not deserted. The summer staffers had gathered around a picnic table, laughing and singing. April knew that they would all come and help with the canoes. There would be lots of cheerful confusion with no time for a private talk.

Suddenly a shout broke into these thoughts, and

April saw some of the staffers run across the open beach. A dark shape emerged from the trees and slumped to its knees on the sand.

"Paddle hard," April ordered Josh.

In a few moments they were pulling up on the sand, just as one of the staffers had run to the water's edge, calling her name. She jumped out of the canoe, leaving Josh to beach it, and hurried over to the knot of people. The little group parted as she came, and April saw a boy, perhaps sixteen or seventeen, looking shaken and exhausted, a large blue backpack at his feet.

"I am a New York State Forest Ranger," she said, forgetting all her own concerns, trying to sound reassuring and confident. "Please tell me what has happened."

Christopher suddenly appeared behind her. "What's going on?" he asked in a low voice.

"I don't know yet."

The boy shivered, and in a few swift motions Christopher unsnapped his own down vest and wrapped it around the boy's shoulders.

Slowly, haltingly, the boy told his story, and it was not nearly as bad as April had first feared. He and a friend had been backpacking, and his companion had fallen, breaking or spraining an ankle. They had waited for a day, but it was early in the season and the middle of the week, and no other hikers had come by so he had left his friend at their little camp and had come for help.

"That was just the right thing to do," April tried to reassure him. "Now, tell me exactly where he is."

He told them. "How far out is that?" Christopher asked her.

"Two days. Maybe a day and a half, but that's pushing it," she answered. She took a breath and started to organize things. "Faith, will you take him up to the bunkhouse, get him something to eat, and find out exactly what food and equipment his friend has? Evan, we'll have to go in after him."

Evan started apologetically. "I'll be glad to go, but I've never backpacked before. They hired me for the lifesaving and the boating."

April bit her lip and looked around at the five or six other summer staffers. Why hadn't this happened after Memorial Day? By then, all the summer staff would be here, including several boys she knew from last year. They were experienced hikers, strong enough to carry a stretcher if they had to.

"What's wrong?" Christopher asked quietly. He must have noted the concern on her face.

"Nothing much," she answered untruthfully. "We're a little short-staffed, that's all, but I can call one of the other parks."

"I'll go if you need me," he said immediately.

"We all will," Steve added, and Josh nodded his agreement.

April looked at the three of them. They were all tan, capable, and strong. It was hard to believe that they were attorneys who sat behind desks most of the year. They would certainly solve her problem.

"But you just came back," she protested.

"We were going to go out again in a day or so," Josh pointed out. "We might as well do some good while we're at it."

"But this isn't a pleasure trip; we'll be trying to get in and out as fast as we can. It will be work, and you are on vacation." April felt that she really couldn't take advantage of their good nature.

"We're on vacation from desks and libraries," Steve said. "We honestly don't mind."

Then Christopher spoke, directly and bluntly. "Let's not dance around here. Would it help if we went or not?"

She looked at him gratefully. "It would help a great deal."

"Then it is settled. How soon do we leave?"

"There's no point in traveling at night," she said. "We'd just wear ourselves out without making good time. So let's leave just as soon as it's light tomorrow. I'll be up at your campsite by four-thirty. Don't pack up; we'll go over the equipment so that we don't take duplications."

Chapter Six

It was still dark the next morning when April drove up to the lawyers' campsite, but they were all up and about. The men had spread out their gear. They had expensive, but clearly well-used, equipment. Their cooking utensils and tiny one-burner stove were smaller and lighter than April's so she pulled hers out of her pack, making it several pounds lighter. "My first-aid kit is better than yours so leave this here," she said. "And we certainly don't need to take three tents for four people. We may have to carry the boy out—"

"Now, wait a minute, April," Christopher spoke. "Please don't be offended, but we were all thinking that perhaps the three of us could travel a lot faster without you."

"No," she said bluntly, looking directly in his green eyes. She tried to ignore the hot wave of anger, which threatened to flood over her. What did they think, that she would be a burden, a nuisance, out on the trail? Didn't they remember yesterday, how superior her canoeing had been to theirs? Of course, they were now only thinking about physical strength, but still. . . . Why did she keep having to prove herself to him? She shook her head. "That is simply out of the question. You don't know the trail, and the safety of visitors is the ranger's responsibility." She tied the last fastening on her pack and hoisted it up on the picnic table so that she could slip into the shoulder straps. "Anyway, I won't hold you up."

April hadn't had her pack on this season, and it took her several hours to get used to the feel of wearing it. The pack had an aluminum frame that extended almost from the top of her head to well down on her hips so that her whole back supported the weight of the pack. The shoulder straps were padded with foam, and another strap buckled around her hips to keep the pack steady. She had chosen the pack carefully, and it was so well designed that carrying all her own food and provisions was not nearly as exhausting as it might sound. In fact, April really did enjoy backpacking; it was such a complete break from the civilized world. At an established campground like Frank Lake, there were at least showers and running water and usually a small grocery store within a few miles. But out on the trail a hiker had to be completely self-reliant. April realized that she had almost made a symbol out of backpacking trips: They proved that she could take care of herself.

If the trip had been one of pleasure, they would have gone leisurely, stopping whenever there was an interesting wild flower or when the trail turned and looked out on one of the striking mountain views. But they were trying to make good time, and all of those intriguing sights had to be ignored.

April was taking the lead. She had done so unthinkingly; after all, she was the ranger. But then she had noticed the three men exchange glances. They had silently agreed among themselves that she should go first; that way she could set the pace and she would not fall behind. But April knew that, although she was by no means muscle-bound, her endurance was excellent. She could keep going as long as they could. At least she hoped she could.

After a few hours she stopped. There was an old trail, no longer maintained or marked on the maps. The Park Service had abandoned it because it involved a very steep climb. But Mike had suggested that they take it. It would save them eight or nine miles, nearly a day's journey. If they used it, they might be to the boy by nightfall.

"Of course," she pointed out, "there's no reason to think that he's in any danger, just uncomfortable, so we don't have to do anything foolish."

But when they were assured that someone had hiked the old trail early last fall—Mike had told two of his nephews about it—the three men were eager to try it.

At first the old trail was as easy as the regular one. The incline was gentle, and it gave April a curious pleasure to know that no human had been on this path since last autumn. No one had yet seen these particular masses of white starflowers. The graceful fronds of these ferns had brushed against no human leg. For a sudden, aching moment she wished that she and Christopher were alone so that they could stop and she could share these thoughts with him.

Would they ever have a comfortable relationship—one in which she could talk to him like that? She knew that he would be glad of it. After all, he did like her and enjoy her company; that sort of warm friendship was probably exactly what he wanted. Except that it would have to be a little more than a friendship; he also wanted to take care of her, give her money, make decisions for her. April tucked her hands under the shoulder straps of her pack. Christopher's parents had given him everything else he wanted, she thought unhappily; why hadn't they thought to give him a sister too?

April's thoughts were making her unhappy enough that she hardly noticed how difficult the trail was getting. Fallen logs, some rotting, lay across the path, and green branches thrust out over the trail, brushing against their arms and faces. The forest had gotten so dense that only a faint whisper of sun filtered down to light the uneven trail.

She stumbled through an unnoticed spiderweb, its sticky threads gluing to her face and hair. She tried to brush them off without breaking stride, but Christopher, walking right behind her, must have noticed how she was twisting her head.

"April, what is it?" he asked.

"Nothing," she answered, running her hands through her curls. "Just a spiderweb."

A touch on her pack stopped her. "That's an awful feeling, isn't it?" He came around in front of her and, with a handkerchief slightly dampened with water from his canteen, gently cleaned off her face. The touch of his fingers on her face might have pleased her at any other time, but standing there with her face obediently turned upward, she felt like a small child having the cereal washed off her face. She did indeed feel like his little sister.

When he finished, he shook out the white square and said, "I'll go first; the trail is getting pretty tough." Ahead of them the path loomed nearly as steep as a staircase.

And April would have liked to cry out that she was the ranger, that she was the one who was supposed to know the forest, that she should bear the brunt of it, that she should go first. But she knew that it would make no impression on him.

It was just after two when they broke out of the forest back onto the new trail. They had already been hiking for longer than most backpackers do in a normal day. Steve suggested that they stop for lunch, and Christopher and Josh immediately agreed.

April spoke quickly, not wanting them to get their packs off. "There's a campsite about a mile and a half up the trail. There might be some people there and if they are on their way out, they might have passed the boy and know something. I think we should push on until we get there."

Christopher had been unbuckling the hip strap of his pack. He paused, his fingers still hooked in the nylon webbing. Then he tightened the strap across his jeans. "That makes sense to me."

April was a little relieved that they were willing to follow her advice. "There's some gorp in the upper right compartment of my pack if someone wants to get it." Gorp was the high-energy snack that backpackers nibbled on: It was made of nuts, little chocolate pieces, and raisins.

Steve got the gorp out of her pack and as they walked they passed it around. The trail was wider and brighter. They could walk more closely, nearly two abreast, and the men started talking about business at their firm. April didn't really understand what they were talking about, but she found it interesting to listen. It soon became clear that Josh was junior to the other two, and April began to suspect that rather than working *with* Christopher, he worked *for* Christopher. She wondered about Beth, who was several years younger than the men and so might well work under one of their supervision. For Beth's sake, she hoped it wasn't Steve. That would be too much to have to work for a man you loved.

April had felt rather bad that morning when they had all been getting ready to go. Beth had been cheerful and very helpful, pouring rice and cocoa out of their original containers and into the plastic bags that packed more easily, but April knew that Beth had not wanted Steve to leave again.

In no time at all the hikers reached the campsite, and as April had predicted, it was inhabited by people who had seen the boy. In fact, the white-haired, obviously retired man came down the trail to greet them and tell them about the boy. "If you are heading north," he said, "there's a young man up at the end of the long meadow."

April stepped forward and introduced herself, explaining that they were on their way to go get him. "We left Frank Lake this morning, and we hope to get to him tonight. How is he? Can you tell us exactly where he is?"

"What?" The man's wife had come up. "You left Frank Lake this morning, and you're here already? That's impossible; you must be exhausted." And she started bustling around them like the motherly sort of person she seemed to be. She urged them over to the campfire and helped them off with their packs.

And suddenly April did feel very weary; the climb had been hard. She let her pack slide down to the ground and sat down next to it, leaning against it, closing her eyes for a moment.

Mrs. Horton, as the woman told them her name was, looked at her with concern and then turned to the men.

"Why did you bring a girl out on an expedition like this?"

"Actually, ma'am"—Christopher, also leaning against his pack, was trying not to laugh—"she brought us. She's the forest ranger; we're just her gun-bearers."

Mrs. Horton looked again at April, noticing for the first time the green uniform shirt. "Well, I am behind the times, aren't I?" she laughed.

"Oh, things haven't changed that much," her husband mused. "I don't know a time when a girl as pretty as Miss Ramsey here couldn't get three men to follow her anywhere."

April blushed.

The Hortons insisted that the four of them eat the fish they had been frying for themselves. "We caught so much fish that we still have lots of food even though we were out two days longer than we had planned."

It turned out that they had come on the injured boy shortly after his companion had left, and they had stayed with him for the past two days. "We hated to leave him, but it's just a sprain and it's getting better," Mrs. Horton said. "If we stayed out any longer, our children would have all had fits and probably would have called the Marines to come find us."

April wasn't really surprised that these two people had completely rearranged all their plans when they had come upon the boy. Out on the backpack trails people tended to be very generous, making all sorts of extraordinary efforts to help others.

"But it took us a full day to get here from his camp," Mr. Horton said. "He's not in danger. Why not stop here and set out in the morning?"

April was startled when she saw the men looking at her, letting her make the decision. "No, the trail isn't too hard from here, and most of it is through the long meadow so it won't get too dark to walk until about nine, and if we push, we'll be there by eight thirty."

"He'll be awfully glad to see you," Mrs. Horton put in. "He was pretty nervous about spending the night alone."

"Then that settles it," Christopher said, and as they were putting their packs back on, he came over to April and said softly, "Why don't you stay here for the night and catch up with us tomorrow?"

She knew that he was concerned about her, but she still found it a little insulting. "I can make it."

But it was hard. They were all tired and walked without talking. With April in the lead again, the afternoon slipped away slowly, punctuated only by occasional brief stops for a drink of water or to tighten a bootlace. The shadows lengthened and then the sun sank behind the tree line, but the sky was still light, and once they were in the meadow, they could see well enough.

Finally, nearly an hour before she expected, Christopher touched her shoulder and pointed to the edge of the meadow. "Isn't that a light over there?"

And more than a mile away, just before the forest began, April could see a tiny campfire and the dark shadow of a tent. "Yes, that must be him," she said. "We've certainly made good time. I would have thought we had nearly another hour to go."

"You set the pace," Christopher responded.

As soon as they were a little closer, Josh cupped his hand and called out the boy's name. They all heard a thankful, happy shout in return.

"We are the rangers," April called out, and then to her complete surprise, Steve and then the others burst out laughing.

"What's so funny?" she asked, trying to look over her pack at them.

"I don't know," Steve answered. "But it suddenly seemed like we were all in a western movie, the brave cavalry riding in to rescue the stranded settlers." The men laughed harder, and April tried to join them.

"Look here, friends," she said. "If we have to carry this boy out, you're going to wish that we were on horses."

This moment of silliness lightened their hearts and quickened their paces, and they soon reached the boy's tent.

Pete Gardiner, as his name was, had crawled out of his little green pup tent and was hoisting himself up on a rock. Even in the fading light April could see that despite the feverish relief he felt at their coming, his young face was drawn and exhausted. Although she had been on several rescues before, she herself had never been stranded or injured out on the trail; it must be frightening to feel so helpless.

"Hi there," she said brightly, trying to summon up her best cheerleader manner. He would hardly be reassured if his rescuers dragged in, looking in worse shape than he was. "We heard you needed a bit of help."

"Gosh, yes," he sighed. "But how did you get out here so fast? I figured there wasn't a chance of anyone getting here for at least two more days—if Tom could even get anyone to come."

April felt a quick pang of sympathy. He'd probably been lying here all day, calculating just how long it would take his friend to get to Frank Lake, and then just when the rescue party might set out.

"Of course, we would come," she said. "And we'll get you out."

April was relieved to see that he was a slight youth. He was seventeen and certainly weighed a great deal less than the men. That would make it easier if they had to carry him out, but if it was just a sprain, maybe he would be able to hobble in a day or so. She started to unbuckle her pack. Christopher was standing behind her and helped her ease it off her back.

She knelt down and looked at the boy's ankle. It was, as the Hortons said, a sprain. Mr. Horton had taken a cooking pan and a plastic garbage bag and rigged up a container deep enough for the foot, and the boy had been faithfully soaking his ankle. When the Hortons had been there, he had alternated between hot water and cold, but since they had left, getting the water hot had been too much trouble to do very often.

Just as April was about to ask someone to heat some water, Christopher brought over a pan full of it. He asked her what else she needed, and she had him dig the first-aid kit out of her pack.

As she took out an elastic bandage, a wave of exhaustion swept over her. For a moment, her hand still on Pete's ankle, she closed her eyes, thinking about everything that still needed to be done in the dark: dinner made, dishes washed, tents put up, sleeping bags unrolled, teeth brushed...The list seemed to go on and on. She just wanted to curl up in her sleeping bag.

She stood up quickly, trying to give herself some new energy. She had been tired before, much more tired than this, and she had always managed to work that one extra shift, to study for one more exam. This wouldn't be a problem.

And then she realized with a sudden flood of relief why she had wanted to come with experienced hikers. The three men had not been sitting around, resting, waiting for her to give directions. The two tents were up, and Josh was dishing some steaming concoction into their mess kits. Gratefully, she took a plate from him and sank cross-legged on the ground. How glad she was that the three of them had come!

And although she was grateful for Steve's and Josh's presence, it was toward Christopher's tall form that her eyes strayed.

He had just finished splitting some wood and was unrolling the sleeves of his shirt, brushing them down his arms, and fastening them at the cuff. He pulled a dark sweater over his head and after settling the collar of his shirt, he took a plate from Josh. The other man said something, and Christopher laughed, his head tossed back, the firelight flickering on the column of his throat.

April knew that she might soon regret having seen him again. She might have to go through the heartache and anguish of leaving him all over again, but right now she didn't care. She was just glad that he was here.

"You aren't eating." Christopher's voice was low in her ear. "Come on, you have to eat something."

"I know," she said, picking up her fork.

He had said that before. "You have to eat something." In the first months of her pregnancy when just the sight of food made her sick, he would encourage her to eat in a voice so distant, colored by only the most formal concern, that she would force herself to swallow something just in hopes that he would sound like himself again. At least there was none of that formal detachment in his voice tonight. She wasn't sure what had replaced it; some sort of mild affection, she supposed, certainly not love. Or perhaps his quiet tones were just a mirror of exhaustion; he was probably nearly as tired as she was.

Dinner was a freeze-dried beef stew, easily made by adding boiling water. Trail food had improved enormously even since April had started backpacking, but still she was just as glad to be too tired to taste it. She shook her head when Steve offered to make coffee. She could hardly keep her eyes open, but she planned on going to bed as soon as the dishes were done.

Pete, on the other hand, was not sleepy at all. He was excited to see them, and after a long lonely day he was eager to talk. Christopher silently indicated to the rest of them that he was willing to stay up a little longer with the boy, and so, leaving him with the dishes to do, April went over to her tent.

It was a little pup tent with openings at either end, wide enough for two people to sleep comfortably and designed so that a tall man could sit upright. April could kneel, and even when sharing the tent with another woman, she had never felt too cramped or closed-in. She quickly unrolled her foam pad and started to spread her sleeping bag out. She was so weary that it took her a moment to realize that although the bag she was holding was a down-filled bag covered in navy-blue nylon, this one wasn't hers. She switched on her flashlight, shining it around the tent. There next to an unfamiliar clothing sack was her own sleeping bag.

Confused, she stared down at the cover she had pulled off this bag. The flashlight shone on a name inked across its side. RAMSEY. Her name. She didn't understand.

Then it was all clear. She wasn't the only Ramsey here. These things were Christopher's. The morning seemed like so long ago, but she now clearly remembered herself saying that they didn't need three tents for four people. Whoever had put up the tents had quite naturally put Christopher's belongings in with hers. Obviously she had to share a tent with one of the three men. There was simply no question that it would be Christopher. When the men had been pitching the tents, they wouldn't have even had to discuss it. "Where do you want April's tent?" Steve or Josh might have asked Christopher, automatically assuming that that was where he would sleep.

What on earth had she been thinking of? What had possessed her to say that they only needed two tents? How was she going to get a minute's sleep if she was lying next to Christopher? If watching him split wood took her breath away, how was she going to manage sharing a tent with him?

But April knew that she had been acting rationally. They would certainly have to carry Pete's belongings out, if not Pete himself; space would be at a premium. And so what if she had to share a tent with Christopher, she told herself resolutely. They would both be zipped up in their separate sleeping bags, and she could just turn to the tent wall and pretend to be asleep. It wouldn't be the first time she had lain next to him, pretending to be asleep. Certainly their sharing a tent for a few evenings in an emergency made a great deal more sense than her trotting off to New York to live with him as his sister.

Had it only been yesterday that he had suggested that? It seemed so much longer ago than that. April sighed, deciding that she simply wouldn't think about it, and she quickly changed into the light sweat suit that she slept in out on the trail. She rolled out her own sleeping bag, crawled into it, zipping it up around her, but before she could start pretending to be asleep, she fell asleep.

The sound of the tent's zipper woke her up. Christopher eased into the tent.

"Hi," she said sleepily, rolling over to face him. He was a dark mass, sitting cross-legged on the bag she had laid out for him.

He looked down at her, her cheek resting on the down vest she was using as a pillow, her curls falling around her face. "Blast," he said softly, "I was hoping to do this without waking you."

April burrowed into the warm cocoon of her sleeping bag, the soft, thick down feathers holding her body heat in. "What time is it?"

"After midnight," Christopher answered, his voice muted by the sweater he was pulling off. "Go back to sleep."

"There's a hook in the center of the tent if you want to hang a flashlight up," she said.

"You don't mind?" April could hear him fumble for a minute, and then her eyes blinked against the sudden light.

He was wearing a khaki-colored safari shirt. He started to unbutton it.

"You still use just one hand," April mused, tucking her own hand under her cheek.

"What?" He looked down at her blankly.

"You use just one hand to unbutton your shirts," April explained.

"Oh, I suppose I do," he said, looking down at his half-buttoned shirt. "I've never really given it much thought."

"I always thought it looked..." April was suddenly not sure what to say. "Very efficient." That was not at all what she really meant.

He laughed lightly. "Well, if you behave yourself tomorrow, maybe I'll show you how it's done."

April liked this, lying here so close to him in this cozy tent, talking about nothing. It felt very married. "How is Pete?" she asked, trying to prolong the conversation.

"He seems fine. I think he was really glad not to have to spend the night out here alone."

"Then I am glad we came all the way today," April murmured.

Christopher finished taking off his shirt and started to rummage through his clothes bag. The flashlight swaying from its hook cast a moving circle of light that glittered on the blue nylon of the sleeping bags and then softened to a pale bronze when it danced across his back.

April longed to reach out and touch his back, to rub the tiredness out of his neck and shoulders, to explore the texture of his skin.

When they had been married, he rarely allowed her to rub his back, even when his neck and shoulders would ache from hours of studying. She would try, always eager to please him, and he would at first relax, giving himself up to the soothing sensations, luxuriating in the feel of her hands on his tense muscles. But then in a moment he would stand up or roll over, saying politely, "Thank you, but you don't have to do that."

At the time April hadn't understood. He had so clearly appreciated it; why had he made her stop? Now she suspected that it was the casual intimacy of such moments, the husband-and-wife familiarity, that had made him uncomfortable.

She supposed that it might make him just as uncomfortable now, probably more so. And she couldn't honestly say that she would just be doing it to please him. It was what she wanted, to touch him, to feel the hard warmth of his back and arms as she had felt them before.

She kept her hands tucked in her sleeping bag.

"April?" Christopher spoke without turning back around.

"Yes?" she murmured.

"I think I owe you an apology."

April raised herself on her elbow and looked at him curiously. "I can't imagine why."

He glanced back at her, holding a gray sweat shirt in his hand. "We were all wrong about you, saying that you wouldn't be able to keep up. You were simply extraordinary. I've been out with plenty of men who could have never kept going as long as you did. You did a terrific job."

April had to blink frantically to keep the tears from rolling down her cheeks. This was, quite simply, the most flattering thing he had ever said to her. Of course, he had praised her for the way she looked, but she couldn't really take much credit for that. This was a tribute that she had earned.

"Thank you," she said softly. "And I can understand why you were concerned," she continued, although at the time she had not understood at all. "There certainly was a time when I couldn't have done it."

"I don't know." He pulled the sweat shirt over his head. Black letters spelled out the name of his college. "You were always so fit. That was one of the things I found the most excit—that I liked about you; you always had so much energy." He brushed a hand over his hair, which had been ruffled up by the sweat shirt. "You know, it's really remarkable how a woman can have a simply stunning figure, and then later you find out that she hasn't got a bit of muscle tone or—" He broke off. "This is a strange conversation to be having with your ex-wife."

"I didn't start it," April pointed out, not certain whether to be pleased that he had been dissatisfied with other women or jealous that he had the opportunity to find out about their, well, their muscle tone.

"Then why don't you change the subject?" he returned.

That wasn't a problem. April had been meaning to ask him something all day. "When did you start backpacking? You've obviously done it a lot," she asked.

Suddenly his face tightened and in the glare of the flashlight April could see it go blank. "In law school," he said abruptly. "The summer after my first year, the summer after you left. I didn't want to go home or even clerk in a law firm so I flew out west and spent the summer in the Sierras."

"That must have been wonderful," April said awkwardly, knowing that her casual question had brought back some painful memories.

"It was and it wasn't" was all he said.

He was obviously done talking and pulled the rest of his sweat suit out, but April felt like there was something she had to say. "Christopher, I owe you an apology too."

"Oh?" His tone was blank; he would have sounded more interested if she had told him his watch was thirty seconds off.

But she was going to go through with it and so sat up, the thick folds of her sleeping bag spiraling down around her waist. "What I said yesterday about—" She took a breath and started over. "I was very angry, and I know that I said some things about men and husbands that made it sound like our marriage had really twisted me and made it impossible for me to have a normal relationship. I really don't think that any of that is true."

His eyes were so dark and shadowed that she had no idea what he was thinking, but she persevered. "It's true that I haven't remarried, but I've just not met anyone; it's not that I hate men or don't believe in marriage."

His lips parted slightly, and she could see the tip of his tongue touch his teeth. "Why are you saying this?"

Suddenly she was almost angry and impatiently jerked her hands out of the folds of her sleeping bag. "Because, Christopher, I don't want you to go on feeling guilty about me. I'm fine. In fact, I'm much better off than I would have been if I hadn't met you." She was speaking firmly, emphatically. "And I know that you've convinced yourself that I was absolutely miserable the whole time we were married, but let me tell you, I wasn't. I was excited about the baby, I loved her, and I—" April broke off, aghast at what she had been about to reveal.

"And you loved me." Christopher's voice was almost harsh. "That's what you were about to say, wasn't it?"

April stared at him in amazement, "How—"

He gathered up her hands in his. "How could I not know? How could I not see what was happening? You were like a flower, slowly blossoming. At first I thought it was just because you were pregnant, but I had to face the fact that it was because of *me*." His voice had a question in it, a confusion in it, as if he could not understand how she could have loved him. "Each day you would try harder to do what you thought I wanted. Each afternoon you were happier to see me. You started smiling again; you were happy again. I knew what an affectionate, sweet nature you had; I knew what it had to all mean."

April shook her head, her loosened curls brushing against her cheek. "I had no idea that you knew."

"Imagine how I felt. Your love seemed like such a precious and exquisite gift that I had no right to because I couldn't return it. Believe me, April, I would have loved you if I could. I tried, I really did, but you always seemed so young."

Suddenly April felt very vulnerable, very exposed, because he had known her secret. How he must have pitied her, a young girl he couldn't force himself to love. Unconsciously she tried to pull her hands away, but his grip on them tightened.

"I think I felt the worst at night," he continued, obviously needing to talk about what he had surely never said before, "knowing that you were turning to me out of love, and that I just wanted you because you were so very beautiful. And there would be times—" His green eyes seemed to be looking through her, not seeing her, but back into the past, seeing a host of intimate memories. "There would be times when you would be lying under me and you'd touch my shoulder and just whisper my name, as if that was all you would dare let yourself say. And although you had just given me the most incredible pleasure, I couldn't—" He faltered. "I knew I should stop using you like that, but I just couldn't keep away from you."

"But, Christopher," she whispered, starting now to realize the full depths of the guilt he had been enduring, "I never felt used."

He didn't seem to hear her. "And then when you left... You wouldn't have gone off without a word like that if you hadn't loved me, would you?"

She had to admit that he was right.

"You would have come to me, talked to me, and we would have worked things out."

"I know, Christopher, I know I should have done that, but I just couldn't."

"April, I understand that, and I did at the time. That's why I didn't hire someone to find you. And I understood why you sent back the money. The only thing you wanted from me was love, and you didn't want anything without that. I'm surprised that you even kept my name."

She looked away, suddenly shy, unable to explain why she had not gone back to being April Peters. At the time she had told herself that it was more convenient not to change her name. Now she realized that she was desperately clinging to the last relic of her marriage.

Christopher misunderstood the pain in her eyes, and his voice was suddenly urgent. "April, did you understand about the divorce? I didn't do it in anger: I wasn't trying to get rid of you." He shook his head, his lips tight and white. "I felt like such a heel. I couldn't help but think that any decent man would let his wife divorce him, but I didn't know what state you were in, what the divorce laws were there. And I didn't know if you had enough money for a divorce. I had to believe that by then you had stopped loving me."

April couldn't stand the anguish in his voice. "Christopher," she breathed softly, "all this happened so long ago, and you didn't do anything that you could have helped. You can't go on torturing yourself like this."

He raised her hands to his lips and gently kissed each one. "April, you are so unbelievably sweet. Don't you understand that I would do simply anything to try to make up for the hurt I have caused you?"

April couldn't speak and touched her hand to his cheek. He covered it with his own, and when she looked up, she saw a flicker kindle in the depths of his eyes, and she recognized it for the smolderings of desire.

For a moment neither moved. Then slowly his hand guided hers down his face, his throat, until her fingers curled around the neck band of his gray sweat shirt. Her fingertips brushed against his collarbone, and she slipped her hand under his shirt.

At first she only allowed her fingers to graze his shoulder, tentatively, uncertainly, but as the memory of his warm, hard flesh returned, she flattened her palm against him, savoring the fuller contact. A hot wave of desire flooded over her, its sharpness followed by a willing languor. Just the feel of her hand brushing under his shirt, touching his shoulder, had aroused her more than anything another man might have done. She closed her eyes and leaned toward him.

Two strong hands gripped her arms, forcing her away from him, jarring her hand loose from his shirt. She looked at him questioningly. His features were taut with desire. He might have pushed her away, but he felt just as she did. She touched his lips with her fingers, felt the movement against them. Then he bent his head and kissed her.

The touch of his mouth was soft, but so achingly familiar that a quiver shot through her. This was Christopher, no longer a memory, a dream, but a real man, here with her in this tent, breathing quick and hard, his lips against hers, his hands crushing her arms, his body tense with longing for her. He took her hand again, pressing it along his leg, up his thigh, across his waist, urging it under his shirt again.

But he kept the kiss soft, just brushing his lips against hers as if he couldn't admit to himself that it was a kiss of passion. His mouth moved gently across her face, involuntarily becoming more caressing, making her aware of the shape of his lips, the warmth of his breath. Then he caught a little bit of her soft cheek, almost biting it, sending a tiny sharp thrill through her that made her moan with pleasure.

At her sound he abandoned the pretense, finally admitting to himself why he had taken her hand and pressed it to his body, why he could barely keep his hands on her arms, longing as he did to slide them across her body, lingering at her curves, brushing aside her clothes. He knew he wanted to explore this new fullness of her breasts, to feel them move against him as he had seen them move under her shirt. He hungered for the feel of her nipples hardening under his fingers; he needed to feel the pleasure shuddering through her when he would tease her, circling the rosy points with his lips, stroking them with his tongue, even catching at them with his teeth, gently, just threatening an exquisite pain. He wanted to lower himself on her, to feel her body beneath his, her legs shifting for him, opening for him, eager for him to sink into the smooth, moist mysteries of her.

He remembered her; he had forgotten nothing of what she wanted. He could please her as no one else ever could have. If there had been others, he would drive from her mind every thought of them. And surely there had been, during those six long years, men she had shared her graceful, golden body with. He would vanquish the memory of their hands and bodies, so completely obliterating them that it would be like none of them had ever existed. Everything would be as it had been six years before when she had known only him, when no other man had ever heard her soft gasps.

And so for the first time in his nearly thirty years Christopher Ramsey felt the white-hot sting of jealousy. It sickened him. What business had he to feel this way? Yes, he had married her, but the marriage, a small attempt to right the great wrong he had done her, hardly gave him the right to feel possessive about her. Only love would give him that—only if he could love her, only if he were prepared to try to meet *all* her needs, not just those of her lovely body, could he rail at other men for trying where he had failed.

He thought of how she must have been when she first left Charlottesville, lost and alone, turning to other men for what she wanted from him. How vulnerable she must have been, how easily she could have been used.

Suddenly it was as if he saw April as he had seen her so often in the hospital—her dusky hair tumbled across a white pillow, her blue eyes looking up at him, moist with hurt and betrayal, but this time she was peering at him over some other man's bare shoulder.

His own images, in their guilt-induced vividness, repelled him. Abruptly he thrust her from him, and without looking at her, said roughly, "It's been a long day. Let's get some sleep."

He had done little more than touch his lips to her cheek.

Chapter Seven

But sleep did not come easily for April that night. The memory of Christopher's face burned into her—the struggle she had glimpsed in his features, the loathing he felt for himself because he still wanted her without loving her. Yes, she couldn't help but be pleased that he desired her. Surely that would dispel those brotherly feelings she so resented. But she hated to see him suffer, to know that he was condemning himself so harshly.

She lay quietly, listening to the sounds of the forest, the wind rustling through the trees, small animals scrambling around the dried needles. But the sound she was most conscious of was the irregular rhythm of Christopher's breathing. And she knew that he wasn't sleeping either.

How she longed for him! And not just for the weight of his body on hers. If only they could talk. If only she could say, "Yes, I loved you then, but I was a child. I am a woman now, and I love you even more." She would plead for him to forget the past and try to look at her fresh without the filtering shades of dark guilt. If only he could just stop thinking of her as April Peters, the pretty, lively, childlike girl he had seduced. If only he could stop thinking of her as young Mrs. Ramsey, the ex-wife he hadn't been able to force himself to love. If he could see her as she was now—that was the only way he could ever start to love her.

But April knew how impossible that was. A man and a woman cannot pretend away their past. Christopher would never be able to admire her new strength, her competence, without remembering the difficulties that she had endured, without blaming himself for the suffering that had made her strong.

She doubted that talking would actually help. She felt as if she had said everything except that she loved him still. And to say *that* would only make him feel worse, make him feel guilty for having divorced her while she still loved him, guilty for leaving her now to face a long, lonely winter, trying, for a second time, to teach herself not to love him. Nothing could make him suffer more than knowing that she loved him.

So April lay next to him quietly, knowing that that was the only thing to do. And it was many, many hours before the long hard day finally overwhelmed her and she slept.

When she woke the next morning, Christopher had already left the tent. She heard voices and the clatter of pans. A fire had been built, and someone was frying bacon: The two smoky scents curled into the tent. April slipped out of her sleeping bag quickly, a little guilty that she had not been the first one up. She felt as though she should have been.

She dressed hurriedly and stepped out into the bright, clear morning. As she had feared, all the men were up, busy about the morning chores. "Good morning," she said sheepishly.

Steve, Josh, and Pete greeted her cheerfully, teasing her about sleeping so late. Christopher looked up from the fire and said formally, "I hope that you slept well."

April sighed. This would be a very long, difficult day if Christopher was going to revert back to his formal, distant manners. "Very well, thank you," she answered, although he knew perfectly well that she had slept poorly.

Josh looked at them curiously, and April saw Christopher notice the look. Surely he understood that if he continued to treat her like a debutante at a tea dance, their awkwardness would poison the day for everyone. Apparently he did realize it because she saw him tighten his lips for a moment, and then turning back to the fire, he told her ungallantly that the part in her hair wasn't straight.

That was certainly more the way that good hiking buddies should talk to one another, and April was willing to play the game if it would ease the tension. She wrinkled her nose at him. "How do you know that it isn't just the latest fashion that hasn't hit New York City yet?" And he laughed.

She went over to Pete and asked him about his ankle. "It's much better, Mrs. Ramsey," he said politely, and as she told him to call her April, she saw Christopher looking up from the fire, a startled look on his face. Well, she thought, why should he be surprised that Pete assumed that they were married? After all, they shared a name and a tent. Lots of women didn't wear their wedding rings out on the trail.

As she started to unwind Pete's bandage with her ringless hands, April felt the tiny curl of pain that still stung at her whenever she thought of her wedding ring. She had left it behind in Charlottesville, thinking that

that, more than anything, would convince Christopher that she considered their marriage over because he had, quite surprisingly, realized how much the ring had meant to her. She remembered one evening when she had poured him more coffee, he had touched her ring. "You are fond of that, aren't you?"

She had blushed and turned away, confused. "Yes, very."

The ring had not been purchased out of love. In fact, Christopher had not even been planning on taking her with him when he bought it, but when she didn't know her ring size, he had said, "Then I'm afraid that I shall have to trouble you to come with me." It was one of the first moments of stilted politeness that she remembered.

And the session at the jeweler's hadn't been much better. April, having simply no idea of the extent of Christopher's financial resources, had been shocked by the prices of precious stones and, in one of the very few times she had ever stood up to him, refused to let him buy her a diamond. Therefore, he certainly must have been surprised when she had grown attached to the simple gold band that he did buy.

But no, he wouldn't have been surprised; April now reminded herself of what he had said last night. He knew that she loved him; he would find it natural then that she would treasure the ring he had given her.

That had been such an amazing revelation. She realized that it would change the way she had interpreted so many things that had happened during their marriage; almost all of her memories would have to be pulled out and reexamined.

But she wasn't going to do it now—she had the whole winter during which she could remember. Right now she was going to savor the present; the past could have its turn another day.

She forced herself to concentrate on Pete's ankle. It really was much better. The swelling was nearly gone.

"I can probably walk today," Pete said, "but these guys wouldn't let me try."

April agreed that they might as well wait another day. "Perhaps you can walk"—she smiled—"but I can't. Not after yesterday."

She offered to take over the bacon frying. "No way," Steve said, spearing a crisp strip with a pocket knife. "We've decided that you deserve the day off."

"No more than any of you," she protested. She had unfastened her hair and was trying, without the aid of a mirror, to part her hair straight.

"It's just that we're taxpayers," he teased, "and don't want you putting in for too much overtime."

April laughed, running her fingers across the top of her head, trying to feel if her part was right. "Does that look straight?" she asked Steve.

"Sure," he answered, without looking at all. April gave up and fastened her barrettes.

"By the way," Christopher said, "do you get paid overtime? You certainly seem to put in more than forty hours a week."

Was this the start of more complaints about her job? April started searching for a coffee cup, rather than look at him.

"We all do," she explained. "Work more than forty hours, I mean. But we only get paid extra for things like fighting forest fires."

"Forest fires!" Christopher exclaimed. "Forest fires! April, I'm not sure that I want you fighting forest fires."

This was not the way friends spoke to one another.

This was how a man might speak to his very young wife. Or to his little sister. "Don't worry," April said, as she poured herself some coffee, now looking at him intently, trying to signal to him not to make the others uncomfortable. "I can't say that I want to fight them."

"How do you want your eggs?" Steve called out. As usual, he did not sense that anything awkward had just happened.

"Fried," April laughed a little nervously.

"Or boiled," Christopher put in. His voice, April noted almost resentfully, seemed quite relaxed.

They both knew perfectly well that the eggs were powdered and there was little else to do except scramble them with some dried skim milk and think about something else when you ate them. But Steve had crumbled the bacon into them and added little bits of cheese and dried onion, and their breakfast seemed to taste as good as any fresh eggs ever had. April knew that there was something about a crisp mountain morning that made everything taste wonderful.

"What does everyone want to do today?" Christopher asked after they had finished breakfast and were lazily waiting for the dishwater to heat.

"Pete is going to soak his ankle all day," April announced, swirling the remains of her coffee around in the enamel cup, "and I am going to take a bath and spend the day puttering around the campsite."

"Then I think I'll watch April take a bath," Josh said brightly.

"I think you won't." Christopher set his coffee cup down with a little bang, and April had to wonder if Josh had made his suggestion just to provoke Christopher into such a response.

April knew that there was an old beaver dam back in

the woods that, at least in years past, had provided a nice little pool for bathing. When the breakfast dishes were done, she got her clean clothes and announced that she would shoot anyone who came to visit her during her bath. As she walked away the men were cheerfully discussing under what possible circumstances a forest ranger could legally shoot one of the visitors to the park. They all, even Christopher, sounded relaxed and happy in the bright morning air.

The little pool was still there, and although the water was cold enough that the first dipping was a bit of a shock, April quickly got used to it and floated around for a while, letting the freshness swirl against her naked body. The green boughs from the trees dipped down into the pool, and her slender form gleamed white through the dark water. She felt like a wood nymph in an illustration from some lush, old-fashioned picture book; she felt graceful and elegant as she moved through the water, feminine and free.

Sometimes she got tired of wearing jeans and boots all the time, and she longed for filmy negligees and floating dresses. But where would she wear such things, and more important, who would see them? Still, she sighed a little wistfully, it would be nice to have something pretty to wear today. Julia Breeland would probably have the perfect outfit for lounging around the campsite, something that was both casual and alluring, her tight white jeans perhaps, or a stylish little sundress, or a denim prairie skirt and a quaint ruffled shirt that she would undoubtedly wear unbuttoned to about her waist. All April had was a pair of shorts and a T-shirt that had been rolled up in the corner of her pack in case of hot weather. They were certainly casual: She just couldn't be sure how feminine or alluring they were.

She dried herself as well as she could on the little towel—a decent-sized towel took up too much room in a pack—and pulled on her shorts. They were shorter than she had remembered, but before she had time to decide if they were *too* short, she heard Christopher's voice.

"April, are you decent?"

She quickly picked up her white T-shirt from the mossy bank and slipped it on. "Over here," she called out and turned toward the sound of his voice.

He appeared out of the forest, one hand lifting aside a tree branch. He froze for a moment, his arm dropping slowly, very slowly, as he stood there looking at her, a slim figure in a white shirt.

April looked at him curiously, wondering why he had stopped so abruptly. His gaze was emerald and intense, and her eyes dropped. It was then that she realized that the thin, white shirt was clinging to her still-damp breasts. He took a step toward her, and her heart began to pound furiously.

But he recovered his poise quickly. "That's not exactly your ranger uniform, is it?"

She tried to match his light tone—even though she felt as if she could hardly breathe. "You all said that I should take the day off."

"Take the whole week off if you're going to look like that." His voice was deep and, April thought fleetingly, not at all brotherly.

She blushed, a hot fire spreading across her flesh. She swallowed and tried to change the subject. "Was there something back here you wanted?"

Christopher raised his eyebrows. "Maybe you ought to rephrase that."

The passion in his eyes was so naked that April had

to look away, and she was suddenly conscious how her nipples were hardening under the damp shirt. Nervously she plucked the thin cotton away from her body, hoping that he had not noticed.

But of course he had. He came over to her and rested his hands lightly on her shoulders. "It's nothing to be ashamed of. Believe me, I feel the same way."

His gesture had pulled her shirt taut again, and April longed to take his hands and press them to her, letting him feel her breasts swelling, letting him know for certain that she had become a woman.

What would he do if she did? Would he step away in surprise or would his eyelids drop lazily, hooding the flicker in his green eyes as she had seen so often six years ago? Would he, for a time, forget all about guilt and obligation and sink down with her onto the soft moss?

Unconsciously April leaned forward and as she gently swayed from side to side, the tips of her breasts brushed against the warmth of his shirt.

For an instant his hands tightened on her shoulders, gripping her, quickening her movements, and she sensed more than saw a faint shudder run through his body. But then, his arms quickly dropping to his side, he stepped away and cleared his throat. "This isn't easy, is it?"

April couldn't answer; she just couldn't be as frank about everything as he was. The whole time they had been married they had never spoken about their desire for each other. April had simply taken it for granted, although, as he had said last night, knowing that she turned to him out of love had made it much more complicated for him. And so she found herself shy, not quite able to admit in words to this man whom she loved that she wanted him.

She didn't know how long they stood there, but finally she was able to turn away and pick up her other clothes.

He then explained why he was out in the forest. "I came to find something to make a cane or a crutch for Pete."

She helped him look, and together they found a sturdy young sapling that had been uprooted in some winter storm.

The rest of the day was just splendid, one of the happiest, most relaxed days April could remember in years. The sun shone warmly, and she was comfortable in her light clothes. The easy manner Christopher assumed as soon as they returned to camp was not hard to match. After all, it was not a pose for her. She enjoyed being with him, and their casual dealings seemed to her like the natural, comfortable way to treat him.

Of course, sometimes the look in his eyes when his gaze would turn up from the crutch he was making and rest on the sun-browned flesh of her legs or arms was hardly casual, but April refused to allow complicated thoughts about love, guilt, and desire to fester and darken the brilliant day.

She was struck with an urge to cook, and using some freeze-dried chicken that the men had brought and all sorts of spices from her own pack, she made a chicken curry for lunch. Pete obligingly ate all the chocolate out of one bag of gorp so that they even had a moderately authentic raisin and nut condiment to sprinkle over the rich yellow curry and the mounds of steaming white rice. Josh and Steve had spent the morning fishing so after lunch April set them to work picking up green twigs for Pete to lash into a rack for steaming fish. As the shadows lengthened, April sprinkled the fish, gutted but still whole, with a tangy sauce she had made of soy sauce and dried spices: ginger, garlic, and hot peppers. Then she steamed the fish for fifteen minutes. It was a technique she had learned in a Chinese restaurant she had once worked in. The original recipe had also called for shao-sing wine and fermented black bean paste, but the fresh mountain air would just have to substitute for those.

"My word, Chris," Josh said after they had finished dinner, "if she can cook like this out of the stuff she carries on her back, what does she do in a real kitchen?"

"And why on earth did you let her get away?" Steve put in.

April smiled, already a little sleepy. "Believe me, I couldn't cook one thing when I was married to him." She had hardly known how to make egg salad when she had been married, and she was honest enough to admit to herself that part of her cooking fit today had been an effort to impress Christopher with how much she had learned.

"What I need right now is a glass of port and perhaps a thin, fine cigar." Christopher stretched lazily.

April looked at him, the way his sweater pulled across his chest as he stretched. "What you are going to get is some fine, hot dishwater," she pointed out.

"Oh, well," he laughed, "I would rather have that any day." And within a few minutes the men were up and busy. Josh was washing the dishes; Christopher was starting to pack things away, and Steve was helping Pete get ready for bed. April was quite uncharacteristically not doing a thing. She just sat, her arms wrapped around her knees, happy and content.

When Pete was comfortable, Steve came and sat beside her. He looked up at the darkening sky and pointed out the first star for her, a tiny diamond on a field of dark blue velvet. "I don't want to go back to the city," he sighed, shaking his blond head slowly.

Josh looked up from the plate he was washing. "Then why are you going? And you too, Chris," he said over his shoulder. "When are the two of you going to realize that neither of you belong in Manhattan?"

Christopher carefully knotted the string on the little denim ditty bag that April carried her spices in. "You're just saying that because you think you've got a better shot at being made a partner if we're gone."

"Well, sure." Josh grinned, but April suspected that under his light tone, he was saying something that he really believed. He ran the dishcloth around on another plate and then continued.

"Sometime Christopher D. Ramsey the Third has got to go back to his old hometown and face the fact that at heart he is still a Virginia aristocrat with all sorts of notions about privilege and responsibility that are much too decent and old-fashioned for our firm. And you, Steve." Josh snapped the dishcloth at Steve, flicking drops of water on him. "Why don't you move to some little town up here and open up a practice, writing people's wills and settling dog-bite cases? You wouldn't make a bit of money, but you'd be a lot happier."

"Dog bites? With my fine legal skills?" Steve asked with exaggerated outrage, treating it like a joke, but April had felt him stiffen while Josh was speaking; perhaps these remarks had come uncomfortably close to some dream of his.

"And as long as you are at it," Josh went on, "why don't you take Beth Market with you? She knows the area, and you could hang out a little shingle, 'Webster and Market, Attorneys-At-Law.'" Steve was very quiet; April could almost feel the knots of tension in his arm.

Christopher spoke slowly, as if sensing some of Steve's discomfort. "Perhaps the lady would want it to be 'Market and Webster.'"

And April knew perfectly well that Beth would prefer it to be "Webster and Webster." She just hoped that Steve was learning that that was what Beth wanted. April stood up. "While you gentlemen try to sort out each other's lives, I am going to bed. We're back on the trail tomorrow."

"I'll be in soon," Christopher said in a tone so casual and husbandlike that waves of nostalgia followed April into the tent.

He came in sooner than she had expected. She had sat on her sleeping bag, thinking about the day and about how wonderful things were when Christopher was like his old self. So she had just started to change when he came in. She had the jacket of her sweat suit on, but she was still in the jeans that she had put on when the afternoon had grown cool.

She was not going to sleep in her jeans. Sleeping in one's daytime clothing was a mistake few experienced campers made. The perspiration trapped in the fabric cooled, and the sleeper had a damp and chilly night.

She was not going to make herself miserable in the name of modesty, particularly considering that this man had been looking at her legs all day and had certainly seen the rest of her before. Her underwear, although of a bikini cut, was serviceable white cotton, not some transparent little wisp. And she was, by necessity, sitting down. She would just slip out of her jeans and slide into her sweat suit.

As she unzipped the jeans, she tried to be casual about it, as if it were simply a matter of complete indifference to her that she was taking off her jeans in front of him, and Christopher, ever the Virginia gentleman, busied himself with his pack as soon as he realized what she was doing.

But he must have looked. For suddenly she felt a strong hand grasp her arm, pulling it away from her body, exposing her to the flashlight's glare.

His voice was the even, almost too casual tone she had heard often before, the voice he used when trying to hide something. "You forest rangers must lead an interesting life," he said. "That's an odd place to get knifed."

She looked at him blankly, not understanding, and then followed his gaze down to her abdomen and the thin line, once red, now faded to rose, that April was so used to that she hardly ever thought about.

"It's my cesarean scar," she said quietly. "From the baby."

He was silent for a moment, tinkering with the zipper on her sleeping bag, opening it, closing it. "Oh, yes," he finally said. "I had forgotten."

"Forgotten!" The light glittering off the shiny blue nylon of the sleeping bags was like little arrows of ice. "Forgotten!" April had to bite her lip to keep from crying. "Oh, Christopher, how could you forget about our baby?"

"Oh, April, no, God, no," he groaned. "It was just your operation I wasn't thinking about. I haven't forgotten about the baby." He reached over and put his arm about her, drawing her to him. "And I never will. I go back every November," he whispered into her hair.

Perhaps it was that his chest beneath her cheek was so firm and warm, but April didn't understand. "Go back? Where?" She leaned back against his arm.

"To her grave. I take flowers to her every year."

"Her grave?" April had never asked what had happened to the baby's body. She had wondered, but she was desperately afraid that her mother or the Ramseys would just say that they had told the hospital to dispose of it in some respectful manner.

Christopher looked down at her gently. "Didn't anyone tell you? I suppose I should have, but you were so sick for so long, and then you were gone. I took her back home; she's buried there with the rest of the Ramseys." He was silent for a moment and then slowly, haltingly, went on. "April, it's not easy for me to talk about these things, but losing her was very hard on me. I loved her too. Maybe not before she was born, like you did, but the minute I saw her, so tiny and frail and as beautiful as her mother."

April leaned against him, tears freely flowing down her cheeks. No one had ever used the word *mother* in relation to her before; she hadn't even herself. But he was right; for a few hours, hours during which she had nearly been in a coma, she had been a mother.

"I thought that you didn't care," she breathed. "Your parents—"

His hand was soothing against her hair. "Yes, I know." His voice was almost apologetic. "They didn't care, and they were happy when you left." He let go of her and briskly pulled his sweat shirt out of his pack. "I just can't forgive them for either of those things. I don't have a lot to do with them these days." He pulled off his sweater and began to unbutton his shirt.

"But Christopher," April said softly. She had lost her daughter; did the Ramseys have to lose their son too? As cold and bitter as his parents had always been to her, she didn't want them suffering too. "You are so precious to them. You must learn to forgive them. Hasn't there been enough heartache?"

He didn't answer, and April reached for the rest of her sweat suit, feeling like there was still something left to say, but she just wasn't sure what it was. Outside, the wind was picking up. The tent ropes creaked, and the trees rustled, their branches swaying, scraping against each other. April shivered.

And then she heard his voice, although his head was still turned away and he seemed busy taking off his shirt. "What I can't understand is how you can forgive me."

"Christopher, it was easy. I loved you."

Suddenly, before she realized what he was doing, he turned swiftly and bent his head, pressing his lips to the scar.

The touch was at first just a gentle one, but it was such an extraordinary gesture, so very intimate and personal, that the rest of the world, the wind in the dark forest, the crackle of the dying campfire, everything, dissolved, and April was aware of nothing but the two of them in this little tent and the feel of his lips against her flesh.

She touched his hair, then his shoulder. As her fingertips moved across his skin, tracing the crescent of his shoulder blade, she could feel his lips start to warm against her. What began as a gesture of respect, as a tribute to their loss, to their long years of suffering, flamed into passion.

The hand resting on her hip tightened and then slid

down, caressing the softness of her thigh, the length of her leg. He lifted his head and gently pushed her down onto the sleeping bag. Seeing neither fear nor refusal in her eyes, he eased down the zipper of the jacket, whispering, "I've wanted to do this all day."

He smoothed the fabric away from her, pushing it down over her shoulders, off her arms. He looked down at her, a slender white shape on a pillow of dark blue down. His eyes followed the soft curve of her waist, the shadows in her shoulders, the warm fullness of her breasts. "My God, April," he breathed. "You are the most beautiful woman I have ever seen."

"You don't mind the scar?" she whispered, her fingertips tracing the thin, raised line.

His hand covered hers. "Oh, no." His voice was gentle. "It just shows how perfect you are in every other way."

As he spoke, April could feel his breath against her breasts. The warmth was like a promise, hinting of further caresses, of greater passion, and April could feel her breasts swelling as if they were reaching out to him.

And suddenly she was no longer embarrassed by her body or ashamed of her desire, no longer confused. Everything was simple. He was her husband, and she loved him. She reached up, touching his face, and then tangling her fingers in his thick dark hair, she pulled his head downward, urging him. And she sighed as his lips closed around her breast.

He gathered her up, his arms encircling her body, his hands roving and caressing. He pressed her to him, fitting her body to the hard strength of his own, and finally she felt just as she had longed for that morning, just as she had waited for six years, his quick, hard breaths against her.

If she wondered before whether he had noticed the changes in her body, she now had no doubt. His hands explored the new softness, tracing the deeper valley between her breasts, sculpting the curve of her hip down to the velvet skin of her thigh. "You've changed," he murmured against her, his lips burning a trail across her breasts, his hand warm and demanding on her leg.

"You remember?" she breathed.

With a little groan he shifted his weight, pulling her under him. "Remember? If you know how often I thought about having you just like this, dreamed of what I would do if I ever saw you again..." He let his body settle on hers, pressing against her, his scorching need awakening an answering fire in her.

But against the smooth skin of her legs she felt only the rough denim of his jeans. She shifted, moving herself against him, exciting him, almost beyond what she knew he could endure, and when she felt his arms loosen and ease out of the circling embrace, she knew that he was only moving away for a moment. And she remembered how sometimes his hands would drop to his waist slowly, leisurely, freeing the leather of his belt from the brass clasp, the movements of his fingers deliberate, controlled, tantalizing her, teasing her, until she would cry his name.

But tonight he was impatient, his fingers jerking at the belt buckle with a quick tug, his longing for her revealed in every gesture.

It had been six years, but the feel of his body was astonishingly, achingly, familiar: the firm shoulders, the flat plain of his chest, the hair-roughened muscles of his legs, the dark mass of his hair as his head bent over her body. This was the man she loved, and she yearned for him as much as he did for her.

But as she felt the remembered, treasured motions, the quick, confident movements that would bring him to her, a silvery thought shot through the whirling warmth.

"Christopher, wait," she gasped.

He misunderstood, thinking she was not ready for him. His weight shifted from her. "I'd never rush you." His voice was low, just a ragged breath disturbing her curls. "You know that."

He wanted to please her, and remembering her body, her needs, as he did, he could. He caressed the slope of her shoulders, the small of her back, her thighs, her breasts, his hands moving slowly, but with a strength, a certainty, a purpose that left her already willing body moist and urgent. And the silvery thought intensified into something more physical than thought, the pure sensation of silver brightening until it exploded into a spray of diamonds, a heightened rapture coming from an awareness of all that his body might, at this very moment, be giving hers.

Afterward, as Christopher eased himself from her, April felt as if her body had become velvet, rich, soft velvet, and for a long time she lay in his arms, her cheek against his chest, listening to the beat of his heart as it slowed.

Finally he released her, letting her slide onto her back. He propped himself up on one elbow, looking down at her.

He trailed a hand down her, shaking his head.

"What's wrong?" she murmured lazily.

"Nothing." His voice seemed softly puzzled. "Nothing at all. That's what's so remarkable. After all this time you are still..."

She sensed what he was trying to say: that, for all his

experience, this time had been special. His halting expression convinced her that his pleasure was truly greater with her. If he had been able to tell her, in some smooth and practiced way, that she was the best, she wouldn't have believed him.

"We aren't exactly strangers." She smiled.

April couldn't believe that it was anything that she had done, any way she had moved, any particular feature of her body that was superior to another woman's but, quite simply, that she loved him. Surely her love brought an extra richness to their joining, a richness that perhaps he could not explain, but that he felt and responded to with an extra measure of pleasure.

His green eyes were so soft, so full of gentleness, that April could hardly look at them, but when her eyes slid from his, they blinked at the white pool of light from the forgotten flashlight still swinging on its hook.

"We should have turned off the flashlight," April whispered. "I'm not usually so careless about the batteries."

"Maybe you had better things to think about." Christopher smiled at her and rolled over to turn off the light. As he reached up he said idly, "I assume you are on the pill. I forgot to ask, didn't I?"

April went rigid, a sharp stab of tension flashing through her. She thanked God that Christopher was not looking at her.

"Yes," she answered, praying that he would leave it at that.

But Christopher had been trained as a lawyer. "Yes, you are on the pill, or yes, I forgot to ask?"

She didn't answer.

His hand fell away from the still glowing flashlight, and she heard him draw a sharp breath. "April, what are you saying?" He turned and stared at her. "My God, that's why you asked me to wait, wasn't it?"

She nodded.

He closed his eyes as if a wave of nausea had hit him. He gripped his forehead, hiding his face in his hand. "This isn't happening. Tell me this isn't happening. Not again." His voice was strangled.

April ached for him. She didn't care about herself, but she couldn't bear to have him suffer.

"April, I don't go around doing this." He lifted his head and looked at her. "I just don't. Do you believe that? Since I was in college, since that first time with you, I have *never* been with a woman without protecting her. Never. I don't know what it is that makes me be so... when I am with you."

April's heart sank. If this was going to reawaken all his guilt, make him hate himself more, then it never, never should have happened.

She sat up and forced him to meet her eyes. "Christopher, this just isn't like before. I'm a grown woman. I knew what I was doing. *I* chose to take the risk."

He made an exasperated noise. "What were you thinking—that you wouldn't get pregnant from just one time? Surely you of all people know better than to count on that."

"I wasn't thinking that at all." She tried to keep her voice calm. She didn't want them to fight about this. "It is as I said! This isn't like before. Don't you understand? My mother knew everything about me. Everything. More than I knew about myself. It was no random accident that she chose that particular night to go to Richmond. But I know my body now; it just isn't likely that anything will happen."

She knew that she was making it sound like she had

made a carefully calculated decision. She had not. Nonetheless everything she was saying was true; there was very little chance that she would get pregnant.

He was leaning back on his elbows. "Still I wish it hadn't happened."

"I don't," she said calmly.

Indeed she wasn't sorry at all. In fact, a little nagging part of her said that what would make her sorry was if she did *not* get pregnant.

He took a breath. "You do see that this changes everything: that if you are pregnant, you will *have* to come to Manhattan."

"We'll see," she said, not wanting to get into that subject now.

They lay quietly, and in a moment Christopher reached up and snapped off the flashlight. As her eyes adjusted to the faint traces of starlight that filtered through the tent fabric, she listened to the whisper of the wind and the trees.

She wanted to speak. She could not endure a repeat of last night, with each of them lying sleepless, locked in a prison of tumultuous thoughts.

"Do you hear the wind?" she whispered. "Learning all about air currents and low pressure systems in school never stopped me from wondering where the wind comes from. Sometimes it seems enchanted." It was easier to talk about nature, about the magical world of the forest, than to talk about their own human troubles.

Christopher didn't answer, and she looked over at him. He was lying on his back, staring upward, his hands linked behind his head.

"I know," he said finally. "I can understand why you took this job. You must be proud to be responsible for preserving the forest. It would be easy to believe that what you are doing is important.''

"Yes, it is.'' As she settled in her pillow April remembered what Josh had said about Christopher's old-fashioned notions about privilege and responsibility, and she knew what he had meant. With the sort of privileges and advantages Christopher had always had, wealth, intelligence, health, education, came the responsibility to use them for the sake of others less fortunate. And those responsibilities were sometimes a privilege; a person had the luxury of knowing what he was doing was important. "Don't you feel that way about your work?'' she asked. "Lawyers can do a great deal of good.''

"They can,'' he answered, "but sometimes it seems like our firm is more interested in its reputation and its profits than anything else.''

Then go back to Virginia, April wanted to say. But that subject was too personal. She curled up in her sleeping bag and tucked her hand under her cheek. "Didn't we have a lovely day?'' she murmured.

"Yes, April, yes, we did.'' His voice was quiet, reflective. "Let's just hope that we didn't let today's pleasures ruin too many tomorrows.''

Chapter Eight

As none of them were sure how well Pete would do on the trail, they tried to leave as early as possible the next morning. He carried his own empty pack, and they divided up his belongings among their four packs. April noticed how different things were from when they set out from Frank Lake two days before. The men no longer engaged in silent conspiracies to make allowances for her supposed weakness. No one suggested that she not carry a share of Pete's things; they listened to her advice about the trail and the pace. She had proved herself.

Pete was able to walk pretty well. They were going down the mountain, not up, and Christopher had fashioned a pair of crutches for him, padding the tops with T-shirts and towels. The boy could put some weight on his injured foot so that while their progress was slow, they weren't crawling.

Actually April enjoyed the leisurely pace. It wasn't so much that her pack was unusually heavy, but that this was the way she thought backpacking ought to be. You shouldn't be rushing to get somewhere as they had had to do on the trip in. The hiking should be as much a pleasure as the evening around the campfire. Today they had time to appreciate their surroundings: the tall pines and the graceful white birches, their bark gleaming silver against the dark forest. Trees that had fallen were now soft shapes grown over with moss, and the ground was covered with ferns of every variety, maidenhair ferns, ostrich ferns, wood ferns, with fronds as lovely as their names. The stream gurgled along beside them, sometimes dancing around rocks, sometimes flowing in a smooth swath of dark crystal.

At such a slow pace they could all talk. April walked next to Pete. Although he never complained, she knew that it was going to be a long, tiring day for him. She talked brightly to him, finding out about his school, his plans for college, his girl friends. She teased him a bit, flirted just a little, and generally was cheerful and breezy, trying hard to entertain him.

When they stopped for lunch, April sat a little apart from the others, finding a tree to lean against. She was tired of talking, she felt like she had chattered the whole morning. She hoped that the men hadn't found the sound of her voice irritating or, if they did, that at least they understood.

But Christopher brought his plate over to sit next to her, and she did not find it at all hard to talk to *him*. They had resumed their comfortable relationship as soon as they had emerged from the tent this morning. April thought it was all very much like a good marriage should be. Whatever the private joys or anguishes, the two people should show an even, happy face to the rest of the world. They chatted about the scenery, and Christopher asked her about an unusual rock formation.

When he had finished eating, Christopher stretched out on the ground, lying on his side, his elbow propped up, holding his head. He was all in blue, his jeans topped by a lighter blue cotton work shirt, and April couldn't help noticing how tall he looked, how his strong body looked as if it stored enough energy to walk all the way from the Adirondacks to the Rockies or the Sierras. April knew her American history: People had done that when the country was still young. Did those pioneers look like this, she wondered, so strong and competent, so, well, so very much like a man ought to look?

Suddenly she noticed Christopher was watching her, and catching his eye, she blushed, embarrassed by her own thoughts.

"What were you thinking about?" he asked. His free hand was idly tracing circles in the loose earth.

"Nothing."

He looked at her carefully. "That's a lie," he said lightly.

She wrinkled her nose at him. "So it is."

He grinned and tossed a little acorn at her. "You know this morning I saw an April I hadn't seen in a long time."

April tilted her head questioningly. "What do you mean?" Then suddenly the warmth of his gaze made her feel a little giddy. "Isn't it too late to see April? Don't you know that it's May already?"

He laughed. "That's what I mean. You used to do that all the time, make little jokes about your name. And all that lively chatter, the sort of wide-eyed innocent flirting this morning," he explained. "That was April Peters, dancing out of high school in her cheerleading uniform." He smiled at her. "It was certainly exactly what Pete needed."

"That's what I hoped. I'm really not like that anymore, but it seemed the right thing to do. Although I was afraid that the rest of you would think that I was awfully empty-headed for a grown woman.''

"Are you kidding?" Christopher drew in his long legs and sat up. "Everyone is relieved that you're managing to keep his spirits up. This could have been a pretty grim day for him if he had had to talk to the three of us about recent Supreme Court decisions.''

"Good heavens, that would be a grim day for anyone,'' she returned.

Christopher seemed less tormented by what had happened last night, April thought with relief. Her relaxed, lively manner must have convinced him that *she* was not worrying about any consequences, or—and April was afraid that this was the more likely explanation—he finally believed that he had found a way to get her to New York where he could watch out for her.

And suddenly it occurred to her as she took the last bite of the strange but surprisingly delicious chili they had concocted for lunch out of their freeze-dried food, that perhaps her behavior this morning had done a lot more than just reassure Christopher and keep Pete going. Christopher had just been talking about what she had been like in the past, recognizing that she wasn't that way any longer. It might not be conscious yet, but on some level he certainly did realize that she was no longer the little teen-ager that needed to be coddled and protected.

"Now what are you thinking about?" Christopher broke into her thoughts.

She looked up at him from the corner of her eyes. "Why do you ask?"

"I don't know," he mused. "You just looked so very happy for a moment.''

April smiled at him, a quick, nearly flirtatious smile. "Well, that's because I am very happy. I am"—she clapped her hands together—"about to do the dishes. Wouldn't that make just anybody unbelievably happy?" She reached out for his plate.

He held it back over his head out of her reach. "Oh, come now," he teased. "I don't know anything that is *that* much fun."

She threw him a long glance. "I do."

She could have bitten her tongue for saying something so provocative, but Christopher broke out with a short, surprised laugh. "Does your mother know you talk that way, girl?"

"Does yours know that you address a lady as 'hey, girl'?" she returned. Her former mother-in-law had very rigid standards for manners and behavior.

"No, she does not, Miss—" He broke off, the laughter suddenly going from his eyes. April thought it was as if a cloud had passed over the sun. It must be hard for him to remember that her name was Mrs. Ramsey. He certainly couldn't be comfortable calling her that even in a joke.

"My friends call me April," she said lightly, trying to dispel the grim look that had settled around his eyes.

But he was still serious. "I hope that you think of me as your friend."

"Well, of course," she answered, still keeping her voice as breezy as if she were talking to young Pete. She just didn't want to think about her feelings for him anymore.

But as she washed the dishes she couldn't help it. She worked very slowly—as the whole point of stopping to cook lunch, instead of eating something cold as hikers normally do, was to give Pete a longer rest without him feeling like he was holding up the rest of them. And as she worked she thought.

Obviously Christopher's attitude toward her had changed. Like the others, he had come to acknowledge her professional competence, and as the conversation at lunch indicated, he also sensed that she was no longer the perky eighteen-year-old he had married.

And of course, he also knew that she wanted him, desired him, that he could still please her. But he did not know that she loved him. She was sure of that; otherwise he would not be so easy and relaxed around her; he would not joke with her or tease her. Obviously her feelings were not as transparent as they had been during their marriage.

So Christopher must think she was a very modern woman, able to have the sort of casual relationships, the sexual encounters without commitment, that he had had with other modern women.

Suddenly she felt a little cheap. She wanted him to know that she was a grown woman, but her traditional background was such that she didn't really want him thinking that she was *that* sort of grown woman. Her eyes strayed over to him. He was still stretched out on the ground, twirling a twig, idly talking to Steve. He must have been conscious of her gaze for the twig stopped and he turned his head. When their eyes met, he smiled, a smile that seemed affectionate and warm, and April didn't feel cheap anymore. Indeed, her desire for him had been paid for dearly; her heart was quite a high price.

But where did this get her, his realizing that she wasn't a child? Certainly he wouldn't ask her to come live with him as his little sister again, but what else? April simply saw no signs that he loved her. Certainly there was affection and passion, but she had had those from him before. He did respect her now, but he just didn't love her.

But what it might accomplish, April suspected, was that, if she were not pregnant, it might free Christopher to love someone else. He would no longer have to remember her as a sad face in a hospital bed; he could keep track of her; he wouldn't have to wonder or worry about her. He could love again.

How pleased Julia Breeland would be! April had done exactly what Julia had asked her to: cut the rope of guilt that bonded Christopher to her.

"Are you all right?" a deep voice asked, low in her ear. It was Christopher. "You looked concerned about something."

April stared at him for a moment, her eyes wide. How sensitive he was to each change in her expression! She would have to watch herself. "Oh, I was just a little worried about some erosion I saw this morning."

"Erosion? I didn't see any."

"Perhaps you didn't know what to look for."

April immediately regretted speaking so crisply. She was still a little on edge.

Christopher shrugged and picked up a dish towel. As they worked together, they talked about afternoon plans, about how much longer Pete would be able to travel and where they should camp. April quickly recovered her poise and was able to talk to him easily.

Then suddenly, glancing over his shoulder to see whether the others were in earshot, he changed the subject. "When we got back from our first trip, Beth Market said that she spent a lot of time with you."

"Yes, I really enjoyed her," April answered. "It didn't seem to matter that she was a lawyer working for that high-powered firm of yours. We seem to have an awful lot in common.''

Christopher twirled the dish towel, turning it into a little rope. ''Look, I don't want you to break any confidences, but do you remember the things Josh said last night?''

''Of course,'' April said, thinking first about how clearly Josh had spelled out the reasons that Christopher should go back to Virginia.

''He suggested something about Steve and Beth that I hadn't thought about before. Do you have any sense that there is some sort of attachment there? But,'' he added hastily, ''don't tell me anything that you shouldn't.''

''Beth and I never talked about it.'' April glanced around the site, checking to be sure that she had gotten all the dishes. ''But I feel very sure that she cares a great deal for him. I don't have any idea how he feels about her, and I don't imagine she knows either.''

Christopher was silent for a moment, and then he began to put the dishes back in the pack. ''Well, that's very interesting.''

''Isn't it?'' April replied rather cryptically. She couldn't help thinking that there was another case of a woman caring a great deal and a man seeming less interested. But no, she had to remind herself, the two situations were hardly comparable. The love growing between Beth and Steve seemed so fresh and uncomplicated by guilt and memories while— She stopped herself; she just wasn't going to think about it anymore.

April threw the dishwater out, and after rinsing the pot out and drying it, she handed it to Christopher. ''You know, Christopher, some of the other things Josh said also made a lot of sense.''

He didn't pretend that he didn't know what she was

talking about. "About me, you mean? I don't know," he scoffed, jerking at Josh's pack as if he wished it were Josh himself. "He made me sound like something out of a kid's history book. As if the family owned the whole county and sat around on the veranda in white suits, drinking mint juleps all the time."

April had to laugh.

But she was very pleased when on a rest stop later that afternoon, he turned to Steve and said, "I think that we all deserve a good steak after this. Why don't you and Beth join April and me for an evening in town?"

Steve lifted his blond head in surprise. "Well, sure," he said slowly, "we could do that." And then he added more decisively, "Yes, it sounds fine. It would be fun."

"Is that all right with you, April?" Christopher turned to her.

She handed him a little bag of gorp. "I'll have to check the duty roster," she said sweetly, knowing perfectly well that Mike McKenna would close the campground and throw all the campers out on the highway rather than have her miss an evening with Christopher.

And Josh, who had, in April's opinion, already shown himself to be nobody's fool, said nothing about the fact that he might deserve a good steak too.

The rest of the trip back passed uneventfully. They stopped for the night at the same campsite they had seen the Hortons in a few days before. As April and Christopher pitched their little tent, he said, "Look here, April Ramsey, we're going to behave ourselves until we get back to civilization."

And April promised to fall asleep promptly. "Does that count as behaving?"

"Only if you don't look too good while you're doing it," he returned.

So that night, unlike the other two nights they had shared that little tent, they simply talked. April lay curled up on her side, one hand under her cheek, while Christopher lay on his back, occasionally turning his head toward her. They didn't talk about themselves: That subject was too volatile. Instead he told her about old friends she had lost track of; they talked about movies and books; she described the problems the park system was having trying to get money out of the state legislature. Just as she was finally drifting off to sleep, April thought such conversations as this, two people talking in the dark, must be one of the best parts of a good marriage. They hadn't ever had them before.

They broke camp nearly at dawn the next morning because they wanted to be certain of getting back to Frank Lake that day. So it was still early afternoon when they approached the end of the trail.

Although her pack was starting to feel very heavy, April wasn't too sure that she wanted this little adventure to be over. So much had happened. She and Christopher hadn't just become lovers while they were out in the forest; they had become friends, better friends than they had ever been before. And although friendship was not all that she wanted from Christopher, even if it was this trip that made him able to love another woman, she knew that she would remember these pleasant days all her life.

The trail emerged from the forest down at the Frank Lake beach, and Evan, the boat attendant, was the first one to know that they were back. Word spread rapidly, and soon the beach was full of the park's staff, Pete's family, and of course a few campers who had no idea what was going on, but enjoyed the commotion.

The Hortons, the couple they had met on the trip in, had had the good sense to tell Mike that they had seen both Pete and the rescue party so no one, with the possible exception of Beth Market, had worried at all. April looked around her. None of the three lawyers who had stayed behind, Beth, Ben, and Julia, were on the beach, and April wondered if anyone had told them.

Just then Ben's silver car drove up, and Beth tumbled out, followed more elegantly by Julia and Ben. Beth darted over to where the five hikers had draped themselves across a picnic table. Suddenly she slowed, apparently shy, and then first spoke to April. But within a few moments, under the noise of everyone else's chatter, she put her hand on Steve's arm and, looking up into his face, said, "I'm so glad that you're back." April glanced at Christopher, who was sitting on the sand, leaning against his pack. Quietly and quickly he gave her a thumb's-up sign.

Yes, they were friends. Whatever barriers of time and guilt still remained, they were friends.

By this time Julia had reached the cluster of people. She was again in her white jeans with a pale pink top that made her long black hair gleam in the sun. She looked cool and fresh, making April feel everything opposite. Her own jeans were dusty; her tangled curls were held back by a bandanna; and her hands, and probably her face too, were streaked with grime.

Julia went straight for Christopher, not bothering to conceal her interest as Beth had. April felt a quick stab of jealousy. She had wanted Christopher to respect and admire her, but not so that he could fall in love with Julia Breeland.

She stood up. If they were all going out on the town, she needed to have a very long session in her pretty bathroom. She quickly helped Pete sort out his belongings, and wishing him luck, she trudged back to the cabin.

Three hours later April felt like a new person and, checking herself in the mirror, was reasonably confident that she looked nothing at all like a forest ranger. Her wardrobe was not extensive; in fact, she felt that it was probably too much of a compliment even to call it a wardrobe, but she did have one outfit that she had purchased for her college graduation. The skirt was a wool challis with such a fine light weave that the fabric floated and swirled as she moved. The print was dark with tones of burgundy, amethyst, and jade. Her blouse was white and Victorian: with a high lace-edged collar and full sleeves gathered at her wrists by wide bands of the same lace. Down the front of the elegant, elaborate blouse ran a few bands of the same lace.

She had brushed her dark hair into a loose knot at the top of her head. A few tendrils escaped down on her face and neck, and she knew perfectly well that by the end of the evening, there would be a great many more such stray curls, but she wanted to feel special, and wearing her hair up always made her feel like something exciting was about to happen.

Standing in front of the mirror, she decided that she looked a bit like something out of a nineteenth-century portrait. But, she reflected, if Christopher felt like a character in a history book, she was certainly prepared to dress the part of his wife.

Mike had been fussing around her for the past

quarter of an hour like a proud papa, and she thought for half a moment, when Christopher came to the door, that Mike would tell him to have her home by midnight. Instead, the gray-haired man stepped around him and gruffly called out to the others to come in for a drink. This startled April. Not only was Mike usually very reluctant to invite people into the cabin, but both she and he drank so little that they didn't keep any liquor around.

Christopher came over to her. "You look remarkable. I'm not sure that I would have recognized you."

She smiled at him. "Is that a compliment?"

"And then some," he answered bluntly. "Steve and I didn't bring ties; the whole point of this vacation was not to wear a tie." He had on a sport coat of Harris Tweed and a dark green sweater over a white shirt.

"It's no problem," she assured him. "Lake Placid is a vacation community. During ski season there are sometimes more leg casts in a restaurant than there are ties."

The door opened, and April was very surprised to see Julia Breeland walk in, dressed in a black halter-topped jump suit, looking more ready for an evening in some stylish New York nightclub than in Lake Placid.

She looked inquiringly at Christopher. He cocked an eyebrow and explained quietly, "Well, she and Ben wanted to come. What could we say? But at least we had to take two cars, so the four of us can drive in together." Then he gestured toward the door. "Look at Beth. Doesn't she look nice?"

Beth did look pretty. The sun had put a soft color in her cheeks, which the quiet peach tones of her dress emphasized.

"Maybe she ought to wear that dress to work,"

Christopher continued. "I don't recall her normally looking so pretty."

April had to smile at his masculine ignorance. First of all, April doubted that it was the dress bringing the light into Beth's eyes, and second, her dress, although very simple, was hardly a work dress. The peach-colored fabric was a soft georgette, and the amount of detail on the dress suggested that it had been very expensive. The bodice was tucked, with many little hand-stitched folds, and all the closely spaced tiny buttons were covered with the dress's fabric. The long sleeves hadn't been lined so the white of her arms peered through the sheer fabric. When April admired the dress, Beth said that it had been worth every cent. It didn't wrinkle so she took it every time she packed a suitcase, even for a camping trip, and it made her feel both like a lawyer and a woman. "And that," she went on, "is not something that's too easy to find."

"Try a woman and a forest ranger," April said.

Beth smiled. "Maybe we ought to find ourselves a new profession."

"Maybe we should," April agreed, only half joking.

By now everyone was standing around a little awkwardly, probably waiting for a bartender to emerge from somewhere. Mike was absorbed in a conversation with Christopher, having undoubtedly forgotten that he had lured people in here with a promise of a drink.

Finally April spoke, "Mike, what were you planning on offering people to drink?"

Everyone laughed at the blank look on his face.

April suddenly felt very happy: Julia or not, this was going to be a wonderful evening. "Well, since the state pays for the Kool-Aid we serve at campfires, we probably shouldn't offer you any of that."

"Why don't we just push on?" Ben suggested, obviously ready for something considerably stronger.

As they filed out of the cabin Ben took April's arm and held her back. "I'm sure," he whispered confidently, "that Julia really wants to ride with Christopher. So how about you riding with me?"

It was times like this that April was very glad not to be eighteen anymore. It took poise and experience to keep from being manipulated by people like Julia and Ben. "That's a lovely idea," she answered sweetly. "But Beth and I really did want to ride together."

Outside, Christopher was stepping into the backseat of Steve's car; Julia was standing nearby expectantly, but April brushed past her, murmuring "Excuse me," and Christopher held out his hand to help her in.

As Steve and Beth opened the front doors Christopher rested his arm along the backseat behind April's shoulders.

"Are you all right back there, Chris?" Steve turned his blond head. "That backseat is not exactly designed for grown men."

"I'll manage." Christopher lightly tugged at a curl that was cascading down April's neck. "I have to sit closer to April than I want to, but I guess I'll survive that," he announced cheerfully.

"I guess you will," Steve returned.

April really liked this feeling, that they were two couples, that she and Christopher were clearly together.

Obviously Beth felt the same way. "This is just like doubledating in high school," she said happily.

Steve slapped his forehead in mock-horror. "And I forgot to ask Dad if I could borrow the car."

They all laughed as Steve started the car and pulled

out of the park. "Well, watch out, Steve," Christopher said, his arm suddenly closing around April's shoulders. "Last time I dated a high school girl, I had to marry her."

"Christopher!" April was shocked, embarrassed. "How can you joke about that?"

"Look, April," he said, serious for a moment. "It happened. It's part of our past; we have to accept it. Many, many people have done things much worse. If that is the worst thing we ever do, then we will be very fortunate."

"I suppose you're right," April said uncertainly. She was very surprised that he was saying this. It suggested that perhaps he was finally deliberately trying to lay to rest some of his guilt.

"This isn't any of my business," Steve said, his eyes in the rearview mirror meeting April's for a moment, "but it sure seems to me that what you two did wrong was not in having to get married, but in not staying married."

"You may well be right," Christopher answered and then was silent.

As they drove across the narrow, winding highway that led into Lake Placid, Ben's silver car followed them. April, glancing out the back window, was sorry to see it. Certainly Julia and Ben would spoil the evening for all the rest of them.

She felt Christopher turn his head and also look back. They were approaching a curve in the road, and he leaned forward and touched Steve's shoulder. "You might take the first turn after the curve."

"Where will that take us?" Beth asked curiously.

"I haven't any idea," he answered.

There was a sharp right turn just around the bend,

and Steve obediently turned, his tires squealing at the sudden maneuver. And after driving down the side road about a mile, the rest of them understood Christopher's scheme. The silver car was no longer following them.

"Now," Christopher said blandly, adjusting his cuff a fraction of an inch, "does anyone know where we are?"

April laughed. "Yes, this road circles around south of town, and we can come in from the east. But Lake Placid isn't all that big; we may run into them."

"Then we'll just blame it on you," he said, picking up her hand out of her lap. "We'll just say that you were showing off, trying to tell direction by the sun or something and got us lost."

Christopher was like that the rest of the evening, affectionate and teasing. In fact, Beth even commented on it when she and April were in the ladies' room together.

"I've just never seen him like this. He's so relaxed and happy. Not at all formal and polite. And Steve and Josh both said that when you were all out backpacking he seemed like a completely different person."

April examined herself in the mirror. As she had predicted, a great many more dark curls had escaped from the cluster at the top of her head. "Well, he is on vacation," she answered.

"Nonsense." Beth shut her purse with a snap. "He and Steve have been backpacking together ever since they joined the firm. It's not just the fresh mountain air that's making him this way."

They ate dinner at one of the hotels that had been built when the Winter Olympics had been held in Lake Placid. They had planned on going to a movie, but when nine thirty came, they were sitting in the hotel's lounge, drinking brandy, listening to music, much too comfortable to move.

It was late when they finally went back to the car, and the drive home was a quiet one. April saw Steve reach across the gap between the front seats and for a moment touch Beth's hand. Christopher put his arm around her, pulling her to rest against his chest. When he felt her hand brush against his leg, he trapped it there, holding it to him.

As they finally turned into the main gate of the campground and Steve stopped in front of the stone ranger cabin, April was very sorry that the evening had ended.

But when she got out of the car, Christopher stepped out with her, and, leaning over the car window spoke softly to Steve. Steve nodded and the car pulled away.

"I thought that they would want a little time alone," he explained. "I'll walk back."

Slowly they walked up the path to the cabin. Christopher had his arm around her shoulders. "You were incredibly funny when the check came," he said.

April laughed. "Do you believe that Beth was about to pay her share?"

When the check had come and Christopher had picked it up, presumably to split it with Steve, Beth had reached for her purse. While April certainly believed that there were times when women should pay their share, this wasn't one of them. She thought that this evening it was important for Steve to pay for Beth. He was so sensitive to everything concerning money, that paying for Beth's dinner, having everyone, including her, automatically expect it of him, would reassure him that their relationship was changing, that they were becoming a couple. So when she saw Beth reach for her purse, April had pointedly folded her hands on the table and stared hard at Beth.

"Do you know why she went along with you?" Christopher smiled. "She probably thought that you couldn't afford your share, and if she paid, it would embarrass you."

April grimaced. "Oh, well, I guess I can live with that," she sighed. "It isn't all that far from the truth."

"She's probably apologizing to him for it right now," Christopher said.

"That should be all right," April reflected. "I imagine that by now even Steve will have the sense to tell her that he enjoys doing things for her and that she should let him do them."

"Which is why," Christopher put in smoothly, "being a woman of great sense yourself, you are going to come on that canoe trip with us this fall."

April had to admire how gracefully he had introduced the subject, but she still shook her head.

He sighed. "April, it is no less true of Steve than me. We both enjoy doing things for the women we care about."

If he had said "love," she would have gone in a minute. "Christopher, you know that things are much simpler between them than between us."

His teeth caught at his lower lip. Reluctantly he agreed.

"Anyway," she said lightly, "money is more important to Steve than it is to you. You've always had it; he hasn't. So how he gets rid of it matters more to him than it does to you."

"You're probably right," Christopher mused, seeming to have accepted her refusal. "I think I'm *practical*

about money. I try to make decent investments, and if
I don't need something, I don't buy it even if I can
afford it. But I've never had any *feelings* about money—
at least I didn't until you wouldn't take it from me."

"Come on," she teased. "I did let you pay for my
dinner. Isn't that enough?"

"No." His voice was rough, and the arm around her
shoulders tightened, turning her to him. He lifted her
chin and, brushing some of the curls off her face, bent
his head and kissed her.

The kiss was gentle, but the arm wrapped around her
body kept her pressed close to him while his other hand
slipped down her chin, her throat, to rest lightly on the
sheer fabric covering her breast. She almost shuddered
at his touch. He felt the stirring in her and pulled her
toward him more tightly.

"Will you come in?" she whispered.

She felt him shake his head. "If I come in, I
wouldn't be able to leave."

"I know," she answered.

In the quiet starlight their eyes met, his green ones
speaking of his passion, his yearning for her, and the
blue softness in her eyes echoed his longing, telling
him that she too needed him.

"I'll be careful," he promised, indicating to her that
the risk they had taken before would not be taken
again.

And afterward they lay in her bed, the quilt resting
lightly over their satisfied bodies, the moonlight floating in through the open window, bringing with it the
smell of the forest night.

Christopher again slipped his arms around her and
spoke, "April, you are so very lovely."

She waited and finally he continued.

"Is there anything I can say or do that would make you come back to New York with me Sunday?"

There was. If he loved her, she would go anywhere with him. But she couldn't say that. She traced the line of his collarbone and spoke slowly, "No, Christopher, I don't want to live in the city."

"April, please, you have to think about your future, and I want to help you."

"You don't owe me anything," she said softly. "You've already given me more than anyone ever has."

She could feel his body tense. "It's not just a question of obligation; I *want* to help you. And if you won't come to New York, I don't know how. Is there anything you will let me do for you? Please."

Love me, she thought, *that's all I want*.

She swallowed and forced herself to say something. "You can give me some new towels. That's the only thing I need."

He smiled briefly at her whimsy. "At least when you leave here, will you let me help you get started somewhere else?"

"No, Christopher." She shook her head gently, her curls brushing against his chest. She knew that she was not telling him what he wanted to hear. But she couldn't lie. Now now. Not lying in his arms like this. "I can't promise that. I am not a child; I want to take care of myself."

He grimaced, obviously struggling to accept her answer, her right to make such an answer. After a moment he said, "You aren't planning on coming to New York even if you are pregnant, are you?"

"No, I am not." She knew it was worthless to try to reassure him. "Christopher, I've been married to a man who didn't love me; I would never do it again. I didn't hate being married to you, but I hated what it did to you. And I would much rather have an illegitimate child than go through that again."

She knew how it must pain him to hear that.

"Will you at least promise me one thing?" His voice was low.

"I probably won't," she said, almost with a smile, "but what is it?"

"That you won't run away again."

Now she could smile. "I won't do that. And if I am pregnant, which I doubt, I will try not to be proud and silly. I will stick you with your share of the bills—not all of them, mind you, just your share. And, in turn, you are not going to treat me like a child who can't do things for herself."

"Have I been doing that?" he asked ruefully.

"Continuously, Christopher, continuously."

Chapter Nine

April woke up late the next morning. Christopher had left before dawn. She hadn't wanted him to leave. He and the others were returning to New York in two days. She had no idea when she would see him after that, and she wanted to treasure the time they had. But he had insisted on leaving, not wanting the whole summer staff to know about her private affairs.

She was just finishing dressing when she heard a frantic knocking at the cabin door.

It was Faith, who was on duty at the registration hut. "Somebody came, looking for one of the campers," she said breathlessly.

This hardly seemed like anything to be upset about. "Did you tell them that we don't know the names of the individual campers?" April said calmly.

In an emergency the staff could go through the registration slips, but those usually only listed the last name of one member of the party.

"No, it was for one of those lawyers up in fifty-three, Julia Breeland," Faith explained. "I've been staring at that list on the inside of the hut for so long that I know all their names."

"Oh?" April was curious. Why was a man here to see Julia? "I wonder what he wanted. Did you send him up?"

"Yes, oh, yes," Faith cried. "I am afraid that I did."

"I don't see the problem." April looked at the girl. She seemed very upset.

"Oh? Didn't I say? I think he had had an awful lot to drink."

April blinked and glanced at her watch. "At nine in the morning? Are you sure?"

"Well, no. At first I just thought that he was acting strange and that his breath smelled funny. And then, after he drove on, it occurred to me that he had been drinking. I am so sorry," the girl pleaded, obviously believing that she had made a terrible mistake. "But I don't drink myself, and so it just didn't occur to me. Anyway, he had these strange, glittering eyes, and he made me feel uncomfortable."

"Don't worry about it," April said evenly, fastening her nameplate to her pocket. "I'll go up and check."

"Oh, thank you." Faith was clearly relieved to have someone else take over.

April was inclined to think that the girl was over-reacting. But as she came to the fork in the trail and turned the pickup toward the campground, she suddenly felt a nervous crawling at the back of her neck, a turning in her stomach, as if something were wrong, as if something hostile, even wicked, had invaded the forest. She tried to dismiss her feelings as silly romanticism. Why should the back of her neck know so much more than the rest of her?

Then she saw the tree.

It was a spruce, a magnificent tree, growing close to the road, towering toward the sky. It seemed indomitable, its needles prickly enough to warn off intruders, its bark a sturdy defense against all attacks.

But just a foot or so off the ground the dark bark was ripped open, and a wide gash had sliced deep into the living wood.

April quickly stopped the truck. The damage had been done by a car—no, by the *driver* of a car. The worst wounds were not from the car's initial impact, but from the careless, impatient way the driver had freed himself, reversing angrily, ripping even deeper into the tree.

April touched the pale wood gently. It was sticky with oozing sap, the tree's lifeblood. She lifted her head, and down the trail she could see at least one, possibly two other trees, defaced with deep, white scars.

She drove slowly up the trail, finding yet another tree damaged by this apparently crazed driver. Her hands were tight and white as they gripped the steering wheel. One tree she could understand. It did happen; the trail was narrow, and sometimes campers had boat trailers that they weren't used to pulling. But four?

Campsite fifty-three was unusually quiet; none of the usual laughter, voices, or sounds of pots and axes spilled out onto the trail. A strange car blocked the entrance, and April had to leave the pickup parked on the trail. She didn't recognize the make of the car—it was low and red—all she saw was how caught under the bright chrome bumpers were shreds and fibers of brown tree bark.

None of the men were there, just Beth and Julia and a stranger. He must have just arrived, for Julia seemed to have just finished introducing him to Beth, and all three were standing there a little awkwardly.

"Hello," April called out to make her presence known.

All three of them turned to look at her. The man looked like such a typical well-to-do New Englander that April might have smiled if she hadn't been so upset about the trees. With straight brown hair and a strong jaw, he was dressed in khaki slacks, a kelly-green Lacoste shirt, and loafers without socks. But he had lost the clean, bright look that he had probably had when he graduated from his prep school. His eyes were bloodshot, and the crisp lines of his features were blurred from years of self-indulgence.

"Oh, April," Beth sighed. "I'm so glad you're here."

April looked at the man questioningly. "This is Tom Breeland," Beth explained quickly. "He's—he's Julia's husband."

So this was the man Julia was trying to free herself from. As April moved nearer she knew that Faith had been right. He had harsh, glinting eyes, and he had been drinking a lot.

To anyone else April would have said something about the trees, but Julia seemed so nervous, her face pale against the swath of black hair, that April did not want to make things any worse. There was already more than just an awkward tension; the air seemed to crackle with a hint of violence that April did not understand. She remembered what Beth had said about this divorce being such a difficult one, with Tom threatening to contest it or to countersue Julia. No wonder, if he was given to drinking, much of his behavior probably was irrational and inconsistent.

He seemed to be spoiling for a fight and was apparently perfectly willing to have it in front of April and Beth. April looked around for signs of Christopher and the others. Tom Breeland might be less likely to quarrel with his wife if there were four other men standing around.

"Where are the others?" April asked Beth softly.

"They went down to the showers just before he got here."

April noticed towels and cosmetic bags on the picnic table. Julia and Beth had obviously been about to shower too. "I'll go get them."

"Don't go." April was startled to hear fear licking at Julia's voice. What was she afraid of? "Please, April, don't leave."

April was surprised by such a direct appeal. Why did Julia feel that she needed her? "Okay," she answered. "They'll be back soon anyway."

"What's wrong, dear wife?" Tom stepped nearer to Julia. "Are you afraid of something?" He picked up a lock of her black hair.

"Of course not," Julia said defiantly. "I'm not afraid of you." She tossed her hair over her shoulder.

The gesture seemed to irritate him. "Oh, you aren't, are you?"

"No. I never have been afraid of you, and I never will be."

"Now, Julia"—his voice was low and threatening—"aren't you worried that if you lie too much, your pretty nose will grow long?" With his forefinger Tom traced the line of Julia's finely chiseled nose.

She knocked his hand away. "Get away from me. You've been drinking."

Tom stared at her for a moment and slowly lifted his arm, so slowly that April wasn't alarmed.

In a sudden slice he hit Julia backhanded across the face, knocking her to the ground.

For a moment April and Beth were riveted, too

stunned to move, so startling was the sight of Julia, always elegant and controlled, on her back in the sandy earth, her hand against her cheek, tears of pain starting to form in her eyes.

Most shocking was the look on her face. It didn't register outrage or anger, any of the fury she was entitled to feel. Instead her features were tight with a bitter disappointment, just, April thought in a pang of shared misery, just exactly how she herself would feel if Christopher suddenly lost control and knocked her down—although in that case, surprise would almost overpower regret.

But Julia was not surprised. Clearly this had happened before.

No wonder Julia was as she was, April thought, hurrying to stand between Tom and where Beth had knelt by Julia. No wonder she longed to control every situation, to manipulate people, to have power over them, if her husband had regularly used a brutish strength to control her. And no wonder she was so attracted to Christopher, who had more self-control than any man she had probably ever met. Tom Breeland obviously had none, trying to compensate for his inability to control himself by knocking her around, by getting her in his power as he was not in his own power.

Beth helped Julia up. Checking to be sure that Tom was leaning against a tree, laughing, his arms crossed, April went over to one of the coolers and got some ice for Julia's rapidly swelling face.

Julia nodded in silent thanks and then raised her head, staring at the man she had married.

"Tom, why are you here?"

"Just to tell you that I am not signing any papers." Clearly he was talking about the final stages of their divorce.

"But the judge says that you must." Julia's voice was weary, exhausted.

"Nobody tells Tom Breeland what to do. No judge, no fancy lawyers, especially not you." Slowly he advanced toward the three women, his arm raised menacingly.

April heard a strange whimper, like a tiny kitten frightened and starving. It was Julia.

It didn't matter that April did not like the other woman. She was a registered visitor at the park, and it was April's job to protect her. And even if there were not professional ethics involved, no woman should ever, April thought angrily, be that frightened by a man.

April moved toward him quickly. As he grasped her arms to thrust her aside, she could smell the swarmy fumes of his breath. Quickly and forcefully she raised her knee to his groin.

Tom sprawled on the ground, moaning in pain.

April sank down to the picnic bench, almost as shocked as Julia and Beth. She had never done that to a man before. Even when drunks had tried to follow her home from the restaurant after the late shift, she had managed to talk her way free.

Tom slowly eased himself upright, breathing hard. "Who are you?" he said in disbelief.

"April Ramsey, a New York State Forest Ranger."

"Wonderful," he panted. "I am glad to know what good uses my tax dollar is being put to." He threw her a twisted grin.

Surprisingly he didn't seem to resent her hurting him, and April suddenly felt a giggle rising up in her. It was hysterics, she thought, trying hard to control it. At the least provocation she knew that Beth and Julia would join her in nervous laughter that would rapidly degenerate into tears.

"Will you go away?" Beth pleaded.

"That doesn't sound like too bad an idea," the man returned with a little self-mocking smile, and under the puffiness, the bleariness of years of drinking, April could sense the charm that must have once attracted Julia.

"No," she said emphatically. "I think you're too drunk to drive. You have already damaged several trees."

"I can always drive," he said proudly and started to fumble in his pocket for his keys. April noticed a key ring, glinting in the sun, apparently having dropped out of his pocket when he fell. Quickly she stood up and unobtrusively planted her foot on top of it. "At least," Tom continued, still searching through his pockets, "I can drive when I can find my keys."

"Tom, don't drive." Julia finally spoke. Her voice made no impact on him. "Please don't," she pleaded.

Breeland obviously liked hearing her beg for things. "So you want me to hang around. Too happy to oblige." And keeping a careful eye on April, he went to his car and leaned against it.

They were like this—Julia and Beth at the picnic table, Tom against his car, and April standing awkwardly on top of his keys—when they finally heard the voices of the four men coming back from the showers.

The men saw the car and their pace quickened. Ben, the most forward of them, came into the campsite first and extended his hand to Tom. Obviously none of them knew who he was.

"Hello, I am Ben Carl..." Ben's voice trailed off as he came near enough to Tom to realize how much he had been drinking.

The other men, more sensitive to the tension in the

three women, looked around quickly, silently asking for an explanation. Julia's head had been bent, her black hair falling forward, but when she looked up, there was no disguising the darkening bruise across her cheek.

"Julia," Josh cried. "What happened?"

Christopher reached her first. He touched her cheek with his fingers. "Did he do that to you?" he asked, jerking his head toward Tom.

"It's nothing that hasn't happened before," she answered, and in response to his startled look, she said, "This is my ex-husband, Tom Breeland."

Tom leisurely acknowledged everyone's glance. "Not quite ex," he answered slowly.

"Did you hit her?" Christopher asked, his voice even and controlled.

"Sure does seem like it, doesn't it?"

Christopher started to move toward Tom with an alertness in his eyes that April had never seen before. She couldn't imagine Christopher violent—for all his strength and fearlessness, he had never, as an adult, struck anyone in anger—at least as far as April knew.

She thought that he just might do it now, but Julia put a hand on his arm, stopping him. "Don't bother," she said. "He won't do it again."

"I certainly won't," Tom said, his eyes flicking toward April. Then he looked back to Christopher. "You must be the famed Christopher Ramsey about whom I've heard a great deal more than I care to."

"I am," Christopher said curtly.

"Well, you don't have to jump in and think you've got call to protect my wife. This lady could stop a tank." And suddenly Tom was at April's side, his hand warm and moist on her arm.

"Get your hands off her," Christopher ordered.

"Excuse me," Tom drawled, "I didn't know that you were so concerned about the welfare of our public servants, however much a particular one might be worth looking after." Tom's eyes trailed down April's form, his hot gaze lingering at her breasts. He noticed the nameplate pinned there, reminding him of her name. "Or is she your sister or something? Just tell me and I'll go away. I try to avoid people's sisters."

"She's *my* wife," Christopher snapped. "So why don't you go?"

"A married man!" Tom whistled. "Julia, my dear, consorting with a married man. How sordid! Well, my dear forest ranger," he said to April, "perhaps we should get them both up on adultery charges. You could probably take him for all that he's worth, and that, I hear, is a great deal."

"Christopher and I are already divorced," she murmured.

"Well, well, then we exes must stick together, mustn't we?" Tom hooked an arm around her shoulders, allowing his hand to settle on her breast. "I like a woman with spirit."

"You didn't five minutes ago," April reminded him softly, and Tom's arm was away from her before Christopher had a chance to knock it off.

Tom shrugged. "I guess I've worn out my welcome. I'd leave, but I seem to be missing my keys."

"You shouldn't be driving," Steve said. He had gone over to Beth as soon as he had seen Julia's bruised face, apparently newly aware of how physically fragile Beth was, how delicate was her small build. Reassured that Tom had not threatened her, Steve was ready to do what he could to get rid of him. "I'll take you into town; you can check into a motel and sober up."

"I'll follow you in my car, and you can take him in his," Josh suggested.

"But, gentlemen, no keys," Tom extended his hands, as if he were a magician, showing them to be empty.

Suddenly April remembered. She bent and picked the keys up. She handed them to Steve. "Here they are."

"Where were they?" Tom asked curiously.

"I was standing on them."

"You are some strange girl," he said admiringly. "Remind me to avoid you," he added, sauntering off to his car.

"What was that all about?" Josh asked curiously.

"Tom was trying to get at Julia a second time," Beth explained, "and April stopped him."

"You did?" Christopher looked at her with surprise. "How?"

"Well," April faltered, a little embarrassed, "it wasn't exactly a fair fight."

The men gradually understood her meaning, their surprise fading into a certain amusement. April spoke quickly to Steve, "Tell Tom that he has a right to report what I did. If he wants to, then stop at the cabin and Mike will give him all the right forms."

Steve looked at her blankly. "If you say so."

The two cars drove off, and Julia covered her face with her hands. Her shoulders were shaking; she was trying not to cry. Christopher sat down next to her, put his arms around her, pulling her to his chest, murmuring something into her hair.

A sudden stab of pain shot through April. If she could be sure that Christopher was just comforting a frightened woman, this sight would not bother her. But was Julia just any woman to him?

It was so hard sometimes to tell what Christopher's gestures meant. All his life he had heard from his old-fashioned southern parents that women needed protecting—not just young girls or wives and sisters, but *all* women. He probably would have behaved exactly as he had if it had been Beth sitting at the picnic table with a bruise darkening her face, or even if it had been a stranger. No, if it had been Beth, Steve undoubtedly would have got there first, but Christopher was quite capable of putting his arms gently around a strange woman and letting her cry against his chest if that seemed to be what she needed.

So it was hard to tell how important it was to him that it was Julia who needed comfort.

"I think I'll be going," April said to Beth in a low voice. "You might be able to sort things out more easily with fewer people around."

Julia heard, and she straightened in Christopher's arms. "April, thank you."

Her voice was sincere, and April, for the first time, met the other woman's eyes directly. She deeply regretted that there had been friction and competition between them. Women ought to be friends with one another, she thought.

"I'm sure that you would have done the same for me," she answered.

Julia smiled tearily and gave a little laugh. "I don't imagine that *your* ex-husband tries to knock you across a room too often."

"No," April acknowledged, ignoring Christopher's little grunt of surprise. "Not too often."

As she was turning toward the trail, Julia stopped her again. "April, there's really no chance that Tom would report what you did. He's not like that. He plays fair."

April suffered for her. To speak like that Julia must still care for him. How dreadful to go on caring for a man when you could not respect him, when you had every reason to be frightened of him. April realized that compared to Julia, she herself was fortunate—for all the unhappiness that her love had brought her, at least she had not bestowed it on someone unworthy.

She glanced over at Christopher, his arms still around Julia. He seemed to be thinking the same sorts of things about her that April had; his green eyes were full of puzzled concern.

As usual Beth Market broke the awkward silence. "Could you have got into trouble, April?"

"Maybe. Rangers aren't exactly supposed to do that to park visitors. But in the absolute worst case, there would be some sort of hearing and it would all work out. Especially now that I know so many lawyers," she added with a smile.

April went directly back to the cabin and told Mike what had happened. Tom had not stopped by to pick up the forms to report her for misconduct, and so Mike said it was best forgotten. "He obviously knew that he deserved it." Then he looked at her interestedly. "I wonder what your husband thinks about the way you handled things."

"Oh, I imagine that he's much too concerned about Julia at the moment to be thinking of me."

"Well, maybe at the moment."

April didn't feel up to one of Mike's little talks about Christopher so she excused herself and went out to one of the shop buildings to get the tree dressing. She went to work on the trees that Tom's cars had gashed. Gently, as if they were injured children, she cleaned and smoothed the wounds, carefully brushing on the tree dressing, tying up some of the worst with burlap to keep the trees from losing too much of their precious sap. She could save the trees from Tom's violence; would anyone be able to save Julia?

It took her several hours to care for the trees. It soothed her to work on them, driving away the memory of Tom's narrowing eyes, of Christopher's hands in Julia's black hair. When she was done, she felt calmer, although drained. The past week had been very stressful: This incident, with its threat of danger and violence, had only been the most dramatic, but other quieter moments, April knew, were disturbing her as much.

As she approached the main gate she saw Faith step out of the registration hut and call to her. "Christopher left a note for you." Christopher was the one camper whose name every summer staffer knew, and April was quite sure that there was a great deal of talk in the bunkhouse about the two of them.

She took it from the girl. It was a sheet of paper, folded without an envelope, and across the front in handwriting April hadn't seen since signing her divorce papers was her name, Ms. April Ramsey.

The *Ms.* surprised her. Not that she wasn't used to it. Most of her official mail came addressed that way, and Ms. was certainly convenient when you weren't a Miss but didn't feel married. She had never really liked it, but she knew her dislike had nothing to do with the politics or the etiquette of the word. She just didn't like being divorced. And she certainly didn't like seeing it in Christopher's handwriting.

What had he thought when he had written her name? April stared down at the flowing black letters traced by a wide fountain pen. Had he been aware of how his writing must have quickened when he wrote out the very familiar last name? Did he remember all the times when instead of writing "Ms. April" he had written "Mrs. Christopher"? No, probably not. He had done it all unthinkingly; he had probably been very rushed.

Slowly she unfolded the paper:

April,
I am taking Julia back to the city to try to get a restraining order to keep Breeland away from her. Sorry to leave so abruptly, but she is distraught. I'll be in touch.

He signed it with his initials.

So Christopher was gone. Without any dramatic fare-wells, without any more efforts to get her to come with him, without any plans to see her again. Just "I'll be in touch."

Would she ever see him again? How ironic, she thought almost bitterly. If she didn't, it would mean that the last time she would have seen him, she would have been paying almost no attention to him; she had instead been concentrating on Julia, her rival.

Julia was still her rival. Even though April felt no more dislike for the girl—in fact, she felt a great deal of sympathy and concern—she was now more certain than ever that she did not want Christopher involved with Julia. Before, April's reaction to Julia had been almost entirely colored by jealousy: She had simply wanted Christopher for herself. But now she was confident that Christopher could not ever be happy with Julia. No man could, not when she was still so confused and tormented by her feelings for her ex-husband.

Well, April tried to tell herself, Christopher was an adult; he could take care of himself. Surely he would have the sense to see that Julia was not ready for a new relationship. But she was as wounded as the trees had been, and Christopher might find her distress enormously appealing.

There was probably so much that he could do for her—get this restraining order, help her sort out whatever legal and financial difficulties remained. And Julia would let him help her in a way that April never had, accepting his help willingly and graciously, understanding that he wanted to do it. Julia would know that it was important to Christopher to have a chance to help people when they were in the kind of trouble that he never got in himself. And April was confident that Julia could take his help without ever making him feel that she was a child or his sister.

April looked at the letter again. It seemed so curt and impersonal, the sort of thing that he might write to anyone. But what had she expected—for him to sign it "Your loving husband"?

Then with a flash of insight April realized that a letter signed that way would probably be worse. That was very likely the way his father signed letters to his mother, with such a meaningless formula. No, this letter, although very abrupt, was not at all the sort of thing that Christopher would write to just anyone. Even his personal letters were no doubt characterized by a certain formality, unconsciously emphasizing the barrier he tended to place between himself and others. But such a quick note as this he would dash off only to someone he felt very comfortable with, someone he felt close to.

But still, she sighed, just because he felt comfortable with her, didn't mean that he loved her.

Chapter Ten

The others left the next morning. They were cutting their vacation a little short, but none of them really felt like staying. Although Julia had not inspired a great deal of affection among any of them, they were loyal to her. She was their colleague; she had come with them; they felt the need to stand by her.

April went up to say good-bye. She liked them. She and Beth could have been lifelong friends if they had been given a chance, and April devoutly hoped that she and Steve would come to a good understanding soon. He seemed like such a good man, marred only by his touching inability to believe that a woman might find him desirable. Obviously Steve was Christopher's closest friend, and thus he was doubly interesting in April's eyes. The two of them probably rarely confided in each other—they almost certainly never had the sort of satisfying talks about feelings and emotions that women had with one another—but they shared their precious leisure time with each other. They liked and respected each other, and except for those moments when Steve had ordered Christopher to stop trying to give money to April and when Christopher had unthinkingly scooped Beth into his arms, they had probably never competed with each other.

Josh, of course, she liked for himself, for his quick insight and ready sympathy. She wondered what would happen to him. Surely he didn't want to spend the rest of his life playing brother to every woman he met. Perhaps someday he would meet a woman he didn't understand at all, and she would probably drive every rational, brotherly thought from his mind.

Even Ben now seemed less offensive. Yes, he was a little weak and competitive, but compared to the viciousness of Tom Breeland, he seemed harmless. Ben could probably solve many of his problems, April thought, if he left Manhattan. The competition was too stiff there. With so many people like Christopher and Steve around, it wasn't enough to be very bright and very capable. Making it to the top in New York City took more than that. If Ben would move somewhere else, he might be the best young lawyer in the office, the most attractive man at any party—and that was what he needed. But he would probably never do it. It took a stronger man than Ben to admit that he was outclassed.

As she came around the final bend in the trail, April could see that Christopher must have taken Ben's car back to town. She idly wondered why he had not driven his own car up to Frank Lake. When she had known him, he had driven a little two-passenger sports car. Perhaps he still did; it hardly made sense to take a car as small as that on a camping trip. He had bought April a larger car, but undoubtedly he had long since sold it. April wondered now how he had managed that; the car had been in her name. That was just the sort of thing that she had not thought about when she left—the various difficulties he might have taking care of matters that might need her signature. Well, that had to be one advantage of being a lawyer; you could figure your way around things like that.

But one thing being a lawyer didn't seem to help on was how to get the equipment that had been in three cars packed into two. Christopher and Julia had left quickly without packing much, and even though Ben's was the smallest of the three cars, April could see that the four remaining lawyers were having trouble packing the cars and the boat.

April smiled and hurried to help them. Soon the cars were packed and they were ready to leave.

This time it took none of Josh's maneuvering to get Steve and Beth together. "Are you riding with me, Beth?" Steve asked for himself. His words were casual, but his voice had an edge of tension as if even now, he thought that she might stare at him in surprise that he could think such a ridiculous thing.

But Beth simply smiled and said, "Of course."

Then he turned to April and asked pleasantly, "When will we be seeing you again?"

"I really don't know," she answered. "Not unless you're planning on coming back to Frank Lake."

"But won't you be down to visit Christopher soon?" Steve asked.

April shook her head, unable to speak. It hurt that his friends were so sure that she had some sort of future with him.

"Oh, April," Beth breathed in pain, and Josh laid a gentle arm around her shoulders.

Their obvious concern telegraphed the situation even to Steve. He spoke haltingly. "April, as different as we are, Chris and I have been friends for a long time. I know him as well as I know any man, and I know that he thinks the world of you. I honestly think that he is proud of you. And," Steve added with self-insight that no one had ever given him credit for, "I am always the last to sense these things. So if I know it, it's bound to be true."

April smiled at him weakly. "I know," she sighed. "He does respect me now, and he didn't before. But, as important as respect is, it isn't enough."

"But are you sure that there isn't a lot more?" Steve asked, clearly unhappy with her answer. "It just seems that whenever he is with you, Chris is just a different person. There was always an abstract, distant quality about him that isn't there when you're around. It just seems like the two of you have a lot going for you."

April shook her head. "No. You have to remember that it isn't as simple as if Christopher and I had just met. We were married, and marriages don't break up cleanly and neatly."

They were all quiet for a moment, thinking of Julia and Tom.

"Then it is too bad," Steve said slowly, "that you weren't meeting here for the first time."

"No." April shook her head. "Everything that I am today, everything that Christopher respects about me, that I respect about myself, is because of our marriage and what happened after that. I would never be the sort of person that I am now if I had not met him."

Josh's arm tightened around her shoulders. "April, I know that this is not going to make any difference," he said, "but you remember what Steve said when we were having that picnic—that any of us would be happy to pay your way if you could come with us this September to Canoe Country?"

April nodded.

"I'm not trying to embarrass or insult you, because I know you won't accept, but I want to emphasize what he said, just so that you understand how we feel about you. You just seem like one of us; you've fitted in from the very beginning, and not just because Chris is much more human when you're around. Even if he weren't coming, the rest of us would want you there."

April felt a burning tightness in her throat at their unreserved affection. Two weeks ago they had been strangers, the curious audience in front of whom she had to cross the campsite and, for the first time in six years, speak to her husband. Now they were dear friends who wished her well.

Everyone looked regretful, and to break the sad silence April spoke quickly. "You better get moving or you'll hit the city just in time for evening rush hour."

They all hugged her, and April whispered softly to Beth, "You will write, won't you?" She had to know what happened between Julia and Christopher.

Beth understood. "Of course."

"Do you want a lift down to the cabin?" Steve asked.

April shook her head. "You would have to tie me to the luggage carrier. I think I'll be safer walking."

They all laughed softly and got into the cars. The engines started and in a moment they were gone.

The site looked terribly empty. It was hard to believe that just yesterday it had been full of tents and laughter. They had left it immaculate, the light sandy soil was covered only with pine needles and footprints, no empty matchbooks or bottle caps. All they had left was a small stack of split wood, the traditional courtesy of one group of campers for the next.

She closed her eyes, remembering Christopher standing in the sunlight, his shirt off, splitting wood. More memories followed this one—Christopher unpinning her nameplate before gathering her up in his arms to dance; him leaning back in the pale armchair of her bedroom, his eyes when he told her that he knew that she had loved him, the strength of his hands, the pressure of his thighs—April covered her hands with her face and cried.

A loud blare from a car's horn startled her, and quickly she brushed the tears off her face. A van followed by another car pulled into the site.

A young man, clearly a college student, jumped out of the van. "Are these sites taken?" he called cheerfully.

"No, no, they aren't," April said and, straightening her shirt collar, went over to talk to this new group about the park rules.

The summer dragged. April was busy: The campground started to be full every weekend and simply overflowed during Memorial Day. But every aspect of each day seemed like a wearying routine, even though the days were sunny and the lake clear, although the wind would whisper through the pines, and the scent of campfires would perfume the air. April felt she would be happier in the hot concrete caverns of New York—if Christopher loved her.

This seemed worse than when she had left him six years ago. Then she felt as if her life were over. Now she knew that it was not. She would probably continue to get up every morning for another fifty years, and she could not resign herself to that much misery and solitude. She had to find something else to give her life meaning, some purpose other than being Christopher's wife and raising his children. But she simply did not know what it was.

She did hear from him. Shortly after they left, she was able to write him a brief, blunt note, saying that she was not pregnant. His answer was typed although the carelessly made corrections indicated that at least he had typed it himself, not dictated it to a secretary. He first said that he was pleased that she was "in good health," which she thought was an odd, but typically Christopher, way of saying it. He told her more about Julia's legal situation than she wanted to hear, certainly more than she understood. The letter went on to tell her about a play he had seen, analyzing the production, the lighting, the direction, not bothering to mention whom he had gone to see it with.

He did say that Beth and Steve were now seeing each other steadily. Steve had said nothing to him, so he was sure that they had made no definite plans, but all the secretaries in the firm were certainly talking like they had.

The letter ended, "Things are quite hectic at the office right now, but I will try to get away for a weekend soon. I hope I don't have to tell you what it means to be in contact with you again."

April jerked at the letter impatiently. What an idiot he was, she thought of the man she loved nearly more than life. How dare he say that? That was the *one* thing she did desperately need to be told—what had it meant to him to see her again. If it just meant that he didn't have to worry and wonder anymore, well, he could have just said that, couldn't he? But this vagueness, it just wasn't fair; it allowed her to hope that he was feeling more than relief.

And why was he talking about coming back up here? Did he want to have an occasional affair with her; was he planning on showing up a few weekends a year for a jolly romp? That seemed out of character; he would probably consider such behavior to be using her. Or did he just feel obligated to come back because they had slept together, to let her know that she wasn't a one-night stand?

Or maybe he wouldn't come at all; maybe this was just one of those things he would always plan to do, but never quite find the time for.

At least he had signed the letter "Christopher." His friends all seemed to call him "Chris" now. People in Virginia had always used the more formal version of his name to distinguish him from his father, and April still thought of him that way. At least he had noticed what name she used for him.

A few days later a huge carton arrived for her. It was full of towels, half in melon, half in jade. They were thick, rich towels, of a better quality than April had ever seen before: hand towels, bath sheets, washcloths— more towels than even an entire family would need.

It occurred to her that Christopher had just walked into the linen department of Bloomingdale's and announced that he wanted to spend as much money on towels as was earthly possible. For it was hard to regard this gift as anything but a ridiculously extravagant joke— Christopher teasing her for her reluctance to accept things from him, mocking himself for his own affluence.

She knew she was right when she opened the card. He had written a single wry sentence, "If it hadn't taken six weeks, I would have had them all monogrammed too."

Monogrammed, she thought ruefully, with what? An *R*—his initial?

She was very tempted to write him how glad she was that they weren't monogrammed so that she could use them if she married again. But she didn't, instead writing, in a mock-seriousness that she knew would make him smile, that she, of course, could not accept such an expensive gift, but she could not afford return postage at the moment. She would start saving up right away and would use the towels until then.

The problem was that every time she used one of the green towels she thought of his eyes—but this she did not tell him.

Although it was only June, April was already starting to dread winter. If summer seemed monotonous and empty, winter would be deadly. Those white days, those long nights: April was wondering how she was going to stand them.

She knew that Mike was worried about her. He had occasionally gone so far as to remind her that there were plenty of people standing in line for her job, that she wasn't obligated to stay. She just smiled and told him not to start getting anyone's hopes up. It didn't look like she was going anywhere.

Beth Market did send her some encouraging news. Although Christopher was spending a lot of time with Julia (Beth did not try to hide the fact that her letter was about the two of them), Josh had convinced Julia to start seeing a therapist, and rumor had it that the therapist was getting her to understand that she was not ready for new relationships; all of her reactions were still too colored by Tom. Naturally it was all rumor, but Julia did seem to have ceased her pursuit of Christopher.

Of course, April had to remind herself, it wasn't as if Julia was the barrier between them. If he didn't love her, it hardly mattered whether he was seeing other women. Six years ago he had tried to force himself to love her. Why should he be able to now?

Then April got another letter from Beth, written when she was so excited that she kept leaving out words and not finishing sentences. She and Steve were getting married at Thanksgiving. They were leaving Manhattan, having got jobs at a smaller firm in Albany, the state capital. The firm had already said that Beth could work part-time if she wanted to have children, which, she assured April, she most certainly did.

The wedding was to be in Rochester, Beth's home-town, and she very much hoped that April would be there. Christopher was going to stand up with Steve.

April was delighted for Beth, but very uncertain as to whether she should go to the wedding. Surely by November she would have stopped thinking about Christopher every day; to see him again would reopen her pain.

And probably make the suffering worse. To see him standing in the front of a church, handing Steve Beth's wedding ring, proposing a toast, doing all the things that a best man does at a big, happy wedding, a wedding so very different from his own. April wasn't sure that she could stand it.

The Fourth of July fell on a Monday that year, giving most people a three-day weekend. Many of them were clearly expanding it into a four-day one because by noon on Friday, all the sites at the Frank Lake campground were taken. The staff let a few people with vans and RVs park in the little overflow lot near the beach, but by the middle of the afternoon, that too was full and they had to turn everyone away, except the backpackers.

April hated having to turn people away; they were always so disappointed. She stayed near the registration hut most of the afternoon with maps of the area and lists of other campgrounds, helping people decide where to go next. She kept in touch with the other parks in the area and sent people to the ones that still had vacancies. When all the state parks were full, she started calling the private campgrounds. The private ones usually had many sites crowded into a small area, but they were better than nothing.

She was working her way through a list of such campgrounds when Don, one of the summer staffers who had arrived after Memorial Day, opened the cabin door and called out, "April, your brother is here."

April stopped dialing. "What? I don't have a brother."

"Oh, I just assumed—" Don stopped. "There's a guy out here to see you, and he's got the same last name as you do."

Christopher! Christopher had come back. It was all April could do to keep from rushing out and throwing herself in his arms.

Instead she carefully placed the receiver back on what she thought was the phone. She missed, and it slipped off the table, dangling by the cord, hitting against the table leg with sharp little knocks. Don looked at her curiously and, replacing the receiver, asked, "Do you want me to finish this?"

"Please."

April stood up and nervously tucked in her uniform shirt. She ran her fingers through her curls and, gulping for air, pushed open the cabin door.

Christopher was leaning against a little sports car, its top open to the warm July sun, the British racing green of its paint a shiny version of the forest's colors. He was still in his city clothes, a navy pinstripe suit and a white shirt. He wasn't wearing the jacket, and the closely-fitting vest gathered in the shirt in a dark line that emphasized the shape of his chest, the trimness of his waist. The slacks were carefully tailored and fitted him nearly as his jeans had.

It was strange to see him dressed like that; even with his coat off, his burgundy tie loosened over the open collar of the shirt, and his hair ruffled by the wind, he was so obviously a successful Manhattan attorney, not at all like the student she had married or the man she had got to know again out on the backpacking trails. He looked unfamiliar and she was suddenly shy.

"Christopher," she said quietly. "Hello."

He had straightened at her approach. "Hello, April." He looked drawn and tired. "I thought that they weren't going to let me in."

"The campground is full," she answered, not quite believing that she was managing to stand here a few feet away from him, talking so evenly.

"You look tired," she heard herself say.

"You don't." But a flicker in his green eyes suggested that he meant a great deal more.

April blushed and glanced away. There was an awkward silence, and just for something to say, she said, "You still have your car."

She wasn't surprised. His family tended to spend a great deal of money whenever they bought something, selecting an item of the very best quality. But then they took excellent care of their belongings and kept everything for years. Christopher must have had this car for almost thirteen years, and it looked as fresh as the day he had got it. His parents had given it to him for his sixteenth birthday, and he had been driving it during that week he had first known April. She had never ridden in a sports car before, and she had almost been as delighted with it as she had been with him.

"Yes," he answered. "They don't make them anymore so it's increasing in value each year. Although it does cost a lot to keep it running."

She tilted her head, looking up at him. "Christopher, why don't you just admit that you love the car?"

He looked down at her, the surprised look gradually warming. "Of course, you are right. It just sounds so irrational to love a car."

Why were they talking about cars? April wondered almost frantically. She cared nothing about cars.

But she continued. "Well, there's nothing wrong with being irrational sometimes."

He reached out and touched her arm. "Again you are right. Are you on duty?"

"Yes, but—" Just the touch of his hand on her arm left her weak, with her mouth so dry she could hardly talk. He must have noticed the little quiver that shot through her, for his hand slid up to her shoulder, turning her, as if he were about to ease her into an embrace.

"Christopher!" April heard a voice cry out and then she felt him step away. Faith, again working registration, had just finished talking to some unhappy would-be campers and had seen the two of them.

"Hello, Faith." Christopher waved to her. "Nice weather, isn't it?"

"It sure is," Faith called back and then glanced longingly over her shoulder to the bunkhouse. April knew that long before nightfall, the whole summer staff would be gossiping about why Christopher had come back.

Why *had* he come? She guessed it was an impulsive decision; it seemed as if he had just left from work, not even going home to change.

She spoke directly. "Christopher, surely you didn't drive all the way up here to talk about the weather."

"No," he admitted and gestured toward the picnic table. "Can you sit down for a moment?"

Again he straddled the bench, resting his arm on the table just as he had done that morning in May, when they had been alone for the first time in six years. When he spoke, again his tone was expressionless, almost professional.

"April, you keep saying that you've changed. I need to know how."

April blinked. At least in May, his questions had been answerable. "What do you mean?"

"In what ways have you changed?" he repeated.

"I am older; I can take care of—" This was no good; she had said all this before, and she felt almost certain that he knew how competent and adult she had become. And if he didn't know, there was no point in telling him. "I weigh five pounds more," she said bluntly.

He smiled. "Oh, I know that," he said, briefly glancing down to where most of the extra pounds had settled. And when he looked back at her face, his eyes told her that he also knew all the things that she had started to say.

"Then I don't understand," she said.

His eyes grew darker, gathering intensity, and his voice almost snapped. "Why were you willing to go to bed with me?"

"What?" April gasped and jerked upright, embarrassed and confused. She recovered quickly and took refuge behind a general answer. "Women have desires too, you know."

"Oh, I know that," he said impatiently. "April, look, a lot of people do foolish things in a passionate, impulsive moment." He gave a short, sharp laugh. "God knows we certainly did. But that last night, after we went out to dinner in town, that was not a moment of uncontrolled irrationality for you."

April breathed deeply. It was one thing to let him feel her passion on a quiet, moonlight night; it was quite another to talk about it in the bright July sun.

Christopher continued. "I think I've done nothing else for six weeks but think about what it means. Of course there are plenty of women these days who'll tell you halfway through your first dinner that they'll go home with you, but you aren't like that. At least you *weren't.*"

"I am still not," April said quietly.

"Then, April, why?" His deep voice vibrated with an urgent quiver. "Why could you invite me in? Why—" He stopped, obviously trying to shake the feeling out of his voice. "Six years ago I would have known exactly what it meant. Six years ago you would have never been so willing unless you—without considerable affection."

April noticed his sudden return to the constrained formality. "Without considerable affection." Why was he so reluctant to say the word *love*? Perhaps her worst fear had come true: He realized that she loved him, and the guilt of not loving her in return was tearing him apart. But, of course, there was another explanation.

He went on. "But then, as you kept saying, you had

changed. And there's no reason in the world why you wouldn't have a much more casual attitude about sex than you once did. And you were always so unruffled and pleasant around me that I had to conclude that you felt about me just as I had felt about you when we were married. You liked me and you wanted me, but you no longer loved me."

There was nothing in his carefully controlled voice to tell her if he thought this good or bad, and she had to know that before she could say anything. "Then, Christopher, why are you here?"

"I'm not sure," he admitted. "But last night Beth had to work late and so Josh and I took Steve out to dinner. We were teasing him about being so slow to notice how she felt, and then Josh suddenly turned to me and said, 'Don't be so arrogant, Ramsey; you aren't much better yourself.'"

April stiffened; she hadn't thought that Josh would betray her.

Christopher didn't notice her reaction. "I thought it strange. I mean, he always uses my first name. I admitted that I hadn't suspected a thing about Beth until he had given us that hint when we were all out backpacking. 'I am not talking about Miss Market' was all he said, but the way he said 'Miss' with such emphasis—you'd have thought he was angry with me—I knew that he was talking about you."

April noted, with a great deal of relief, that he seemed to have forgotten that Julia was also a Mrs.

"I thought about it all night," he continued. "No wonder I look tired. On the one hand, Josh had no idea how transparent you were when we were married, how every single glance and gesture revealed your love—and I simply knew that there had been nothing like that again. That was what had made me so sure that your feelings were not too involved. But on the other hand, you *had* changed—and maybe this was one example of that change." His voice was very tight. "Maybe now you can hide your feelings from me just as Beth hid hers from Steve."

It occurred to April that Josh would have never, ever, come so close to breaking her confidence unless he had been very sure. "Christopher," she said softly, "how can you possibly doubt the way I feel?"

"Are you kidding?" He was obviously so uncertain that he could not hear the reassurance in her voice. "I haven't any idea. Either way makes sense—that I was your ex-husband, whom you liked well enough and since I knew you and your body, I could be counted on to give you a good time in bed, or—" He broke off.

"Is that the way you want it?"

He didn't answer right away, slowly unfastening the cuffs of his white shirt, rolling up his sleeves. April knew that he was again trying to keep his hands busy while his emotions were churning.

Finally he spoke. "No, it isn't. That's the irony of it. Back when you loved me, I tried so hard to love you, and I just couldn't. But now I have a feeling that our positions are reversed. I love you," he said bluntly. "But, April, if you have changed, don't pretend. Don't pity me and try to force yourself. We've had enough of that."

April looked directly into his eyes. "Christopher, many things have changed about me, but not the way I feel about you."

She heard him breathe sharply, and the arm that lay on the picnic table curled around her. But just then another carload of campers drove in, and Christopher was too discreet to do more than squeeze her waist for a moment.

His voice was low. "During those two weeks here all I could think about was how much you needed my help. Then when I left, I finally realized that you didn't. Ever since, I've done nothing but think about how much *I* need *you*." He reached into his vest pocket. "I kept telling myself that I had no right to hope, but I brought you this." He handed her a small white parcel.

It was an envelope, folded over a small hard object. April carefully, slowly, began to unfold the envelope. It was embossed with the return address of his firm.

"I guess I should have got a box," Christopher said. "I didn't think, but then if I had been thinking, I wouldn't have bought it."

April could tell by the shape that the envelope held a ring. Breathlessly she opened it, almost afraid that she would drop it.

It was a diamond solitaire, very generously sized, but not so large and flashy that she couldn't wear it every day. It had a simple Tiffany setting with a delicate pattern of flowers and vines etched on the gold band.

"Oh, Christopher, it's beautiful," she breathed.

"Do you like it?" he asked eagerly. "I saw it in the window of an antique store on the way to work this morning, and it just looked so much like you." He took the ring from her. "I don't remember deciding to go in or even asking to see it, but then when it was the right size it just seemed meant to be. So I bought it and drove up here. I mean, you didn't have a diamond the first time we were married."

"The first time?" April tilted her head and looked up at him through her lashes.

His eyes danced. "Well, there's going to be a second

time, isn't there?" His fingers held out the ring invitingly. "After all, it won't be so much trouble this time since you don't have to change your name, so why not?"

"Why not?" Her casual words were charged with a tremor of deep feeling as Christopher slipped the cool band down her finger. April turned her hand, and the diamond caught the sunlight and sent back a scatter of sparkle more brilliant even than light dancing off the water.

"Does it fit?"

"Yes," she breathed. "How did you know my size?"

Wordlessly he pulled out his gold pocket watch. It had been his great-grandfather's. He had not carried it often when they were married, only when he put on a suit, but now, April imagined, he probably carried it nearly every day. He spread out the chain, and she saw dangling from one link a small gold ring. It took her a moment to realize what it was.

"That's my wedding ring," she gasped.

"It must have broken your heart to leave it behind," Christopher said gently.

"It did," she answered, knowing that he understood everything. "But surely you haven't carried it all this time."

"I have."

"Christopher." She shook her head, deeply touched that he had treasured her ring. "No wonder Beth said you still felt married."

He looked at her curiously. "I suppose on some level I did." Then he spoke slowly. "By the way, you know, don't you, that I haven't always *acted* married? I've never been in love with another woman, but—"

"I know," April interrupted. She understood; she

could accept his past, but she really didn't want to hear about it.

Then she saw in his eyes the question that he honestly felt he had no right to ask.

"Well, no," she answered. "I mean, I was so busy, what with working and going to school—"

"Good heavens, April," he laughed. "You don't have to apologize to *me* for not sleeping around. I think I can manage to forgive you." His eyes told her how pleased he truly was. "Do you remember the night on the trail when I asked you if you were taking birth control pills?" April nodded. "I think I wasn't entirely sure what I wanted your answer to be. If it were no, it meant that you might get pregnant. But if it had been yes, then that meant not just that you had been involved with other men, but that you were probably seeing someone at the time. And I think I might have had trouble dealing with that."

"Christopher, there haven't even been that many men I wanted to go out to dinner with."

"Well, why don't we not talk about it?" He smiled. "If I am at heart a primitive, possessive brute, I'd rather not know about it."

April laughed.

"Speaking of feeling like a brute," he went on, "do you remember the day we bought this?" He picked up the watch chain, balancing her wedding ring on the tip of his little finger.

"Of course."

"Do you know, that was when it first hit me just exactly what I had done to you. I was, of course, planning on getting you a diamond, but then you said that we really hadn't been engaged—not with showers and parties and pictures in the paper—"

April winced, interrupting him. "Did I really say that? That shows what a highly developed notion of marriage I had. Anyway"—she held up her hand, not letting him continue—"I hope you have finally stopped feeling bad about that. A girl can make it through life without bridal showers—especially when she has as many towels as I have now," she added teasingly.

Christopher was also now able to laugh about it. "My dear," he drawled, "I stopped feeling bad about everything when I saw what the price of diamonds started to do. That's the best investment that anyone has ever talked me out of. Just think, diamonds have increased five or six times in value since then."

April touched her wedding ring. "This has increased in value a great deal more."

Christopher's eyes were warm; he let the watch chain slip and trapped her hand, pulling it to him. "What do you know about the price of gold?"

"Not a thing." She smiled. She looked down at her left hand again, admiring the sparkle of her new ring. "You're just lucky that I still wear the same ring size, that none of my extra pounds settled on my fingers."

"April," he said in a low voice, "I know where every ounce of that is." Under the cover of the table his free hand slid caressingly down her thigh. "Let's go inside," he said.

"It's the middle of the day," she protested a little breathlessly.

"Yes, but it's Friday," he said invitingly, as if that's what Friday afternoons were made for.

"I'm on duty," she countered, weakening.

"Then maybe we had better go for a walk," he said immediately and stood up. "We can always throw ourselves in the lake if things get too frustrating." And looking at him, standing there in his dark vest, April wished that he had tried a little harder to persuade her to be less professional.

As they set off down the trail he said, "Now, there are some things I want to talk to you about so wipe that smile off your face and be serious."

"Yes, sir," she said, putting on a mock-serious face.

"First, how much do you mind leaving your job?"

"Well, a lot," April admitted, suddenly sober. "But not as much as I would mind keeping it."

He grinned at her. "That makes just heaps of sense."

"I'm serious," she protested. "Not many people have the chance to leave a life they like for one they will love; I'm lucky to be leaving while I still like it. I might have stayed on until I hated it."

Christopher seemed satisfied with her answer. "But about Manhattan. I know that you don't want—"

"Oh, Christopher, no," she interrupted, the seriousness in her eyes becoming genuine. "I'll live anywhere. I didn't want to go to the city before, but that was because I didn't know whether you loved me." Then she glanced at him from the corner of her eye almost flirtatiously. "And I just couldn't see myself pretending to be your sister."

Christopher shook his head in disbelief. "Did I really suggest that? What an incredibly stupid idea. It would have worked for about four-and-a-half minutes. Then you probably would have done something unbelievably provocative like set your purse down or ask for a glass of water, and I would have grabbed you."

"As I recall," April teased, "you were going to introduce me to your friends. Find some nice boy for me."

Christopher lightly pinched her. "Stop making fun

of a troubled man. I think I was already more than half in love with you, but I couldn't admit it. All I knew was that I wanted you in my home, and somehow it came out like that.''

"Well, it hardly matters now. I want to be in your home, and it doesn't make much difference where it is. I am not a city person, but I'll be happy as long as we are together.''

They had come to the fork in the trail and moved off to the left toward the beach. In a moment Christopher spoke again. "Then what would you say to going home? Back to Virginia?''

"Virginia?'' April stopped dead.

He took her hands in his. "April, we belong there; we both do. Let's go back. Sure, we made a mistake, but it was a long time ago, and anyway, it's nobody's business but our own. Let's not make another mistake by staying away.''

"Oh, Christopher.'' April could hardly believe what he was saying. "I'd just love that. I can't imagine any other place ever feeling as much like home.''

He smiled down at her. "My grandparents left their house to me; we can live there. Or we can build a new place. It doesn't matter; whatever you want—just so long as we fill it with lots of children. I feel like I owe that town another pretty cheerleader.''

April laughed. "I thought we weren't going to feel guilty or obligated anymore.''

"I don't,'' he said, obviously lying a little. "I'm just looking for excuses to spend a lot of time in your bed.''

They started walking again, around the green-painted posts that marked the beginning of the beach. The beach was crowded. Mothers patiently allowed their diapered toddlers to pour little shovelfuls of sand over their feet. Young girls giggled softly in each other's ears, as teen-age boys self-consciously threw Frisbees, awkward under the girls' gaze. Schoolchildren darted in and out, playing tag.

"What a lot of people!" Christopher said in surprise.

"That reminds me," April said. "Just where do you plan on staying tonight, Mr. Ramsey? The park is full."

"I'll manage to find somewhere, I imagine," he said, looking down at her with a long glance.

"But you know that I'm still not on the pill," she returned.

"Well, pretty lady, then you'll just have to take your chances."

April wrinkled her nose at him. "Don't you mean that *you* will have to take yours?"

"No," he said, suddenly serious. "I may have once thought that I had to marry you, but I had no idea what it felt like to really *have* to marry someone. I can't imagine anything that could possibly make me feel more compelled to marry you than I do now—even if you were on the verge of having triplets."

"Triplets?" April grimaced. "I'm not so sure I want to take my chance at triplets."

He laughed with her. "It is a rather sobering thought, isn't it?"

A bright green Frisbee came sailing out of the crowd, grazing against their legs, and landed, half buried in the soft sand. Christopher picked it up and with a lithe, easy gesture, spun it back to its young owner.

"Thanks," the boy called, and then he saw April standing next to Christopher in her green uniform shirt. "Oh, hi, Miss Ramsey."

"Call me Apr—" she started to say automatically when Christopher interrupted her, his arm closing around her shoulders.

"Her name, son, is *Mrs.* Ramsey, and it's going to stay that way for a long time."

Chapter Eleven

"Christopher, if you put it up there, no one will be able to see it. Not everyone is as tall as you."

It was 2:00 A.M., and April and Christopher were hanging pictures. Like every other married couple trying to do some unfamiliar task when they haven't had enough sleep, they were squabbling. Their dining room ceiling was fourteen feet high, and April thought that Christopher was putting the portraits up too high.

"April, you don't understand," he said almost impatiently. "Nobody wants to look at these pictures." He let his great-great-grandfather's gilt frame lean against his long legs. "They are my ancestors, and I don't care whether or not I can see them. Why should anyone else?"

April suddenly laughed. She knew perfectly well that her irritation had nothing at all to do with him. "You're right. Let's just leave him on the floor."

Christopher obediently let the picture slide to the floor. "And what will the tour guide say tomorrow?" He mimicked a feminine, affected voice. "'Young Mr. and Mrs. Ramsey, in the course of doing research into family history, have discovered that great-great-grandpop spent many hours under the dining room table in a drunken stupor and have decided therefore to leave his picture there.'"

April smiled at him and sank cross-legged onto the floor, leaning back wearily against the wall. "Why on earth did we agree to do this?"

It was Historic Garden Week in Virginia. For the next seven days ladies from all over the state would put on silk shirtwaists and low-heeled, sensible shoes and tour some of Virginia's finest homes and gardens. April and Christopher had agreed to let their house be on the tour this year.

"It was the only way to get the house finished," Christopher answered. He stepped over his ancestor and came to sit next to April on the floor. He put his arm around her. "And it worked, didn't it? Except for Kit's new room and this one last picture, we are more or less done."

When they had returned to Virginia three years earlier, they had moved into his grandparents' house. It was a big stone mansion whose walled garden took up a full square block. As beautiful and solidly built as the house was, it had sat vacant since his grandparents' deaths and needed a great deal of work. April and Christopher had had it completely rewired, had remodeled the kitchen, and had added several additional bathrooms.

It was a good thing she liked to camp, April had said often during this period. It seemed impossible to have any normal routine. For two weeks they had had to shower at Christopher's parents' house, and for a month they had had no kitchen, boiling water for their morning coffee on their little backpacking stoves.

But it was finally done—the oak floors had been sanded and stained; the new plaster had cured and been painted with the cool, clear colors traditional to colonial Virginia; the antique furniture had been polished and, where necessary, reupholstered. The only room still empty was the one that had been designated for two-year-old Christopher D. Ramsey IV—or Kit, as he was called—once the new baby was born.

The garden was even more lovely than the house. When plumbers, plasterers, painters, and every other form of workmen took over her home each day, April had taken her baby out to the garden and worked. She had found, among the family papers, a plan for the garden drawn up before the Civil War, and as much as possible she tried to restore the garden to this century-old design. She moved azaleas, pruned magnolias, put in bulbs, dug up dandelions and chickweed. She planted herbaceous borders and saved the rosebed from black spot. In addition to the garden's historic interest, it was beautiful in its own right, and the Garden Club had been eager to get it on the annual tour.

April was a member of the Garden Club. Before coming back to Virginia, she had decided that she would try hard with Christopher's parents. She had thought carefully about Mrs. Ramsey's activities and decided that the Garden Club was the one she would be best able to stomach.

To her surprise, she enjoyed it. The club's activities were not limited to flower-arranging classes and little luncheons. Many of the women felt a deep commitment to preserving Virginia's natural beauties and had eagerly welcomed April's professional experience. She hoped to be more active in some of the club's activities, but at the moment she was pregnant with what she hoped was Kit's sister. Between chasing an active two-year-old and "sleeping for two"—which was her description of pregnancy—April did not have much free time these days.

Mrs. Ramsey appreciated April's efforts in the Garden Club, and if the two women were not close, there wasn't much friction between them. Each had made concessions. Mrs. Ramsey did not criticize April when, on a summer afternoon, she would find Christopher the Third in his backyard, dressed only in jeans, playing with Christopher the Fourth who, in imitation of his father, would be wearing only a diaper. In turn, April always put a skirt on herself and shoes and a little hat on Kit when she visited her mother-in-law.

Christopher's parents might not know much about love, but one emotion they did understand was pride. They had been surprised when April had left Charlottesville because neither of them thought that she had that kind of pride and spirit. Her leaving had earned her their grudging respect, and when she returned, they could see, far more quickly than their son had, the extent to which she had changed.

Of course, she was not as formal or concerned about appearances as they would have liked, but the Ramseys had been deeply grieved when Christopher had moved to New York, and they realized that it was his remarriage that had brought him home. Then when Kit was born—a respectable twelve months after his parents' marriage—the Ramseys had to admit that April was a good mother, even though they had recently heard that now that he was walking, April was allowing Kit to wade in puddles, which they could not quite approve of. But, in truth, they liked her more than they admitted.

For the first time in his life Christopher Ramsey was in a home where love was given generously, warmly, and completely. April loved him with a steady passion that had little to do with the girlish infatuation that she had once felt. And his son, now that he was emerging from the wonderfully selfish world of babyhood, adored him. Christopher had always thought that love was something that had to be earned; this sturdy, little toddler was teaching him that sometimes love was just given.

When his New York friends came to visit, they found Christopher a different man, easier, less distant, more relaxed, laughing more readily and more often.

In one way he had not changed. If anything, his own happiness had increased his sense of obligation to those less fortunate, and he was, in a very quiet way, making quite a difference in the town. At Steve's and Beth's wedding he had met Steve's younger brother, a woodworker with dreams of opening a small factory to build, almost entirely by hand, reproductions of antique furniture. Christopher had persuaded him to come to Virginia and had provided the capital for starting the business. It was doing well, providing the town with some much-needed jobs. Christopher brought in several other similar businesses, each rather small, but doing well enough to give the town a flush of prosperity without luring in the big-city developers. Only his father, his partner in these ventures, completely understood Christopher's role in improving the town's economy, but local businessmen sensed enough to know that it had been a good thing for the town when young Mr. Ramsey had brought his wife back home.

It was, after all, where they belonged.

Readers rave about
Harlequin American Romance!

" ...the best series of modern romances
I have read...great, exciting, stupendous,
wonderful."

      —S.E., Coweta, Oklahoma

" ...they are absolutely fantastic...going to be
a smash hit and hard to keep on the
bookshelves."

      —P.D., Easton, Pennsylvania

"The American line is great. I've enjoyed
every one I've read so far."

      —W.M.K., Lansing, Illinois

" ...the best stories I have read in a long
time."

      —R.H., Northport, New York

"The stories are great from beginning to end."
—*M.W., Tampa, Florida*

"...excellent new series...I am greatly impressed."
—*M.B., El Dorado, Arkansas*

"I am delighted with them...can't put them down."
—*P.D.V., Mattituck, New York*

"Thank you for the excitement, love and adventure your books add to my life. They are definitely the best on the market."
—*J.W., Campbellsville, Kentucky*

Names available on request.